High

GW00598716

by
Sue Hoffmann

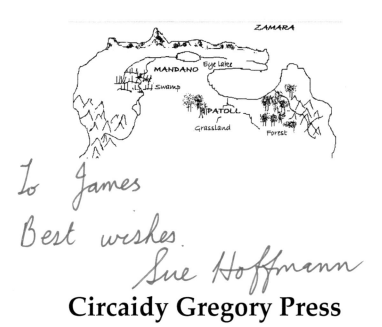

To James
Best wishes.
Sue Hoffmann

Circaidy Gregory Press

Copyright information

paperback ISBN 978-1-906451-80-6
ebook ISBN 978-1-906451-84-4

Printed in the UK
by Berforts Group Ltd

Published by Circaidy Gregory Press
Creative Media Centre
45 Robertson St, Hastings
Sussex TN34 1HL

www.circaidygregory.co.uk

Dedication

For my sister Marian, without whom The Island would
have remained just a legend.

Acknowledgements

Special thanks to Kay Green of Circaidy Gregory Press for her support and guidance – and for believing in Zamara. Thanks also to Cathy Edmunds for her super artwork and sound advice.

About the Author

A teacher for 25 years, with an MA in Language Teaching and Learning, Sue Hoffmann knows all about creating and sharing stories. Her competition successes include 'Game Plan', Winner of Readers' Challenge 107, *The New Writer Magazine* Dec 2011; 'Smoke and Mirrors', 2012 Winner of the New Eastbourne Writers 2nd National Short Story Competition; 'Encounters with Marcia', runner up in The Booktown Writers' Annual Short Story Competition 2012 and 'Red', Runner up in the Fylde Brighter Writers Circle Prize 2012.

She has had a variety of short stories published in newspapers, magazines, online or in anthologies, including the Earlyworks Press fantasy anthology *The Sleepless Sands* and the sci-fi challenge anthology *The Road Unravelled*. As well as the short stories she continues to write, Sue is working on a children's book, *Timothy's Gate* and an adult fantasy, *Focus Stone*, and the Zamara story continues to grow, which will make *High King* the first of a series.

When she is not writing, Sue enjoys reading, gardening, line dancing, tennis and badminton. She's passionate about animals, especially her dog, two budgies and hamster.

Foreword

The Birth of Zamara

Plan an outdoor adventurous activities day...

That was the brief given to me, along with a few leaflets on group problem-solving tasks. Planning the six tasks for our group of students was relatively straightforward and the activities I devised looked challenging and interesting. However, they lacked that special spark that would make them competitive yet fun. They needed a link – a common theme.

I decided to connect the tasks through a quest set on an imaginary island which I called "Zamara". Each activity would take place in a different region of the island – a swamp; mountains; a desert. "Magical spells" would help or hinder along the way.

Thus, Zamara was born.

What began as a one-day project gradually grew into a term's work, all based on the requirements laid out in the National Curriculum of the time.

In response to the students' curiosity about the people and the history of Zamara, I wrote for them a series of stories. "High King" – the first of these stories – has changed and developed since I first wrote the tale, although the original story remains at the core of the revised version. It is now a full length book for adults, but still accessible to younger readers. So, welcome to Zamara – a land of many mysteries.

Sue Hoffmann, April 2013

The Royal House of Almar

Lanna (First High Queen) m. Edron

Six Generations

Drask (High King) m. Sarreen

Jarin
d. aged 20

Marleth m. Trella

Lendra m. Keld
Two children

Ibren m. Aril
One Child

Sharina m. Drient

Brak
d. aged 17

Lantor m. Ryella

Renolth m. Ardelle

Trisella m. Marnlon

Jerram Darrant Amryl

Zenton

Brandell

Contents

Chapter One

A New Land

Zenton ran, shoving his way through bushes, feeling thorny branches tugging at his clothes and tearing skin from his hands and face. Coming at last to open ground he increased his speed. His breath came in gasps. His heart hammered in his chest. If only he could reach the cave he would be safe. It could not follow him in there.

He risked a glance behind him. It was closer now, gaining with every stride. Surging forward again he saw that he had misjudged his position. He was at the top of the dunes and the soft, blue-tinted sand slowed his flight. He was too close to the edge of the high, steep sandhills. Hot, damp, foul-smelling breath brushed the back of his neck and he spun round. Out of a dark, menacing cloud, a hand reached for his throat. Terrified, he stumbled away, fell – and woke.

For a while Zenton lay still, trying to shake off the residual fear from the dream. He'd had vivid dreams before – some of them surprisingly prescient – but never such a terrifying nightmare, not even during the worst days of the plague. The plague! He began to panic. He was sweating and shivering at the same time. Was he ill? Did he have the dreaded sickness? He fought down the terror. There had been no cases of plague aboard the ships for the final two months of the voyage, and certainly none since they had made landfall. He was not ill, just frightened.

He sat up slowly, calmer now but still disturbed and unwilling to go back to sleep. From the faint light filtering into the shelter, he knew it must be close to Oltan's dawn. The camp would be stirring soon, preparing for another day's work. A gentle snore from the rolled bundle on the right of the shelter told him Brandell was still sleeping soundly. Quietly, Zenton wrapped his cloak around himself, gathered up clothes and boots and went out to the wash area to try to scrub away the sweat and fear the nightmare had caused.

Two guards greeted him as he crossed the camp. Zenton took comfort in the order and normality of the site. He washed and dressed slowly, then wandered towards the cook-fires where the morning's meal was already being prepared.

"Zenton!" Renolth was sitting a short way from one of the fires, cradling a steaming cup of banellin. Pleased to find his father alone for once, Zenton went to join him.

"Here," said Renolth, pouring a second cup from a covered jug and passing the drink to his son.

Zenton blew on the dark liquid, cooling it a little, before sipping appreciatively. "Do you think banellin will grow here?" he asked.

"I hope so," Renolth replied with feeling.

Father and son sat in companionable silence for a minute or so and then Zenton asked, "Will we stay here?"

"It's too soon to make that decision," Renolth said. "We've been caught out twice before, have we not? Still, it looks promising. There's no evidence yet of any people native here. Did you know that Irvanyal's search band reported dense forest three days eastwards? They saw wildlife and found edible fruit and fungi." Without waiting for any response, he continued, "Whether or not this place turns out to be The Island, it's saved our small fleet, and we seem to have escaped the plague at last, thank the Light."

Zenton's stomach lurched as he recalled his earlier fear of being ill. He was on the point of telling his father about the dream but Renolth spoke again and the moment passed.

"It seems to be a good land. We should be safe here. When the ships are repaired, I'll send one to chart the coast and see if this is an island or part of some mainland. If we *are* the only people here, and if the land can support us, I'll tell Murl it's time to sail back to the Homeland and lead the others here – assuming there are still some survivors. It's taken us so *long*, Zenton. I never imagined it would take so very long."

"Lantor will keep them safe," offered Zenton, "and I'm sure we'll be able to settle here." There was something special about this place, something that called to him, making him desperate to stay. "When we do send Murl back and Lantor hears of our success –" he began.

"If you can call it success," Renolth interrupted, his tone tinged with bitterness. "Four ships left out of seven! It's a good thing you have sharp eyes lad, or none of us would be here now. How you spotted the channel through that mist still amazes me."

Zenton could barely remember the last time he and his father had sat together and talked like this. It was before the earthquakes had begun, before the devastation of the plague and the horrified realisation of the Almari people that their land was doomed and their race could well be facing extinction.

Maybe he should tell his father it wasn't just sharp eyesight that had enabled him to find the entrance to the harbour. He had felt a strange pull – a sense of something drawing him in the right direction. Perhaps he should say something about it now.

"Prince Renolth, here's your meal."

Renolth and Zenton turned to see one of the cooks standing holding a bowl of tarren and some flat bread.

"My thanks, Jeya," said Renolth, taking the food.

Before he could begin to eat, though, Captain Murl and two other people came to him with queries and he stood up to speak to them. Annoyed at the interruption, Zenton rose quickly and stalked away. With a touch of unwanted self-pity, he doubted if his father even noticed he was leaving.

"Hold hard, cousin!" Brandell was walking towards the cook-fires. He paused to stretch, yawn broadly and rub his eyes. His shoulder-length, dark hair was still tousled from sleep but he was dressed neatly enough and had a travel pack slung casually over one shoulder. Zenton felt a brief stab of envy. Almost three years older than Zenton, Brandell was allowed to join the longer searches while the younger prince was kept to a half-day's travel from the encampment. The two years until Zenton would be sixteen and considered an adult seemed to him to be an interminable wait, especially when he felt he'd done a man's job aboard the *Tennel's Flight*.

"Wait there," said Brandell, tying his hair back with a leather thong. "I'll get us some food. You haven't eaten yet, have you?"

Zenton sat on a fallen log near the cooking area and made a half-hearted attempt to tidy his own hair. As dark as Brandell's but annoyingly wavy, it had so often defied being tied back that he now wore it short. He watched as his cousin dumped the travel pack, collected two full bowls and came to sit by him on the log.

3

"Oh, good," muttered Brandell, handing a bowl to Zenton, "tarren again. I had a choice you know – tarren or tarren. I thought you'd prefer tarren."

Still vaguely unsettled by the nightmare and unreasonably irritated by being denied more time alone with his father, Zenton was in no mood for Brandell's levity.

"Jeya said last eve we have only two sacks of tarren left," he reported, "and only one satchel of seed. If that doesn't take here you won't have to worry about being sick of tarren again, will you?"

Brandell stared thoughtfully at the congealing porridge in his bowl. "I suppose not," he agreed amicably, seeming not in the least bothered either by his cousin's tone or by the threat of starvation.

Hungry despite his ill humour, Zenton ate his morning meal hurriedly before grudgingly wishing his cousin a good search and heading off to the main meeting area to see what his own duties for the day would be. He discovered he'd been assigned to a group whose task was to continue searching the grasslands south of the main encampment, mapping the area and gathering samples of plants which might prove edible or medicinal. Zenton smiled. The day was starting to improve. He knew that food, water and medicines were the main concerns for the Almari at present, but a search of the grasslands would also enable him to study any wildlife he found. Guessing that Renolth had arranged for him to be included in this particular search band, Zenton put aside his earlier resentment and hastened back towards his shelter to fetch his travel pack.

Find the cave.

Zenton turned quickly to see who had spoken. No one was close to him. He stood for a moment, puzzled. The voice had been quiet, almost a whisper. Perhaps he'd imagined it, or maybe he had simply overheard a snatch of someone's conversation. He walked on.

Donar and the others were waiting for him by his shelter. "Hurry along, lad," said Donar. "Oltan's well risen and the Smaller Sun's on its way. We should be well on *our* way by now."

Zenton ducked inside the small shelter and hastily gathered up his pack. He checked that one of his precious sketchpads and some charcoal were securely in place, fastened the straps and joined his team.

Find the cave.

"What did you say?" he asked Donar.

"I said, 'Hurry along'."

"No, I mean just a second ago, when I came out of the shelter."

Donar frowned at him. "I didn't say anything. Come on, if you please, Prince Zenton. We'll collect our supplies and head south and east today, following the main stream back along its course."

The group turned to leave. Donar started discussing the land's plant life with Merret, and Slen and Lissanne were bickering amiably as usual. Zenton trailed after them, expecting at any moment to hear the faint voice again. He listened intently, but the only sounds were the normal chatter and bustle of the busy encampment.

Chapter Two

Light and Shade

Brandell hunched down under the scant protection of a broad-leaved, grey-blue sapling and pulled the hood of his cloak farther forward in a vain attempt to keep the rain from his face. The waterproofing had long since ceased to be effective and he was soaked to the skin.

Accustomed to the heavy but brief downpours of the Homeland Isles, Brandell found the steady, relentless drizzle of the past two and a half days depressing in the extreme. He tried to take comfort in the fact that at least the weather was warm, but chewing at soggy rations during a mid-suns rest stop when neither Oltan nor Bardok was visible through the blanketing greyness of lowering clouds was not his idea of the best way to spend his time. Truth to tell, he resented sitting here in the rain for what he thought was an unnecessary halt. Walking in this appalling weather was bad enough but stopping to eat and rest in such conditions rather than eating on the move seemed to him to be bad judgement on Irvanyal's part. Still, she was the leader on this search and he didn't feel like trying to exert any 'royal' authority over her at present. He doubted if she'd take much notice anyway. There was a great deal less formality now between the princes and the rest of the people than there had been before the voyage. Brandell supposed that was inevitable, considering all they had been through together, but he missed the comfort and security of the time before the earthquakes had begun.

He'd had a good life, back then. Oh, there had been some sadness, of course. His mother – younger sister to Lantor and Renolth – had died along with her husband when Brandell was just five years old, but Renolth and Ardelle had taken him into their family and had always seemed more like his real parents. Being a member of the royal household had suited him well. He'd loved the riding and the sailing, the state visits and the feasts. He'd enjoyed having fine clothes, and servants to wait upon him. Then everything had changed.

A few drops of water from the leaves above splattered onto his nose, ending his reflections on the past and bringing him back to the waterlogged present. He sighed, stood up slowly and shook some of the wetness from his cloak.

The light rain finally eased as the search band pressed on eastwards. Oltan began to dip towards its night's rest; the skies cleared and a steamy warmth enveloped the land. The forest they had entered about a half-hour ago was denser here. Thick undergrowth made their chosen way impassable at times, forcing them to keep changing direction. The rays of the setting suns filtered through the canopy above, turning the great woods into a world of contrasting patches: first brilliance then deep shade. The place was alive with insects and birds, strange calls and flashes of movement adding to the mystery. Some of the plants, birds and insects were familiar to the search band but there were many they had never seen before.

"Zenton ought to come here and study these," Brandell commented to Chandrane. "It's his area of interest."

Chandrane nodded agreement but did not reply. He, like the rest of the group, had been virtually silent since entering the forest. Their voices seemed out of place: unwanted sounds from uninvited guests.

Brandell watched as Chandrane made his way carefully past a low-growing tree with spreading branches bearing delicate, creamy, conical flowers and sharp, bright-crimson thorns. Despite the weight of a heavy travel pack and the difficulty of the terrain, Chandrane moved with an easy grace. Brandell recalled seeing him training with Slen the evening before they had left the encampment. A little taller than Brandell, though almost a year younger, Chandrane was broad-shouldered and, but for the privations of the voyage, would have been of muscular build. At present too thin for his height, he was nevertheless strong and energetic. He showed promise of being Slen's equal or better with sword and bow.

Finding a small grassy clearing ringed by towering arantha trees, Irvanyal called a halt for the day. Brandell shrugged off his travel pack and dropped it on the ground. Something large, grey and furry shot past his feet and disappeared into the undergrowth.

"Nad's shadow!" he exclaimed in shock.

Irvanyal glared at him. "Prince Brandell," she said reprovingly, "startled you may well have been, but I see no cause for such language."

Brandell crouched to unstrap his pack. "Whatever that was, it must have been hidden in the grass. I almost dropped my pack on it. No wonder the poor thing fled." He grinned, recovered now from his fright. "Sorry if I offended you Irvanyal, but it's only a saying."

"An unpleasant saying. Remember: He'll wake if you call him."

"That's another unpleasant saying," retorted Brandell, "and has just as little meaning. I distinctly remember being scared half to death by that one when I was about six years old." He rose and stretched his weary muscles. "Look, we're all tired, and the light's not going to last much longer. I'll see if I can find some dry wood for a fire and I'll prepare the evening meal, if you like, while the rest of you organise the camp."

Brandell's newly acquired cooking skills were far from being finely honed but Irvanyal nodded and gestured to the other four members of the search band to begin setting up the small travel shelters.

Later, after a passable meal, the group sat quietly around the small, stone-ringed fire, listening to the changing sounds of the forest as full dark swept in like a restless black tide. Peculiar, trilling calls sounded in the distance and occasionally there came sudden, piercing shrieks.

Chandrane shuffled a little closer to the flames. "Do you really believe what you said earlier?" he asked Brandell, who was lounging next to him, a dim shape lit fitfully by the flickering blaze of the cook-fire.

Brandell took the tough grass stem he'd been idly chewing out of his mouth. "What did I say?"

"You know. Sayings about... about... Well, that they have no meaning?"

"Sayings about Nad?" Brandell sat up and flung the grass stem into the fire, sending a brief shower of sparks dancing like tiny glowflies. " 'He'll wake if you call him'. 'The Evil One sleeps, don't disturb him'," he quoted softly. "I've heard people say 'Nad's shadow', or 'Nad's black cloak', and other such expressions, many times. As have you, no doubt. I've not seen much evidence of it

8

making any difference to anything, apart from allowing people to relieve their feelings. Have you?"

"Well, no, but –"

"Don't tell me you believe he's real?" Brandell said scathingly.

Chandrane didn't answer immediately. He leaned forward and fed a few small twigs to the hungry flames. "I've never given it much thought before," he said at last. "Back in the Homeland I suppose I'd have agreed with you. Here, though, I'm not quite so certain."

Brandell reached for his bedroll. "Well, if this *is* The Island, we should be safe enough, should we not? All our legends say The Island has beauty and power, and it's supposed to be a sanctuary for us. Light knows, we certainly needed one." He chuckled as he shook out his bedroll. "Let's just hope Nad doesn't know how to find it!"

Chandrane roused Brandell to share the last watch and, thankful for a dry morning at last, the prince rose and ambled across the clearing. He leaned against the trunk of a sturdy arantha, staring out into the inky darkness, trying in vain to make out any shapes beyond the range of the flickering firelight. He had slept well enough yet did not feel fully rested. It was hard to summon his usual enthusiasm for facing the coming day.

The sky brightened almost imperceptibly. The dawn light of the First Sun forced its way into the denseness of the vegetation, reaching out to wake the trees and bushes like a mother gently rousing her sleepy children. For a brief time the forest was silent, then a bird high in the canopy sang its welcome to the new day and its song was joined by the voices of others until the whole forest came alive with chirping and whistling calls.

Entranced, Brandell shrugged aside his tiredness and listened to the sounds around him. Something landed lightly low down on his left arm, causing a sudden itching sensation, and instinctively he clapped his other hand hard across his wrist. Feeling a slight stickiness beneath his fingers, he looked down and, in the brightening light, saw the squashed body of a sail-wing. He stared at the harmless creature, noticing how similar it was to those back in the Homeland Isles, its gauzy, fragile wings huge in comparison to its tiny body. The Homeland sail-wings were usually blue or green but the broken insect on Brandell's arm had wings of silvery grey, shot through with violet threads.

A fluttering movement just to the right of his head caused Brandell to turn. Three sail-wings were flitting around the side of the clearing, two of them circling and dancing together while the third darted from leaf to leaf, hovering briefly before moving on, as if searching for something. Brandell felt an unexpected twinge of remorse. He had acted spontaneously, thinking he was being bitten or stung; he'd not meant to cause harm. Brushing the dead insect from his arm, he went to start preparing the morning meal.

Chapter Three

Searchers and Watchers

It was several months before the storm-damaged ships were seaworthy once more. Renolth's priority had, of necessity, been the welfare of those in his charge. Only once food and water had been found, a long-term encampment established and searchers had found no evidence of habitation within a three-day walk had he sanctioned full time repairs on the ships. Shortage of skilled labour and initial difficulty in finding repair materials had delayed the work, but now all the vessels had been careened and re-caulked. Planks, masts and spars were mended, and sails had been sewn and re-fitted.

Like Zenton, many people believed this place was indeed the legendary Island. Renolth still reserved his judgement. However, the land seemed welcoming, fertile and safe, and he deemed it time to launch a final rescue mission to bring more Almari here, away from their doomed Homeland.

The *Horizon's Edge*, presently anchored at a rocky outcrop which formed a convenient quay, was to remain, her services needed for deep-water fishing. The crew aboard the *Waves of Oltan* would shortly set sail to begin charting the coastline of the new land. The other two ships were loaded for the long voyage back to the Homeland Isles. Navigational charts were copied in readiness for the journey, along with detailed soundings and information about sea-currents around the dangerous reef near the harbour entrance.

Despite the hazards the voyage would undoubtedly present, there were more than sufficient volunteers to crew the returning vessels and Zenton watched with the rest of the Almari settlers as the *Tennel's Flight* and the *Star's Reach*, under the commands of Murl and Jedron, weighed anchor, raised sail and headed for open sea. It seemed strange to see so few people aboard the two ships. The crews would find the vessels spacious after the overcrowding of their last voyage. Those on shore waited quietly as the ships drew away, gradually shrinking into the distance and disappearing into the mist which seemed a perpetual shroud around the harbour entrance.

Near to Zenton, a baby girl who had been born during the last days of the voyage began to cry loudly, a demanding wail of hunger. Her mother rocked her gently as she turned and walked back towards the shelters to feed her. Others followed and the crowd slowly dispersed, returning to tasks they had left to watch the ships depart.

Zenton bent to pick up his travel pack, excitement reasserting itself after the solemnity of seeing the *Tennel* and the *Star* leave. By dint of much persistence on his part, and with Donar and Brandell arguing on his side, he had finally managed to persuade his father to allow him to go on one of the longer searches. He was to accompany Brandell as part of a band assigned to explore the region to the north. Bidding farewell to Renolth, he hastened to join the group assembling near the rowboat that would carry them across to the rocky coastline which formed the northern boundary of the natural harbour.

Brandell rested on his oar and studied the jagged shoreline. "Well, so much for that plan."

Donar nodded and scratched thoughtfully at his beard. "There's no way for us to land anywhere along here," he said. "We're going to have to do this the hard way."

"Row all the way back and then walk instead?" asked Zenton.

Brandell laughed. "You wanted to come, cousin. Don't start complaining now."

"I'm not," said Zenton. "It's just…"

"What?"

"Nothing. It doesn't matter."

Brandell chuckled again and passed his oar to Zenton. "Here. Your turn."

With six in the group and the boat large enough to carry ten, there was room to change places easily. However, just as Zenton stood up, a sudden, forceful swell tipped the rowboat to port and he almost overbalanced. His hasty grab at the gunwale, along with Brandell's helping hand, averted mishap.

"Careful," Brandell warned light-heartedly. "We don't want to have to tell Renolth we lost you overboard on your first full search."

12

Zenton dredged up an answering smile as he changed places with his cousin and sat down alongside Chandrane on the centre thwart. Chandrane grinned at him but Zenton just sighed. He didn't want to go back and start the search again overland. There was something to the north that he needed to find and now he was going in the wrong direction. Forcing down the urge to protest, he bent to his oar.

Taking shifts with the rowing, the search band headed back to where the harbour sands ended and the rocky terrain began. Here they beached the boat well above the high-water mark and resumed their journey on foot, heading northeast towards the towering cliffs which were visible from the main encampment.

Although the way was steep, it was a fairly easy climb and the light breeze blowing off the harbour waters kept the searchers pleasantly cool. After a while the ground levelled out and the group found they were travelling eastwards with the glistening water far below them to their right. They camped overnight in a sheltered hollow and at Oltan's dawn on the following day they set off northwards, stopping at frequent intervals to map their route, record landmarks and collect samples of vegetation for the healers and the cooks to study on the band's return.

"There's a huge stretch of water over there," called Brandell. He had wandered ahead of the group and now came bounding back to them. "I could see it from that next high ridge. It looks to be about an hour's walk away." His enthusiasm was infectious and the searchers headed in the direction he indicated.

A light mist formed across the land as they walked and the apparent nearness of the water was deceptive. It was over three hours before they reached a grassy hillock just south of what was clearly a vast lake. A gentle, steady breeze dispersed the thin mist as they left their packs in a small cluster and walked to the water's edge.

The shingle beneath their feet was grey-brown, with just a hint of the strange blueness of the harbour sands. Tall reeds fringed the lake, their pointed, dark-green leaves swaying gently in the light breeze. Small insects, striped red and brown, buzzed industriously around the reeds' bulbous blue flowers. Wherever the shingle gave way to muddy soil, grasses grew, intermingled with spindly, pink flowers. Wide-petalled, cream-coloured water plants bobbed just offshore and insects with long, dangly legs flitted across the rippling surface, iridescent wings shimmering in the reflected light of the suns.

One by one the members of the search band moved a few paces back from the edge of the lake and sat down on the warm grass. They sat for perhaps a full quarter-hour before Brandell broke the silence.

"How about a swim?" he suggested.

Donar shook his head. "It's tempting but there might be water creatures who could object to us invading their habitat. Perhaps later, when we've studied the lake a bit more."

Something large and dark broke the lake's surface, snatched up one of the long-legged insects and plopped back underwater.

"Point taken," said Brandell, and Donar laughed.

"We'll need to map the area," Tegran reminded them.

"Yes," agreed Donar, "if it doesn't take us too long. Renolth's 'three days search and then turn back' rule is still in force, remember?"

"Makes sense, I suppose." Tegran stretched his long legs out towards the water and rested back on his hands. He glanced at Lirreth, seated to his right, and sighed. She was at least a decade older than he but seemed far less tired.

Donar looked up at the sky, judging the daylight hours left to them. "We'll set up a base camp here," he decided. "After we've eaten, we'll split into two groups. Lirreth, you take Tegran and Brandell and head west along the lake shore. Chandrane, Zenton and I will go the other way, mapping the lake. Turn back as soon as Oltan begins to set. We'll meet back here before Bardok's light goes."

"Wouldn't it save time and energy if each group camped on the way and then continued the mapping on the morrow?" asked Tegran.

"It would indeed," agreed Donar, "but it might not be safe here come full dark. I want everyone together." He rose slowly. "I know it's hard to leave this place but we've work to do. Let's get moving."

The search band reassembled in time to share a late meal as the Smaller Sun's rays faded from the sky. Two of the moons were soon visible, lending light and shadow to a countryside bleached of colour. With the night's watches organised, four of the searchers settled to sleep while Donar and Zenton kept first guard.

14

Tired though he was from the day's activities, Zenton felt restless and too alert to sleep. He was glad of the chance to sit alone for a while. He could see the humped shapes of the small travel shelters and, not far away, the still figure of Donar standing on the lake shore gazing at the moons' reflections in the polished surface of the calm water. All was serene and quiet, the night sounds soothing. Zenton flexed the weary muscles of his shoulders. A search without carrying heavy travel packs would certainly be more enjoyable. He yawned, finding after all that the lethargy of impending sleep was creeping up on him. Mentally, he shook himself awake. Falling asleep on watch would be embarrassing in the extreme. He could well imagine Brandell's comments.

A faint prickling sensation between his shoulder blades brought him fully awake and he froze in place, listening for any change in the sounds around him. Nothing seemed amiss, yet Zenton knew with absolute certainty that he was being watched.

Chapter Four

A Little Thief

He sat perfectly still. There was no feeling of danger, no trace of the terror of the nightmare in which he had been stalked and chased, just a sense that *something* was staring at him. The feeling diminished and he turned slowly, scanning the moons-lit campsite. Seeing nothing unusual, he rose and walked towards the banked fire, treading softly to avoid waking those in the travel shelters. He could still see Donar by the lake, a shadowy shape unhurriedly patrolling near the water's edge.

Zenton shrugged. His over-active imagination was playing tricks on him. A covered jug of banellin had been left to keep warm in the fire's embers and he reached into his pack to take out his cup. Something wrapped itself firmly around his thumb. With a startled yelp, he withdrew his hand fast.

The constriction around his thumb increased and his instinct was to shake whatever it was free. Controlling his fear, he lifted his hand and looked down to see what had ensnared him. Two bright, silvery eyes regarded him steadily and Zenton blinked in astonishment. A little creature had coiled its tail firmly around his thumb and was dangling head down, staring at him with huge, round eyes. Zenton's trepidation turned to delight and amusement. He could not make out the colour of the small animal's fur but he could see quite plainly its heart-shaped head and chubby body, and its four stubby legs ending in dextrous, four-digit paws – a front one of which grasped his polished metal cloak brooch.

None of the sleepers had been disturbed by Zenton's cry of surprise, but Donar had heard him and was hastening towards him. The little creature's tufted ears twitched at the sound of approaching footsteps. Its button nose quivered and its long, fine whiskers trembled as if in a stiff breeze. With a chitter of protest, it swung itself up onto Zenton's wrist, unhooked its prehensile tail, shot up his arm and dived down the front of his tunic. The brooch clasp

16

scratched his chest as the creature turned and snuggled against his shoulder, clinging to tunic and skin with a vice-like grip.

"Ouch! Stop that!" He unfastened the top buttons of his jacket and reached carefully inside his tunic. "Come out of there. No one's going to hurt you."

Donar stared at him. Clearly believing Zenton was talking to himself, the search band leader spoke gently, as he might to a timid child. "Prince Zenton. Just wait calmly. I'll wake the others and we'll sort this out."

Zenton laughed and then winced. "Ow! That hurt! No, Donar, don't wake them. We have a night visitor, but I doubt we're in much danger from it." Finally managing to extricate the small, furry bundle from its hiding place, he held it out for Donar's inspection.

Fascinated, Donar bent closer. "What is it?"

"I've no idea. I found it in my pack."

Apparently deciding it was not in mortal peril, the creature settled itself in Zenton's cupped hand, curled its long tail around its body and promptly went to sleep. The prince gently pried the cloak brooch from its small hand. "I'll keep it with me until it wakes," he told Donar, "then I'll set it free away from the camp."

Donar smiled and nodded. "Very well. I'm just glad nothing was wrong. You had me worried there for a moment." He wandered off back towards the lake shore.

Zenton bent to pick up his cup. He stood with the cup in one hand and the little creature in the other, wondering how to pour himself some banellin. The animal solved the problem for him. It woke and clambered swiftly up his arm and onto his shoulder where it clung tenaciously to his jacket collar. Moving carefully, Zenton took a cloth from his pack to wrap around the jug's handle before filling his cup and setting the jug back down. Carrying his drink, he walked back to the small hillock where he'd been sitting and resumed his watch. Once he was seated, the furry creature settled itself down against his neck for an extended nap and barely stirred again for the rest of his turn of night duty. So quiet and still did it remain that he had all but forgotten its presence until it sat up quite suddenly as Chandrane came to take over the watch.

"What is *that*?" asked Chandrane softly, staring at the small animal with its too-large round eyes and gently twitching ears.

Zenton laughed softly. "That's what Donar wanted to know." He lifted it from his shoulder and stroked the short, silky fur. "I don't know what it is. I found it – or it found me. I'd better set it free now."

"I suppose you'd better," Chandrane agreed. "It *is* a wild creature, after all. Not that it looks very wild right now. Go on," he urged as Zenton hesitated. "You need to get some rest."

Zenton put the little animal down at the base of a leafy bush. It sat staring up at him for a moment, indignant at being deposited on the grass. Chattering crossly, it turned its back on him and reached out to grab a large berry from a low branch. It stuffed the berry into its mouth and chewed contentedly, dark juice dribbling from the side of its mouth. Resisting the temptation to pick the delightful creature up again and take it with him, Zenton stifled a huge yawn and headed for his shelter.

Only when he came to reorganise his travel pack the following morning did he find his cloak brooch missing once more. A trail of tiny, smudged, sticky handprints gave testimony to the identity of the thief. Zenton counted the lost clasp a small price to pay for the brief friendship offered by the enchanting, mischievous animal.

By the time he joined the others for their early meal, Donar and Chandrane had related the encounter, leaving Zenton little to add. He decided against mentioning the pilfered item. His night visitor was welcome to its stolen treasure.

Hoping the little creature might still be near the campsite, he wandered around looking for it before the day's search began. Disappointed to find no sign of it, he ambled down to the lake shore where his cousin was standing staring out across the water, much as Donar had stood the night before. There was rigidity in Brandell's stance, a tension unusual in the young man who tended towards a casual and relaxed attitude, and Zenton hesitated, wondering what was wrong.

His cousin turned as he approached. "I heard about your new furry friend. Sorry I missed all the excitement. Have you sketched it yet? I'd be interested to see what it looked like."

"No, I'll draw it later when I've more time. I'd like to see it in daylight really, but I can't find it now. It's probably nocturnal."

Brandell nodded and turned towards the travel shelters. "Come on, let's get packed and moving."

"Brandell?"

Brandell halted. "What?"

"Is everything all right?"

"Why shouldn't it be?"

"I just thought you looked as if something was bothering you."

Brandell shrugged. He plucked a thick stem of grass and chewed it briefly before throwing it down. "I slept badly," he said. "I woke when it was full dark, before I was due on watch, and came out of the shelter. There was a dense fog. I couldn't see more than an arm's length in front of my face. I thought I heard someone calling me. Then I woke and realised I'd been dreaming. The worst of it was that I *was* actually standing outside my shelter. I'd walked in my sleep and that's something I've never done before. This time it was really bright. All three moons were full."

Zenton was about to protest that the third moon had not been visible last night, and anyway, three full moons was such a rare occurrence that the whole search band would have been out watching them, but Brandell went on speaking. "I was going to find you to tell you about the moons and about my sleepwalking and then I woke up."

"But I thought you said –"

"Yes, but I mean I *really* woke, still in the shelter. Tegran was shaking me, saying it was my watch." He reached into his pocket for his leather thong, ran his hand through his hair and deftly tied it back off his face. "I never have dreams, not clear ones like you do. You know that. This dreaming that I was awake – twice! – has unsettled me a bit."

Before Zenton could respond, Brandell strode off towards the camp, calling back over his shoulder, "Come on, we'd better help the others. Not that I mind someone else doing my work for me, but Donar might object."

As on the previous day, the search band divided into two groups and set off to map the lake as far as they could in the time they had left before they must, by Renolth's command, turn back to the settlement. Tegran suggested leaving the travel shelters in place since

Donar had decided the group would once again reassemble at the same site by suns-set, but Zenton pointed out that any equipment left behind could attract the attention of wildlife possibly larger than the little nocturnal visitor and might be damaged by such animals. More importantly, in Zenton's opinion, an inquisitive creature could become entangled in shelter ropes or pack straps and might come to harm. In reluctant agreement, the searchers shouldered their full packs once more and set off, leaving little evidence of their overnight stay – except, thought Zenton wryly, a metal cloak brooch somewhere out there.

At times, when they needed to walk in single file, Donar led his small group, with Zenton following and Chandrane bringing up the rear. The terrain did not make for easy travelling but, with the first part of the route round the lake having been mapped the previous day, the searchers made reasonably good progress. Zenton found himself thinking about Brandell's recounting of his dream. The very fact that Brandell had discussed it at all gave evidence of how much it had disturbed him. He seldom spoke of personal matters, even to Zenton. It was probably, Zenton decided, the experience of remembering a dream as much as the actual content that had so unsettled his cousin.

Zenton himself often dreamt with startling clarity, and had done so for as long as he could recall. His first memory of a dream which had impinged upon reality went back to the time he was about five years old. Amryl, High King Lantor's youngest child, had gone missing. Zenton had dreamt that she'd wandered to the underground storerooms in the palace, following a brindled kitten, and had become trapped behind some fallen crates; and so it had proved to be. Amryl and the kitten were found and returned safely to their respective parents. More disturbingly, a half year before the first tremor had rocked the Homeland Isles, Zenton had dreamt of an earthquake followed by the spread of a dreadful illness.

Some time later, Zenton's vivid dream of The Island and the direction the Almari must sail to reach it had influenced Lantor's decision about sending an advance fleet to search for sanctuary. Zenton's 'sight' of the future seemed to have paid off on this occasion, but it still wasn't reliable enough for his liking. Nowadays

20

he seldom mentioned his dreams in case people read into them meanings they simply did not have.

He was just reviewing his nightmare about being pursued as he sought the safety of a particular cave when Chandrane came up beside him and began chatting. Soon afterwards the three searchers came to the end of their mapped route and began once more to note and record the details of their journey.

The rest of the morning passed well enough. Zenton found Chandrane easy company and the friendship which had begun aboard the *Tennel's Flight* seemed destined to continue now they were on land. Zenton was glad of the rapport between them. Brandell, with his ready wit and impetuous ways, gathered friends easily despite his quick temper. Zenton did not find it so simple.

"I doubt we're going to get much farther today," announced Donar, his words breaking into Zenton's musings. The group leader had ranged a short distance ahead of the two younger searchers and now came back to speak to them. "There's a river ahead, flowing east out of the lake."

Chandrane and Zenton followed him to the river's bank. "It's not particularly fast flowing," Chandrane pointed out. "We can probably find a way across."

Donar scratched at his beard, a habit of his when he was deep in thought. "Maybe we could," he said, "but it's mid-suns now and we'll have to turn back in an hour or so." He slid his pack off, dropped it down by his feet and flexed his shoulders. "All right," he decided, "we'll break here for some refreshment and then follow the river bank for a while. If there's no obvious crossing point, we'll look for any section where it might be possible to swim over. No!" he added, seeing Zenton and Chandrane's sudden enthusiasm. "I won't countenance a swim across without the back-up of a full search band. We've no idea of the currents or river creatures."

Reluctantly accepting Donar's decision, Chandrane and Zenton set down their packs and drew out food rations. Conscious of the two suns moving all too quickly across the cloud-dotted sky, the group ate hurriedly before resuming the search. Donar called a halt, however, before they had found either an easy way to ford the river or a place that looked suitable for a later attempt to swim across.

21

Disappointed though they were, neither Zenton nor Chandrane voiced any complaint. Three days out and then turn back. Renolth's word was law.

"You know," Chandrane told Zenton, "when we set off this morning, I had this feeling that we might make our way round to the other side of the lake and meet the other group more or less opposite our night's campsite. So much for feelings, huh?"

Zenton didn't answer. He was too busy trying to quell his own growing feeling that he was walking in the wrong direction. Finding their track narrowing again, he dropped back behind Donar and Chandrane.

Reaching the site where the river left its mother lake, Donar called a brief rest stop. Chandrane sat down on a conveniently flat boulder.

"Where's Zenton?" asked Donar.

Chandrane looked around. "He was following me a moment ago."

"He should have been in front of you!" Donar snapped. "Where *is* he?"

Chapter Five

The Lure of the Cave

Maglin, master cartographer, historian and teacher of the young, studied the map he had drawn on the large sheet of parchment spread out before him. Finding himself sucking the end of his writing implement he hastily withdrew it from his mouth and mentally chided himself for indulging in a habit he strongly discouraged in his pupils. His greying, straggly hair flopped over his face as he bent forward and he brushed it aside abstractedly, as if he were shooing away a persistent and irritating fly.

"Well?" demanded Renolth.

Maglin was not to be rushed. He peered at the open sketchpads spread out on a low, rough-hewn table to his left, then dipped his quillat into the small jar of ink and added a few careful lines to the map. He studied his handiwork for a moment, then rose from his stool and stepped carefully to one side. "See for yourself," he offered, relinquishing his place to the Almari leader.

"Well," Renolth said again, this time in a tone of consideration as he moved closer to the large table and stood looking down at the map. "The southern shore of the lake is curved; we know that for certain. A river enters from the west and one flows out from the east. The search band could see parts of the northern shore; you've drawn those in – and traced a fainter line where the shape is just conjecture."

"Go on," urged Maglin, impatient now at Renolth's apparent obtuseness.

"I don't see... Oh, yes. It looks like an enormous eye." He paused, then added lamely, "Very interesting."

"Yes," agreed the cartographer, oblivious to Renolth's lack of excitement. "It's the symmetry of it, is it not? When are the next searchers due back? And what about the *Waves of Oltan*? I really would like to make more progress with mapping our coastline." Finally noticing Renolth's preoccupation, he asked belatedly, "How is young Zenton?"

"He's with the healers at the moment, but he seems well enough."

"Has he said what happened?"

Renolth sat down on Maglin's vacated stool. "He says he doesn't know. He remembers standing on the river bank, about there, I think." Renolth jabbed his finger down on the map, causing Maglin to jerk forward, not to observe the location but to check there was no smudge on his precious chart.

Apparently unaware of the cartographer's momentary panic, Renolth continued, "He wanted to reach a cave which was due north, so he told me, and he found himself halfway across the river! He's quite a strong swimmer, as you know, but the current caught him and flung him against some rocks. Chandrane went in after him and brought him out."

"So he tried to swim across the river to reach this cave?"

"It would seem so, but he has no recollection of going into the water, only of hitting the rocks. When he realised where he was, he tried to turn back to the south bank. Then Chandrane reached him and helped him to swim back." Renolth stood up and pushed aside the stool. "He's got some spectacular bruises but Silmedd didn't think he'd broken any bones. You'll have to excuse me now, Maglin. I'm going to speak with the healers. I'll return when I can to see how your maps are progressing."

Maglin nodded. He waved a vague farewell as he resumed his seat near the parchment and pored over the sketchpads and large map once more.

Renolth left the shelter and headed across the encampment. He had much on his mind.

The encampment was gradually being transformed into a more permanent settlement. The banellin-bean plants were thriving and the young leaves of a native plant the settlers had called tengra made a pleasant brew. Searchers had recently discovered a bush bearing berries which could be eaten fresh or crushed to make a delightful fruit drink and, possibly, a palatable wine. Although red acronny had failed to grow here, white acronny for bread had taken well, as had tarren. The *Horizon's Edge* crew had fast become expert at deep-sea fishing, providing regular supplies for the settlers. With these

24

achievements, food sources were increasing – but rationing was still necessary and probably would be for some time yet to come.

Thankful though he was for the successes, Renolth was tired. The Almari workers were competent but still sought his approval on almost every decision concerning farming, fishing and building. On his short walk to the small infirmary he had to stop five times to answer queries, discuss the progress of some new shelters and listen to suggestions for further improvements to living conditions in the settlement.

Finally nearing the healers' shelter, he reflected on how fortunate it was for the community that Silmedd and Vemran were amongst the survivors who had reached this new land, for the three other healers who had set out with the small fleet had themselves succumbed to the plague two weeks into the voyage. Silmedd – young, tall and softly-spoken – was quite possibly the most intuitive healer Renolth had ever known. It was, in all likelihood, Silmedd who would be able to determine which of the native plants and fungi could be used for medicinal purposes. Vemran was older, shorter, rather brusque and at times almost intimidating in his manner. Nevertheless, he had the gift of instilling confidence in his patients. Rather surprisingly, considering his general demeanour, he was an excellent instructor and had already begun to train two young people who had shown an aptitude for healing.

Zenton had left the shelter by the time Renolth arrived. The Almari leader took the seat and the banellin offered by Vemran and listened with considerable relief as the healers confirmed their initial impressions that Zenton was not badly hurt and that he would recover quickly. They could not, however, give any explanation for his actions, nor for his brief memory loss. Gratefully accepting the fact that Zenton had taken no serious harm, but still concerned about what had happened, Renolth left his drink half-finished and went in search of his son.

On leaving the healer's shelter, Zenton had made his way to the fringe of the settlement and found a secluded spot amongst the high dunes overlooking the glistening waters of the harbour. He sat for a while, staring out towards the northern region his search band had so recently been exploring. His right side and shoulder were still sore from his collision with the rocks in the river but the worst of the pain and stiffness had eased off during the walk back from the lake and his grazes were healing cleanly. Despite the river incident, he wasn't unduly bothered about his own safety. He *was* worried that his father might forbid him to travel out again on future searches.

Taking hold of the thin chain around his neck, he drew out his medallion and ran his thumb over the raised engraving of a dragon curled round a glittering gemstone. Renolth had given it to him on the fourteenth anniversary of his birth, just hours before they had found the way into the harbour.

The emblem of the Royal House of Almar was a dragon in flight but Renolth had chosen a dragon in a different pose on the medallion and Zenton thought that, despite the supposed ferocity of dragons, this one had a quality of serenity about it, as if it had either just awoken from a peaceful sleep or was about to settle to slumber. He'd been told there had once been dragons on the Homeland Isles but they had vanished long ago. Certainly there was no record of them being seen for five or six generations past. After such a time, reality and folk tales had become so intertwined it was hard to be sure if the dragons were myth or fact. Zenton preferred to accept that they had indeed existed. He hoped someone would eventually find irrefutable proof that they had lived.

Replacing the medallion inside his shirt, he stood up. It was time he returned to the settlement. Renolth would doubtless be looking for him by now and Zenton had no wish to cause his father any further anxiety.

Delayed once again by seemingly endless queries and greetings, the Almari leader had barely begun to try to find Zenton when Merret and Lissanne came dashing towards him.

"Prince Renolth..." Merret was fighting for breath, desperate to give his information. He leaned forward, hands on thighs, head down, drawing in great gulps of air.

Lissanne had been in no better state when the two of them had skidded to a halt by Renolth but she recovered more quickly than her companion. "There's something – or someone – coming across the grasslands towards the encampment," she informed the prince.

Merret straightened up. "Actually, it's a *lot* of somethings or someones," he corrected, "and they're moving fast."

Concealing his shock and the sudden surge of fear which coursed through him, Renolth nodded acknowledgement of their news. "Lissanne," he ordered, "find Slen. He's in the training field. Tell him to bring everyone who can bear weapons and form a line on the southern boundary of the settlement. Then go and sound the Defence Bell." As Lissanne sped off, he turned to Merret. "How much time do we have?"

Merret shrugged. "I'm not sure. Maybe a quarter-hour. Probably less."

"Right. Find Irvanyal – No, wait. She's out on a search. Find Donar, Tegran and Lirreth. Last time I saw them they were on their way to see Maglin. Bring them, and Maglin as well, to me at the southern boundary near the healers' shelter. I'd rather negotiate than fight – if we get that option."

Merret hurried away and Renolth set off quickly towards the appointed meeting place, scanning faces as he passed, hoping to find Zenton and Brandell. He reached the healers' shelter, without having caught sight of his son or nephew, just as the Defence Bell's warning tones rang out across the encampment. There was immediate consternation amongst the settlers but, much to Renolth's relief and satisfaction, no sign of panic. People reacted quickly, moving in the way they had rehearsed once each week since the landing, taking up their stations and waiting anxiously to find out if this sounding signalled an unexpected drill or true danger.

Within a short space of time the Almari were as ready as they could be to face any threat. Slen, sword in hand, stood at Renolth's side, with his small fighting force strung out in an all-too-thin defence line ready to offer what protection they could to the settlers. Renolth saw that Brandell and Zenton had arrived where they were supposed to be, some distance from him and from each other, with Brandell flanked by Merret and a young swordsman called Traggarin, and Zenton by Chandrane and Lissanne. Renolth had no chance to take further stock of anyone's position for a deep rumbling, drumming sound could be heard in the distance. The ground seemed to tremble slightly and Renolth saw those around him turn pale. For one sickening moment he thought an earth tremor was shaking this new land. There was a growing thundering noise, a pounding that shook the ground, and a great, billowing cloud of dust headed straight for the settlement.

Chapter Six

Encounters with Tamans

Renolth was proud of his people. Frightened they might be but no one moved from his or her appointed position. The archers calmly strung their bows, nocked arrows to strings, and waited for Renolth's signal.

The noise grew louder and then, quite suddenly, died away to a faint reverberation. For a full minute the dust cloud rolled on towards the settlers before it, too, died away, sinking gradually to the dry ground whence it had come. There was a gasp from the watching Almari. A few people laughed quietly, nervously. Signalling those around him to remain where they were, Renolth took two paces forward and then stood still, and the whole tableau froze for several long moments.

There was no army confronting the newcomers to the land, no hostile native people, no fearful monsters. As the grey-brown dust cleared and settled, the Almari gazed in wonder and admiration at a herd of magnificent, glossy-coated animals. There were at least sixty of the creatures, perhaps even as many as a hundred, stamping now and snorting, tossing heads and whisking long tails as they regarded those who had come to live in this fertile land. The animals were large quadrupeds, with shaggy manes and sturdy hooves. Even the youngsters in the herd looked hardy and powerful. They bore a strong resemblance to amans – the Homeland Isle mounts, except for one striking difference: these animals had horns that glinted in the light of the two suns.

"Tamans," Zenton whispered.

Chandrane glanced at him. "What?"

"Tamans. Old Language. *Tam* – horned. *Amans* – mounts. You combine the words. Look, they're going now."

Apparently satisfied by the inspection they had made, the animals lifted their heads as if at a given signal then wheeled around and trotted away, leaving behind another cloud of dust and a stunned group of Almari.

Unsurprisingly, little work was done in the encampment for the rest of that day and, quite naturally, the main topic of conversation was the encounter with the herd.

Renolth sent trackers out but the animals moved swiftly and those tracking them returned some hours later to report that the herd could not be found. Though the grassland where the animals had gathered – just south of the encampment – had been thoroughly trampled, some of the tough vegetation was already springing back into place, hiding the prints of the thundering hooves. Amazingly, and whether it was by design or sheer good fortune was the cause of much speculation in the settlement, the areas newly planted with seed crops brought from the Homeland had suffered no damage at all. The herd animals had apparently swerved aside to avoid the sown ground.

Zenton stoutly maintained that the herd's avoidance of the cultivated areas was a deliberate act, and Chandrane concurred. Brandell and Merret took the opposing view. With emotions running high after the earlier scare, a heated discussion ensued. Zenton found an unexpected ally in the taciturn and normally pessimistic Lissanne. After listening to the debate for some minutes, she declared matter-of-factly, "They were headed straight for those fields. They turned on purpose." She walked away, her calmly delivered statement effectively ending the argument.

That night, several hours after the Smaller Sun had set, Zenton woke quite suddenly from a sound sleep. Though he was physically still tired, his mind was racing and he tried in vain to go back to sleep. The evening had been quite cool and a stiff breeze toyed with the shelter but Zenton felt stifled by the air around him. He rose, dressed and left the shelter, fastening a cloak around his shoulders as he wandered through the quiet settlement.

The patrolling guards were there to alert the encampment to any threat from outside. It was not their purpose to question anyone walking around at night, or to prevent anyone from leaving should they so wish. Nevertheless, Zenton avoided those on duty. He did not wish to become engaged in conversation, nor did he want the company and protection they would undoubtedly feel obliged to offer should they see him. Pulling his cloak a little tighter against the chilly wind, he headed past the healers' shelter where glowing lamplight indicated that Vemran or Silmedd was still up tending a patient or engaged in research.

Turning southwards onto the grasslands, Zenton left behind the slumbering encampment. Two moons were not far past full and the third was a pale orange crescent but fitful clouds scudding across the sky intermittently obscured their light. However, Zenton found little difficulty in walking on the uneven ground for his night vision, always good, seemed to have improved further since coming to the new land. He smiled slightly as he negotiated some low, sprawling bushes. He decided there and then against saying anything to Brandell unless his cousin actually noticed the increased ability. Brandell would doubtless make some cutting remark about light eyes and night sight, and Zenton was sick of never having a ready reply. It was hardly his fault his eyes were a strange shade: grey-violet and paler than usual for any Almari. Why couldn't they be like Brandell's – the gold-flecked brown usual in Almari royals?

When the fires and lamps of the settlement were faint sparks in the distance, Zenton stopped and stared out into the darkness, wondering what had drawn him out here. Unlike his experience at the river, he had a clear memory of all his movements since waking but he knew he'd been drawn here in a way similar to that in which he'd been compelled to seek the cave in the northern region. Comparing his feelings then and now, he sensed an excitement, a strange sort of rightness in being out this night, a need to be here but without the terrible, consuming urgency which had assailed him on the river bank just before he'd ceased to be aware of his own actions.

For about a quarter-hour he stood waiting, growing gradually more chilled as the wind stole the warmth from his body. He was about to give up and return to the encampment when he heard the sound of heavy hooves cantering towards him. Out of the darkness came one of the tamans.

Entranced, and only a little afraid, Zenton held his ground as the dark, glossy-coated creature slowed its pace to a purposeful walk and then came to a halt just an arm's reach from him. It was a young animal, not a foal but still smaller than most of those he had seen by the settlement. Its horns were fully-formed, though: one above the other on its forehead. They pointed forwards, wider at the base and

31

narrowing towards the tip. The upper horn was almost the length of Zenton's forearm and the lower just the length of his hand from wrist to fingertips.

For a full minute, prince and animal regarded each other and it seemed neither was quite sure what to do next. Then Zenton tentatively reached out his hand. Though he'd moved slowly, the creature danced away, snorting and tossing its head. It trotted in a full circle around the prince before standing once more in front of him. This time Zenton remained still and it was the animal that moved forward, its nostrils flaring as it snuffed at the prince's hair and clothes before nudging him sharply on the shoulder. His gasp of pain as his bruises protested at the rough touch caused the animal to shy briefly.

"Calm down," Zenton murmured, his own fear gone now. "I didn't mean to scare you." He reached up once again and this time managed to stroke the creature's velvety muzzle. At that instant the light of the moons and stars were blotted out and the land was plunged into blackness. The ground trembled and Zenton froze, petrified.

Within the space of a few heartbeats the night was as it had been, with glittering stars and bright moons visible through thinning high cloud. Zenton was still standing, arm outstretched, touching the creature's soft nose. It tolerated his touch for a moment or two before backing away and stamping a large fore-hoof. Then it turned and trotted off into the night.

Zenton sat down, his mind in turmoil. What was happening to him? He found he was fiddling nervously with his medallion and hastily stuffed it back beneath his tunic.

As his heart stopped pounding and his breathing calmed to a normal rate, he began to think more rationally. There was a reasonable explanation for everything that had occurred. The young animal had seemed unaffected by darkness or tremors, so it must be his imagination playing tricks on him. After all, there had been no unusual incident when he'd held the small nocturnal creature that had raided his travel pack, had there? As for his unexpected swim across that river – well, the earlier nightmare in which he'd needed to find the cave must have been preying on his mind more than he'd realised. He had simply not been thinking clearly when he'd entered the water. Hadn't he been told often enough in the past, not least by Maglin, to stop daydreaming and concentrate on what he should be doing? And that voice telling him to find the cave? More imagination. He must just have caught a snatch of someone's conversation.

Convincing himself he had solved all the mysteries, Zenton rose and stretched. The night suddenly felt strangely empty without the companionship of the large animal and he needed the security of the settlement. He turned and retraced his steps to the encampment. Once there, he headed for one of the night-fires and helped himself to a warming drink of banellin. Not yet ready to return to his shelter, he sat down by the fire, sipping the hot liquid.

Realising he was no longer alone, he said, "You're up late, Brandell. Do you want some banellin?"

Brandell sighed loudly and sat down by his cousin. He spat out the grass stem he'd been chewing. "You knew I was there without even turning round," he accused.

Zenton shrugged. "I heard you coming."

"Nonsense," Brandell countered. "I came up quietly. You've developed Renolth's trick of knowing who's near you before you see them!"

Zenton poured some banellin into a second cup and handed it to Brandell. "You have that ability too," he pointed out.

"Yes, and I've always been far better at it than you – until now. You're growing up, little cousin." Brandell took the offered cup. "I'm out here because I volunteered to take a turn at night duty," he said, changing the subject. "What's your excuse?"

"I didn't realise I needed one," Zenton retorted.

Brandell laughed. "I suppose you don't," he agreed, "but it's very late, or very early depending upon which way you choose to look at it. Are you all right?"

"Yes. I just woke and couldn't get back to sleep, so I went for a walk."

"And?"

"And nothing. I just went for a walk, that's all."

"Fine," said Brandell without rancour. "Keep it to yourself if you want. Just remember I'm here if you need to talk about anything." He stood up. "Now, I'd better show willing and wander round the settlement. Try to get some sleep if you can. That dip in the river didn't do you a lot of good, you know."

Zenton smiled ruefully. "The river was all right. The rocks were the problem." He too, stood, nodded farewell to his cousin and, drink in hand, wandered away.

Nearing his shelter, Zenton paused, pondering the fact that he'd not mentioned the animal on the grasslands. Perhaps, he thought, it was just that he wanted to savour the experience, to keep it to himself for a while before sharing it. Still, it was the first time he could remember ever deliberately keeping something important from Brandell.

Chapter Seven

Safe Harbour, Hidden Knowledge

"I'd like one more attempt before we abandon the search."
Renolth leaned back in his seat and considered Valdrak's statement. Captain of the *Waves of Oltan*, Valdrak had faced the hazards of the voyage from the Homeland Isles with care for his ship, crew and passengers and without any complaint about the dangers of the journey. He was courageous, efficient and experienced but Renolth hesitated, unwilling to sanction another voyage that would risk the lives of Valdrak and his crew yet again.

"I've read your latest report," said Renolth, "but I'd like you to bring the others up to date if you will, Valdrak. Tell us about the charting voyages and then explain the search problems."

The captain looked momentarily panic stricken. He turned to Renolth for deliverance but the prince showed no mercy. "Go ahead," he urged.

"Well," Valdrak began, tugging at his bushy, greying beard, "charting the northern coastline was pretty straightforward. We just had to keep far enough from the land to avoid being driven onto the rocks by the rough waters, near the reef in particular, but there were no real problems."

Renolth, and some of the others gathered in the newly completed meeting hall, smiled slightly at Valdrak's description of the sailing being 'straightforward'. To say that the seas were rough was, according to most of Valdrak's crew, a gross understatement. Even when the wind strength was light to moderate, pounding breakers crashed against the jagged, rocky shoreline and fierce, ripping currents threatened to wrest control of the sturdiest ship from its battling crew.

"Sailing the east and west coasts was easier," Valdrak continued, "so I reckon our charts are pretty good there." He paused to take a deep breath and then ploughed on. "We had the most difficulty with the southern land-line, only managing to sail around there once, but, as I've reported to Prince Renolth, we have determined that our new homeland *is* an island, and on none of our voyages did we see any sign of habitation."

"Our legends tell of The Island that awaits the Almari," Maglin said, standing and slipping into the tone he used when lecturing a group of his students. Though everyone in the meeting hall knew the traditional stories well, Maglin was an excellent speaker and no one minded hearing them again. "The legends say that The Island is beautiful, fertile and welcoming to those who have a right to seek its sanctuary. The legends are wondrous, but most people were settled and content in the Homeland Isles and The Island remained a distant dream, a faint longing. Few indeed left the Isles in search of this dream. Fewer still returned, and those had sought in vain."

"Few indeed," repeated Irvanyal quietly from her seat at the side of the hall, "but are we the ones who have found it?"

"Perhaps, Irvanyal," said Maglin. "Perhaps we have."

Renolth did not stand to speak, nor did he raise his voice, but his words carried clearly across the suddenly silent meeting hall. "Whatever the truth of the matter – and time, no doubt, will let us discover that truth – this land *is* beautiful and fertile, and it has welcomed us. We must repay it by living here in harmony with the land and its wildlife, and with each other."

He saw his words hit home with some of his listeners; a few people stared at the ground or shuffled uneasily. For the most part the displaced Almari had worked well together as they settled their new land but just lately some petty quarrels had marred the unity of the group.

Renolth allowed for a few moments of quiet thought before he requested Valdrak to complete his interrupted report.

The captain pulled at his beard again, smoothed the ends of his curling moustache and cleared his throat. "We still need to sail the waters around this island many more times to chart the sea currents and learn the prevailing winds, and to improve our coastline maps. As far as we could tell, there is no other landing site anywhere around the island. Had Prince Zenton not spotted the harbour entrance for us, we could not have made landfall."

At the back of the hall, Brandell nudged his cousin and whispered a teasing comment about light eyes having their uses after all. Zenton pointedly ignored him.

"I have suggested to Prince Renolth that Kaldrina takes the *Horizon's Edge* to confirm our findings and complete the charting," Valdrak continued. "Both her crew and mine should become familiar with the waters around us. At some stage in the near future though, I'd like another attempt to search south and west for any lands near us. We know from our voyage here that there is no land within a month's sailing to the east, and you'll remember that the *Star's Reach* was blown off course to the north for a week or so before rejoining our fleet so we're pretty sure we have no near neighbours in that direction either. The south and west need further exploration."

Renolth frowned. "You've made five attempts in the past eleven months, Valdrak," he said. "You reported treacherous whirlpools and reefs off to the west. And, on all but that first occasion, you've been forced back by unusually sudden and violent storms whenever you've tried to sail the southern coastline. Localised storms which were felt neither here in the settlement nor by the *Horizon*'s crew out deep-sea fishing. I'm not inclined to sanction further voyages at this time. It's too risky."

Valdrak nodded acceptance of the decision. He sat down heavily and gave his beard some respite from being abused.

Maglin moved to stand near the large map he had fastened to a board at the front of the hall. "With Renolth's permission," he said, "I'd like to summarise what we know of our island." Without waiting to see if he was granted that permission, the cartographer straightened his rather rumpled jacket and launched into his summary.

"The coastline has been charted roughly, giving us the basic shape of the land. The harbour, with its almost concealed entrance, gives us the only calm water area and landing site. We know the harbour region, Patoll, pretty well now. There are extensive grasslands to the south and dense forests to the east. The Eye Lake in the northern region of Mandano has been fully charted. A main river enters to the west of the Eye Lake and leaves its eastern side, flowing eventually down a huge waterfall to enter the sea near the harbour entrance. This is the cataract we saw when we first found our way in to safe water."

Maglin could probably have expounded for some time on the known geography of the land but, as he paused for breath, Renolth stood up, not quite interrupting the master cartographer but effectively taking control of the meeting. "My thanks to Maglin and to Valdrak," said Renolth. "It seems clear that this is a land of many wonders and of some intriguing mysteries. Still, the Almari have never shied from a challenge. We'll continue to remake our lives here in the settlement and to explore our new homeland."

The questions and discussions which followed Renolth's short speech lasted until Oltan's set when the prince called a halt to the meeting. The hall emptied gradually, finally leaving Renolth sitting quietly pondering the discussions and Maglin carefully sorting his maps and charts.

"Your son chose well with the names *Patoll* and *Mandano*," Maglin commented.

Renolth looked up. "*Safe Harbour* and *Hidden Secrets*. I'm pleased the vote went in favour of those suggestions."

"Actually, *Mandano* is more accurately translated as 'hidden knowledge' or, to be precise, 'knowledge hidden'," said Maglin.

Renolth laughed. "I stand corrected."

The cartographer rolled the last of his charts and came to sit beside the prince. "I welcome the use of the Old Language. It seems appropriate here somehow." He placed the chart carefully on his lap. "Zenton has quite a good command of the Old Tongue, you know. There were few enough of us who could still speak it in the Homeland. There are less here now. You've done well to maintain his interest."

Renolth shrugged. "I just encourage him when I can. It was Ardelle who taught him and gave him his love of learning – with your help of course, old friend."

"Your lovely wife was a talented linguist and a gifted artist." Maglin placed a hand gently on the prince's arm. "You must still feel her loss deeply."

"Every day, Maglin," Renolth replied softly. "Every day." He rose abruptly and left Maglin alone in the meeting hall.

Chapter Eight

Temptation

Leaning against a tree, Brandell drummed his fingers impatiently on his thigh as he watched Merret rearranging Halden's travel pack. The prince sighed inwardly and closed his mouth on a critical comment. Halden was a man grown, accepted as adult well over a year ago. Merret fussed too much – and Halden let him. Brandell chewed thoughtfully at his lower lip as he waited. He supposed it was understandable really, since Halden had nearly died of the plague back in the Homeland. He *had* recovered though – one of the few people to do so – and he certainly looked to Brandell to be strong and healthy; quite healthy enough to sort out his own pack.

Brandell pushed off from the tree. "Let's move on," he said, signalling to Drent to take the lead and thinking as he did so that Drent was not much older than Halden but was certainly more mature in his attitude.

The going was easier than it had been during the morning, the undergrowth less dense and the trees spread a little more thinly. The search group would have to turn back soon but Brandell still wanted to know what had made the prints near their campsite last night and Drent was proving an able tracker.

The forest around them was alive with sound and colour. Birds sang and shrieked high in the branches, some peeking down cheekily at the search band, others flitting away with chirps of protest at the disturbance. Now and again the search team caught glimpses of arboreal creatures clambering aloft or swinging nonchalantly from tree to tree. Furtive rustles sounded often in the shrubbery and the barks and whistles of larger creatures could sometimes be heard.

Brandell thought it strange that none of the forest creatures ventured close. They could never have encountered people before. Why should they fear this small group of explorers? He scratched at an insect bite on his neck. He had no objection to the birds and animals but he bore a strong resentment towards insects that bit or stung.

Drent stopped abruptly and hunkered down to study something. Brandell narrowly avoided tripping over him.

"I wish you'd warn me before doing that," the prince complained mildly.

He waited with more patience this time, using the halt to check that the others were keeping up. He could not see Lirreth at the rear of the group but she was reliable enough and wouldn't be far away. Merret and Halden were just behind Chandrane.

Drent reached out and tapped Brandell's leg to gain his attention. "More prints," he said, gesturing to some indentations in a small patch of mud beneath a huge, yellow-leafed tree.

Brandell crouched down by him. "What made them?"

Drent shrugged. "You asked me that before and I still don't know. Could be feline or canine. Your guess is as good as mine. They look pretty recent though so we're probably on the right track."

"Whatever it is, it's big and has claws," observed Chandrane, peering over the prince's shoulder.

Brandell grinned up at him. "Scared?"

Chandrane grinned back. "Yes."

"Well," said Brandell, straightening up, "you'll be pleased to know we're unlikely to find 'whatever-it-is'. We only have about another half-hour or so before we'll have to turn back." He eyed Chandrane speculatively. "You *have* been noting our route, have you not?"

Chandrane looked aghast. "Er... I... I thought Lirreth was doing it."

Brandell's temper flared. He'd learnt quickly in his two previous visits to the forest that it was all too easy to become lost here if you were careless. Chandrane had been on search here before too; he should know better. "No, Chandrane. I asked *you* to do it today."

Chandrane paused, then with a flourish lifted a detailed sketch from the top of his pack. "Now you come to mention it..." With a swordsman's reflexes, he swayed aside to avoid the blow Brandell aimed at him.

Brandell's temper cooled as quickly as it had risen and he laughed. "You almost had me believing you there," he admitted.

Ostentatiously rubbing the side of his jaw where Brandell's fist had so nearly made contact, Chandrane said lightly, "And you almost knocked me cold. I thought royalty had others do their fighting for them."

Brandell's expression hardened and the atmosphere became tense. Then he laughed again and the tension eased. "I prefer the personal touch," he said. "However, I think I may need a little more practice if you can dodge me that easily. Come on, my intrepid little band. Let's see if we can track down our night visitor before we head back."

The 'whatever-it-is' eluded the search team with consummate ease. Noting the changing angle of the suns' rays through the dense forest canopy, Brandell conceded defeat and the group retraced their route, using Chandrane's sketch, to camp at the same site they had used the previous night. It was Halden's turn to prepare the meal but Brandell noticed without much surprise that Merret did most of the work. Still, Brandell cared little who cooked so long as the food was sufficiently palatable.

Hunger and thirst satisfied, the prince strolled across the small clearing to join Lirreth. Older and calmly self-sufficient, she had been assigned to the group by Renolth. Brandell had chosen the other band members and had not particularly wanted Lirreth but, as always, Renolth had the final say. He required more details about plants and animals in addition to search routes, and Lirreth had been sent along because of her skills as an artist. Chandrane was more than competent when it came to sketching though, and Brandell had thought his inclusion sufficient. Still he had to admit to himself that Lirreth had been an asset rather than a hindrance and he quite enjoyed her company and dry wit.

"What's that you've found?" he asked, seeing her studying a small, black and yellow striped lizard clinging to a low branch.

"I think it's a different 'whatever-it-is'."

Brandell chuckled. "At least Chandrane shouldn't be scared of this one." The little lizard twitched its tail and hissed, opening long, pointed jaws to display tiny but viciously sharp teeth. "On the other hand..." amended Brandell, backing away.

Lirreth smiled. "It seemed friendly enough a minute ago," she said. "Perhaps it's overawed by your royal presence."

Brandell snorted in irritation. What was it about this search that was causing him to suffer so much teasing about his rank? He chose not to dignify the jest by responding. Informality was all well and good, until it was taken too far.

"You have first watch, do you not?" he asked, a little more curtly than he had intended.

Lirreth nodded. "Indeed I do, Prince Brandell."

His tone had obviously not gone unnoticed. Briefly, he regretted the sudden loss of the shared companionship that had existed a few moments ago. He shrugged off the feeling. It did no harm to give the occasional reminder of his status – such as it was these days.

He felt a disquieting pang of homesickness, a longing for the luxury and security of the royal palace in the time before the earthquakes. He quelled the urge to dwell on the past. At least conditions here were improving. To say that the first few months had been hard would be an understatement. Most people had needed to learn new skills and tackle unfamiliar jobs but it had seemed wrong to Brandell to see Renolth, Almari leader and brother to the High King, labouring alongside former servants to build shelters or plant crops. Brandell had done his share of manual work but he much preferred exploring. Nowadays Renolth was more involved with administrative tasks: a sign, perhaps, that some semblance of normality was at last beginning to return to their lives.

Leaving Lirreth to commune with the ill-tempered lizard, Brandell went to his sleeping mat. The warm, dry weather meant they had no need to erect travel shelters, and leaves dropped onto the campfire caused enough smoke to provide some protection from insects that wanted a handy meal of blood. Brandell slipped off his jacket and boots, rolled himself in his blanket and lay down. Tired though he was from travelling, sleep did not come easily. Exciting and intriguing by day, the forest took on a more sinister aspect as night descended. The moons' light etched strange silvery patterns on swaying leaves and branches and cast weird shadows that moved as if with a life of their own. In places where tree branches interlocked like giant clasping hands the light was shut out completely, leaving areas of utter blackness. The sounds changed too; peculiar howls, grunts and screeches and the ever-present hum of night insects set Brandell's nerves on edge. He would rather have the northern region with that huge lake or the grasslands south of the harbour, vast open spaces with plenty of sky.

He was not aware of having fallen asleep until a voice woke him.

There's something you should see.

Brandell sat up slowly. He had no idea how long he had slept but his companions had settled for the night. Some sleeping shapes were visible in the flickering firelight. He could not see who was on watch, nor could he tell who had spoken. Mystified and somewhat annoyed, he stood up and pulled on his boots. A movement at the edge of the encampment drew his attention and he wandered towards it, finding as he did so that the side of the clearing to which he was heading seemed to be growing brighter, as if dawn was breaking there but nowhere else. The light had a strange quality about it: hazy and faintly greenish. Brandell hesitated, puzzled and wary. The forest was worryingly silent.

It's just over here.

Like the light, the voice was odd. Brandell found it hard to put into words how it sounded but it made his skin crawl. Nonetheless, the mystery intrigued him so he took a step forward. Ahead of him in a dense thicket the green glow shimmered and coalesced into a vague, disturbing shape which he could not quite identify.

You're standing by it now.

The voice had come from the green shape. Brandell halted.

Look down.

Brandell obeyed. At his feet was what appeared at first to be just a chunk of wood. Closer examination showed it was a rough carving. Its form was familiar and after a moment's thought he realised that it reminded him of Zenton's medallion – the one with the raised image of the sleeping dragon.

Take it.

Brandell bent and reached out a hand, then changed his mind and straightened up. There was something tantalising about the idea of picking up the wood, of taking it and making it his, but he'd felt quite sick when he'd bent down and the momentary queasiness had unsettled him.

Take it.

Brandell shook his head. "No."

There will come a day when you will want to do so.

"I don't know what you mean," said the prince, turning and trying to make out the figure shrouded in the peculiar light.

The green glow shimmered and vanished.

"Brandell?"

Someone was shaking him awake. He looked up to see Chandrane kneeling by him. Thoroughly confused, Brandell sat up.

"Are you all right?" asked Chandrane. "It's way past Oltan's dawn and you said you wanted an early start."

Brandell ran his hand over his face. The clearing was bright with the First Sun's rays. Lirreth and Drent were serving morning rations. The forest creatures were calling and singing to greet the day. Two scarlet sail-wings were dancing together at the edge of the clearing.

"I'm fine," he lied, and watched as Chandrane walked away.

Taking a few deep breaths to dispel the lingering heaviness in his head, Brandell rose slowly. He had been dreaming, of course. He swore softly and viciously. How he hated dreaming. It had been so vivid, too; he'd been sure he'd actually woken and seen that strange light across the clearing. He stared at the bustling campsite, reassuring himself that he was truly awake this time. It was morning. There was no green glow and no harsh, whispering voice. Everything was as it should be.

Only when he tried to find his boots did he realise he was already wearing them.

Chapter Nine

Devastation

Alone in the storeroom, Amryl smiled as an image from the past came vividly to her mind. This was where Zenton had found her. How old had she been? Certainly not more than three. Jerram said her memories of the incident were the product of imagination based on what she'd been told by others but Amryl disagreed. She could recall quite clearly how she had followed the kitten through the kitchen, past two servants sleeping by the banked fires of the great ovens, down the stairway, along the corridor and into the room where the cheeses were stored. She remembered the smell of the room. The almost overpowering odour of ripe cheese had assailed her nostrils as she had slipped through the open door. She had just picked up the kitten when some crates had become dislodged, trapping her and her furry armful. Too frightened to cry out, she had sat cradling the little animal for what had seemed forever until her cousin had come into the room and called her name.

They *were* her own memories; of that she was sure. She could not remember the kitten's name, or even its colour, but the smell of the few remaining cheeses here on the shelves brought the event back to mind in a fair degree of detail. She wondered if Zenton, himself only five at the time, remembered it too. He had wriggled through a gap under the crates, coaxed her out and then calmly helped himself to a small, round cheese from the then plentiful store before leading her out of the room. She'd never told anyone about the cheese in case one of the adults reprimanded him for taking without first asking.

She shook her head to dispel the gloom which threatened to settle over her. Zenton was still alive; he had to be – he and Brandell and Renolth and all the others. It had been so long, though. Surely they should have found The Island by now – or, if not The Island, *any* suitable land – and sent back a rescue party. Why were they taking so long?

A sudden tremor shook the building, sending dust and debris slithering from already damaged stonework.

"Not again," Amryl prayed quietly. "Light, please, not again."

Whether her plea was answered or it was just the natural course of events, the shaking of the walls ceased almost as soon as it had begun. The same could not be said of Amryl's limbs – which continued to tremble alarmingly. Drawing in a deep breath to calm herself, and coughing slightly in the dust-laden air, she forced her unwilling legs to carry her from the room, forgetting completely the cheese she'd meant to fetch. Closing the storeroom door behind her, and noticing in a somewhat absent way that it seemed a mite loose on its hinges, she hastened back along the passageway, climbed the narrow, stone stairs and stepped out into the huge kitchen where she stood for a while to regain her composure.

The silence of the kitchen did little to help. It seemed wrong for it to be so quiet, so deserted at this hour. Mallavette should be here, organising the evening meal, ordering everyone around with her usual mixture of firmness and praise. Amryl sighed, and coughed again. It was useless to wish for things to be as they once were, Jerram kept telling her. She knew he was right but she couldn't help it. She wanted Zenton and Brandell here with her. She wanted Mallavette back and she wanted the warmth and comfort of the kitchen fires and ovens. It was too dangerous now to have the roaring cook-fires. Fire spread all too quickly during an earthquake, even in a building as sturdy as the royal palace. Amryl sighed aloud. This kitchen used to ring with laughter. It was hard to recall the joy any more. Too many things had changed and too many people had, like Zenton, Brandell and now Mallavette, gone from her life.

"Amryl? Amryl, are you all right?"

For a fleeting moment she thought it was Brandell calling her, so like him did Darrant sound as he came running into the kitchen. Amryl dredged up a smile. "I'm fine," she assured him. "Is everyone else all right?"

Her brother nodded. "The quake was only slight. There wasn't any real damage this time. No one was hurt." He reached out and wiped a smudge of dirt from her face. "Did you find the cheese?"

"Oh! The cheese! No, I forgot. I'll go back and get it."

46

Darrant drew her gently away from the stairs. "I'll go. You have a look round here and find some plates. Feldrick's brought some bread for us."

"Feldrick?"

Darrant nodded again. "He and his wife used to work in the gardens, remember? He was short and somewhat rotund –"

"And his wife was tall and stately," finished Amryl. "Yes, I remember now. His wife died, did she not?"

"In the last quake, yes. He and some others have set up a small bakery near the well in the Old Quarter. Some of the buildings there are still relatively safe." He turned and headed down the stairs.

For a moment or two Amryl stood where she was, bitterness welling up inside her. It was all so unfair. Why did the earthquakes keep happening? Why did the plague continue to ravage an already destroyed land? Why had she recently spent the thirteenth anniversary of her birth cowering in an underground cellar with her family and their few remaining servants, sheltering from yet another tremor? She should have been celebrating with her friends. It was *so* unfair.

The thought of her friends brought her sharply out of her mood of self-pity. Two of her closest companions had died last month, in the quake that had claimed the life of Mallavette and many others, and only four days ago she had learned that Linnelli – bright, vivacious Linnelli, who had been more like a sister than a friend – had succumbed to the dreaded plague. What right had the favoured Princess Amryl to be feeling sorry for herself? At least her parents and brothers were alive and well, and she had a home which was habitable despite the earthquake damage. People from the towns and villages around the palace brought them what food they could spare (and, she suspected, sometimes *more* than they could spare) and servants still helped out where they could. She ought to be grateful and satisfied with what she had. Amryl's eyes filled with tears. She brushed them away with a dirty sleeve and went in search of plates.

Lantor sat down heavily in his favourite chair and gratefully sipped the drink his wife handed to him. "You look tired, Ryella," he observed in concern.

Ryella laughed. "That, my dear, is a case of the rip-tide calling the whirlpool rough."

The Almari High King smiled. "I suppose you're right," he admitted. He took a longer draught of the lightly spiced wine. "That tremor had me worried for a moment."

"It's strange, is it not?" Ryella said. "We've had almost four weeks without a quake. How quickly we forget the absolute terror."

Lantor's smile did not reach his eyes. "And how quickly we feel it again at the slightest earth movement."

Ryella nodded. "We do indeed. I saw Darrant and Amryl a short while ago. Where's Jerram?"

"I asked him to check on our ships and then make arrangements for a final sweep of the Isles."

"You've sent vessels and messengers out three times already," Ryella pointed out gently. "All who are going to come will be ready by now."

Lantor shrugged wearily. "I have to try one more time. Maybe some of the messengers will find people we missed in the inner villages."

"They'd all have made their way to the ports before this, would they not?" She poured a drink for herself and sat down near her husband. "There will be some who won't come, you know."

A deep sigh escaped Lantor's lips. "I know. They'll cling to the hope that things will improve, that everything will be back to normal again one day. They're wrong." He shifted position, trying to ease the bone-deep ache of fatigue. "I could order them to leave."

"That would be pointless, would it not? They're hardly likely to obey if they're bent on staying and we certainly don't have the resources to enforce such an order."

"True," agreed Lantor, stretching and leaning back in his chair. He fingered the ring on his left hand, twisting it round, surprised it still fit snugly despite his loss of weight. "The royal seal: symbol of the sovereign's authority," he murmured. "I should have given this to Renolth."

Ryella frowned. "Given it to Renolth? Why?"

"It embodies the royal family powers, does it not? Such as they are these days. Renolth stands a better chance of survival than we do. I should have given it to him."

48

"You sound as if you've given up hope, my love," Ryella chided gently. "That's not like you."

"Given up? Not entirely. Not yet, anyway. I just have this feeling the ring shouldn't be lost here. It needs to be in whatever new land Renolth finds."

Ryella smiled. "Oh, so you *do* think he'll find us a new homeland."

Lantor shrugged. "Maybe. At least I'm sure he's still alive."

Ryella set her drink down on the small table next to her chair. "Then shouldn't we wait a little longer? Just a week or two, perhaps."

"No." Tired though he was, Lantor's answer was quite definite. "I've waited too long already. We should have set sail weeks ago."

He had considered leading out the fleet two months ago but had opted to delay a while longer. The rescue ships, he had reasoned, must surely be on their way to lead the rest of the Almari to whatever safety Renolth had found. He had waited – and an offshore quake had sent yet another tidal wave, this one more powerful than any before, swamping ships out at sea, smashing vessels in the harbour against what was left of the jetties and sea walls and flooding a long stretch of the coastline. Fully half the pitifully small fleet – ships that had been saved from previous tidal waves and storms and made ready to set sail – had been sunk or damaged beyond repair. From a once proud armada, a mere fifteen deep-sea vessels remained. The tragedy of it was, Lantor thought bitterly, these would probably be more than enough to carry the survivors from all seven islands.

"If we delay further, we probably won't even need fifteen vessels."

Not until he saw Ryella's shocked expression did he realise he had spoken aloud. He grimaced and set his cup aside. The drink was palatable enough; it was the taste of despair that fouled his tongue.

Jerram leaned against the doorway in the limited shelter of a dilapidated building which had once been a thriving jewellers. He watched morosely as driving rain swept in from the sea. He was tired – tired of the earthquakes, the plague, the constant anxiety and, most of all, the waiting. His father should have given the order to leave weeks ago. What use was there in staying? Renolth would have sent help by now had he been able. How likely was it anyway that they would actually find the fabled Island? Jerram had believed in it once, when he was a child, but no longer. He wasn't even sure if he believed in the Light any more. How could a power for good allow such appalling suffering to come upon the people of the Homeland Isles? They weren't evil people, were they? Just ordinary mortals, some better than others, going about their ordinary lives. What was so wrong in that? It wasn't as if they were out to conquer other races. The Almari of old might have called down the wrath of the Light by their warlike ways, but that had been in ages past. They were traders now, or had been until the quakes had begun.

As if in response to his memories of the first earthquake, a tremor shuddered through the ground. He clutched at the nearest timber post for support. Regaining his balance, he moved prudently away from the building in case the thing collapsed on him. The ground steadied but he remained where he was. It was better to be wet than crushed.

"That was a short one."

The prince turned as two sea-captains approached. It was Gaveldi, the younger of the two, who had spoken. Small and wiry, with flaming red hair, Gaveldi was barely older than Jerram himself. Promotion came quickly in times such as these, the prince reflected. He chose not to comment on the brief quake, asking instead, "Why the delay, gentlemen?"

Harrilton, older than Gaveldi but not much more experienced, jerked a thumb towards the expanse of ocean. "The wind's changed," he pointed out.

"I had noticed," Jerram returned mildly. "I'd also noticed that Kessie organised row boats to take *her* vessel out of the harbour."

In a whispered aside which Jerram could hardly fail to hear, Gaveldi muttered to his colleague, "I did suggest that." He turned back to the prince. "You want us to do the same?"

Jerram smiled. "Yes. Another large quake and we'll have more ships wrecked against the harbour wall or the jetties. We'll bring them back in when everyone's ready to embark."

"Right you are, your highness. Come on then, Harrilton. Let's see which of us can clear the harbour first!"

50

His mood lightening as he watched the young men race off towards their ships, Jerram turned from the harbour and headed back towards the palace. It still felt strange, even after all these months, to be walking without an escort of guards. At first he'd enjoyed the freedom but now it seemed just another reminder of how everything had changed. Amryl was still escorted, of course, on those few occasions when she was allowed to leave the palace grounds, but both he and Darrant had too much to do to go in search of a palace guard or two every time they went out.

Darrant had grown up quickly, Jerram mused as he negotiated a pile of rubble. He'd had to, with all that had happened. What age was he now? Almost sixteen? It was difficult to keep track when birth anniversaries were no longer celebrated and sometimes not even remembered in the midst of the every-day struggle to survive. Jerram gave a short, humourless laugh as he realised somewhat belatedly that yesterday had been his own anniversary. He was twenty-two. He should have been travelling the Isles, meeting the rulers, learning to govern in preparation for when he became High King. Instead, here he was trudging alone up the steep street which led to Palace Way, picking his route around fallen buildings and pools of filthy water. At least they would be leaving soon. Three more days, that was what his father had decreed; three more days before they gave up on Renolth and set sail themselves. It couldn't come soon enough as far as Jerram was concerned. They should have left months ago.

Running footsteps behind him caused him to spin round, his hand dropping to the knife at his belt. This was one of those moments when the presence of guards would have been welcome.

"Prince Jerram! Prince Jerram!"

Jerram relaxed as he saw a young girl hastening towards him. She wore the red sash of a messenger, though surely she could not have been more than ten years old. The sash was torn and grubby, and the child's face and hands were none too clean either, despite the rain, but she straightened the cloth symbol of her job proudly as she drew to a halt.

"Prince Jerram," she gasped as he motioned for her to speak, "there are two ships at the harbour entrance!"

Jerram was not impressed. "Really? And you've been sent all this way to tell me that?" The child looked so deflated that Jerram felt the need to explain his curt reaction. "I've just sent two vessels out, messenger." The girl stood taller at the use of her job title. "I'm somewhat surprised they've made the entrance already, but then they *were* making a race of it."

"No, your highness. You don't understand. Two ships are coming *in*. Captain Gaveldi said to tell you they're from Prince Renolth's fleet!"

Chapter Ten

Departure

"What kept you?"

The High King's tone was mild and he smiled as he spoke but there was no doubting the underlying reproof. Having seen even in the short journey from harbour to palace that conditions in the capital city of Ashkantin had gone from merely desperate to utterly catastrophic in the time they had been away, Murl and Jedron stood in silence as they faced their monarch.

Rising from his chair, Lantor walked slowly forward and clasped Murl's hands in his own. It was several seconds before he could control his emotions sufficiently to be sure his voice would not falter and betray him. "Welcome, old friend," he said. Releasing the captain's hands, he stepped back. "Your presence must surely mean the Light has not abandoned us entirely. What news have you?"

There was a note almost of pleading in the question and Murl took a moment to overcome his shock. Lantor appeared to have aged ten years or more. His dark hair was greying, lines of strain and fatigue were etched into his face and his gold-flecked brown eyes were shadowed and haunted. He was, as ever, neatly dressed, but he had forgone state robes and embroidered garments in favour of a plain, dark-green shirt with black trousers and jacket. The only evidence of his rank was the exquisitely crafted ring on the middle finger of his left hand: the royal seal with the Almari monarch's emblem of a dragon in flight.

"I'm neglecting my duties as host," said Lantor, mistaking Murl's hesitation for weariness or hunger. "Come, sit with me and tell me all your tidings while refreshment is brought for you." He nodded to Darrant to find one of the servants.

"Finding a servant will be a great deal easier than finding enough fresh food for guests," Darrant muttered to Amryl as he passed her on his way from the room.

"Have you found The Island?" Amryl burst out.

No reprimand was forthcoming for her speaking without invitation in a meeting.

"I don't know, Lady Amryl," Murl said honestly. "We *have* found a land. A good land for our people." He paused at the intake of breath from his listeners. "Whether or not it *is* The Island I cannot say, although Prince Zenton believes it to be so."

Darrant returned then and echoed his sister's question. Murl was about to repeat his answer but at Lantor's insistence he waited until bread, cheese, apples and wine had been served. Lantor thanked the servant and gestured for the two captains to help themselves. Neither had the chance to take more than a few much needed sips of wine, however, before the questions began again.

"What *did* keep you so long?" Jerram wanted to know. "It's been over a year and a half, Captain Murl."

"That I know all too well, Prince Jerram," said Murl. "It was difficult to find land where we could take on provisions during our search – land that was not inhabited." He looked directly at the High King. "Your orders *were* obeyed, Sire, though it proved hard for Prince Renolth to enforce them." Lantor nodded and Murl went on, "After the first ten days of sailing, the plague no longer seemed to spread as it had, although there was still the occasional case aboard one or other of the ships until the last two months of our voyage." He took a quick sip of his drink and gestured for Jedron to continue their tale.

"We thought we'd found a suitable land – not just for provisions but for habitation also – just seven weeks after leaving here," said the younger captain. "Prince Renolth sent search bands out and initial reports were favourable. The place became our home for almost a month and then, on the very day ships were due to return to lead you from the Homeland, a nearby island we'd not yet explored proved to be a fire-mountain."

"It erupted?" Jerram surmised.

"Indeed it did," said Murl. "We barely escaped with our lives. We lost one vessel, though we saved most of her passengers and crew. We sailed on – sometimes southwest but mostly westwards because of the winds and the currents. We managed to take on fresh water and some food on several occasions but there was nowhere we could safely stay until another three months or so had passed."

"So you'd finally found The Island and yet still you delayed in sending vessels back?" Jerram persisted.

"No, Prince Jerram," Murl responded patiently. "This was before we found the place which *might* be The Island."

"Go on, Murl," prompted Lantor, with a quelling glance at his elder son.

"Well, Sire, we disembarked and made camps. We began charting the land and it seemed to be part of a mainland, cut off from the interior by a range of high mountains. Prince Renolth was wary of sending for you too soon this time and he was right to be cautious."

"Some people argued that rescue vessels should set sail after a few weeks had passed," Jedron put in, "but the debate was halted when we had to leave again."

"Another fire-mountain?" asked Amryl.

"No," said Jedron. "There was some kind of insect breeding in the water. We had no idea there was a problem until the things started to hatch and swarm. They were in every pond, stream and river. The sky was dark with them and their sting was vicious. Some of the older people and the children suffered particularly badly. Several people died of the toxin in the stings."

"More casualties," muttered Lantor, his tone a mixture of concern and resignation.

"Seven died, yes," said Murl, "and doubtless we'd have lost more but for the swift evacuation Prince Renolth organised. We sailed on, farther this time, much farther, without sighting land in any direction. One ship went down in a storm and another was holed on a submerged reef. Conditions were desperate aboard what was left of the fleet and we'd all but given up hope when young Prince Zenton sighted land."

"The land that will be our new home?" asked Amryl.

Murl nodded. "It's uninhabited, as far as we can tell, and it's fertile enough to support us. We're building a settlement near the harbour."

"The *Star* and the *Tennel* were dispatched as soon as was reasonably possible, Sire," Jedron said. "We'd charted the voyage but retracing our way was more difficult than we'd anticipated. We've been sailing unfamiliar waters and the winds and currents are strange and capricious. We were driven off course several times. Once, some two months ago it must have been, a storm took us onto rocks. We had to make landfall and see to the damage before we could continue."

"But still –"

"No, Jerram," his father said. "It's enough for now that they are here. I'm sure we'll have plenty of time on our voyage to hear in greater detail all that has happened."

"Sire," said Jedron, "why is there still such terrible hardship here? The Homeland Isles has had trading treaties with Phrata and Barl for generations. Did they not send help?"

The High King's laugh was full of bitterness. "I fear I made a grave error, Jedron. I'd posted signals to warn their ships when the plague began to spread across the Isles, had I not?"

Jedron nodded. Those signals had been in place for some time before Renolth's fleet had sailed. "But surely they could have sent help without actually landing here," persisted the young captain. "They could have sent rowboats from their mainships and just floated supplies into the harbour on high tide."

"I sent ships to both Phrata and Barl," said Lantor. "Our captains were ordered to stand offshore and signal our need. At first both the Barls and the Phratans ignored the vessels. Then, when one of our ships ventured too close to Barl, it was fired upon. We had no resources to retaliate."

"I take it we're no longer granting them trading rights here?" Murl said dryly.

This time the High King's laugh held a touch of genuine amusement.

Lantor stood on the azure sands. He smiled, revelling in the warmth of the suns. A gentle breeze off the harbour ruffled his hair. So this was the new land. His people should be safe here.

The crown he wore suddenly felt strangely heavy. He tried to take it off to relieve the pressure but couldn't lift it. The weight grew, forcing him to his knees. Head bowed, he saw a shadow surrounding him.

I'll take that. The shadow reached out and the crown was gone.

Lantor leapt up. "No," he cried. "The responsibility is mine!"

56

The shadow slithered away towards Zenton.

"Zenton!" Lantor called frantically, "Here! You'll need this." He took off his ring and threw it to his nephew.

Zenton turned to catch the ring, and Lantor woke to find Ryella shaking him.

"What's wrong?" she asked. "You were shouting out."

Lantor sat up. "I should have given it to Zenton," he said. "The royal seal. I should have given it to Zenton."

"Zenton?"

"Did I say Zenton? I must have meant Renolth. It was just a dream that confused me. My mind's still on Murl's arrival and the new homeland. Three days, Ryella. After all this time, three days only until we leave." He reached out and patted her hand. "My apologies for waking you. It's still dark. Go back to sleep."

Ryella settled back. Lantor lay down again but sleep evaded him for the remainder of the night.

The plan to set sail in three days fell apart dramatically and quite literally in the shambles of yet another earthquake. Starting with appalling suddenness at dawn on the second day after Murl and Jedron's arrival, the quake shook the ground like a water-sherran shaking a freshly-caught fish. Though the main tremor lasted just a few seconds and was centred on one of the outer Isles, the radiating shock-waves caused yet more damage to already unstable buildings in Ashkantin. The palace itself, half destroyed by previous quakes, was virtually razed to the ground.

Already aboard the *Tennel*, the High King coordinated rescue efforts and the gathering and embarkation of all the survivors who could be found. With the havoc caused by the quake, it was nine more days before the fleet finally assembled in Ashkantin's huge main harbour. Food and medical supplies were perilously low, and drinking water, brought from inland streams found blessedly untainted by sewage, would have to be strictly rationed. With a heavy heart, Lantor gave the signal for the ships to weigh anchor and set sail.

More people than he had expected had managed to arrive at the appointed sites to join the exodus. Ashkantin's fifteen vessels, plus Renolth's two messenger-ships, were crowded from bow to stern.

Lantor hoped fervently that, with the difficulties of communication, no one who wished to leave had been left behind.

With a fair wind and a clear day to start them on their journey, the vessels would have made quite an impressive sight, Lantor thought sadly, had it not been for the knowledge that they carried all that was left of the Almari race. Jerram's attitude was that at least they *had* a future now, with a new land to go to – whether or not it was The Island of their legends. Lantor envied him his optimism.

Standing at the stern of the *Tennel*, gripping the ship's rail so tightly that his knuckles whitened, High King Lantor watched with Queen Ryella as the beleaguered Isles faded into the distance. Despite the dreadful happenings of the past years, abandoning the Homeland was proving an even greater wrench than he had anticipated. When he had sent out Renolth's fleet, Lantor had believed that at some time in the future, albeit generations hence, the Almari would return to the Isles. He had clung to the hope that his people would one day be able to rebuild their cities, fish the seas and farm the land once more. No longer did he have that belief. The land was too badly damaged, the population decimated. The era of prosperity was over. His beloved Homeland held only memories of ruin and death. He wondered if he would ever be able to think of the past without the terrible pain he felt now. No – there would be no return. The Isles would, if the quakes ceased and the vegetation recovered, revert to the wilderness it must have been before the first settlers came to colonise the island chain. At least the remaining animals would stand some chance of survival, even those that had stayed on the main Isles. Many of the wild creatures had fled when the quakes had begun, some primal instinct guiding them to seek the relative safety of the uninhabited outer islets least affected by the tremors and tidal waves.

The notion of the Isles being returned to nature distressed Lantor less than the distinct possibility that, if the land did make some sort of recovery, Barl and Phrata would doubtless vie with each other to lay claim there. With a momentary flash of pure venom, the High King cursed aloud his former trading neighbours, wishing them everlasting strife if they sought to possess the Homeland Isles. It was unreasonable, he knew. After all, the Almari had conquered the islands back in the distant past, subjugating the inhabitants and turning the land to their own use. The Phratans and Barls were no worse than the Almari had been and they would be taking only the land and not a race living there. Still, Lantor did not recall his malediction.

He stood, balancing with practised ease against the rising swell of the sea, long after the Homeland was out of sight. He told himself it was the stiff salt wind that was stinging his eyes to tears.

Toying with his ring, he murmured, "This will be needed in our new homeland. Sometime in the future, it will be needed there. I should have given it to Renolth."

Chapter Eleven

Coming-of-age

"You are charged to use your time and talents for the good of the community, to bring no dishonour to your family or your friends either by your actions or by lack of action, and to obey the rulers of the land insofar as that obedience lies along the path of the Light and in accordance with the dictates of your own conscience."

Zenton had heard the traditional words many times in the past. He remembered clearly Brandell's coming-of-age ceremony back in the Homeland – celebrated just days before a particularly violent earthquake – and some they had managed to observe aboard the *Tennel's Flight*. He remembered also the three ceremonies which had taken place since their landing. Drent, Brandell's friend, had had his ceremony two weeks after the landing. Five weeks later, Sendri – a girl Zenton barely knew – had come of age, followed four months afterwards by Merret's younger brother Halden. By custom, a senior member of the young person's family led the ritual but since leaving the Homeland Isles Renolth himself had taken that role since the youngsters approaching adulthood had lost many of their family members.

Zenton had always taken the words rather casually – until today. Today was the sixteenth anniversary of his birth and the importance of the words struck home. He was about to be accepted into the community as an adult. His opinions and decisions would carry as much weight as those of any other adult; the responsibility for his actions would be his alone. He swallowed hard against the sudden dryness in his throat. He had not expected to be so moved by this familiar and seemingly simple ceremony.

It had been a strange day. The morning had dawned warm and dry but by mid-suns the weather had turned uncomfortably sultry and Zenton had felt a peculiar tension in the settlement. Tempers had seemed short and he'd noticed several people arguing heatedly. Towards the First Sun's set, as the time for the rite had approached, a cooling breeze had sprung up from the harbour and, to Zenton's relief, the settlement had become calmer.

Zenton glanced across to his cousin. Brandell had helped him prepare for the ceremony and now stood off to one side as father and son faced each other in the centre of the gathered Almari. Brandell's grin brought no answering smile from Zenton.

"Zenton, son of Renolth and Ardelle, Prince of the Royal House, do you accept these charges laid upon you?"

For an instant the well-known and carefully rehearsed response fled Zenton's mind. He had a sudden vision of a huge, magnificent creature soaring high over the harbour, its strange haunting cry echoing across the rippling waters. He blinked and the vision faded as quickly as it had come. He glanced out across the harbour and saw only sea birds wheeling and darting above the waves. His hesitation had been momentary and must have gone unnoticed by anyone else, for Renolth was still calmly awaiting the customary reply.

Zenton stepped closer to his father and gave the time-honoured response. "I pledge to work with the rulers of the land and with the community for the furtherance of the path of the Light and for the good of our people. I accept the charges laid upon me."

"Then be welcomed as an adult in the community of the Almari." Renolth reached out and clasped his son's hand.

Zenton felt the tension he'd sensed earlier return with a vengeance. He tried to speak, to warn his father that something was wrong, but he had no time to form the words. A huge, dark cloud blocked the light and he looked up just as a jagged, green bolt of lightning arrowed down towards him. It struck the ground between him and his father, flinging them both and all near them to the grass. The very air seemed to crackle and shimmer as a tremendous thunderclap resounded across the settlement.

Tingling from head to foot but otherwise unhurt, Brandell was one of the first to react. He clambered shakily to his feet and ran unsteadily to where his uncle and cousin lay.

"Where's Silmedd?' he shouted, his voice sounding hoarse in his still-ringing ears. "Someone fetch Silmedd or Vemran! Hurry!"

"Move aside, Prince Brandell," said a composed voice directly behind him. "Let me deal with this."

Recognising Vemran's authoritative tones, Brandell stepped back and sank to his knees, trying to control his rasping breathing. As Vemran knelt to tend Renolth and Zenton, Silmedd hastened from the outer rim of the crowd and moved to assess the condition of the other five people still prone on the scorched ground.

Within minutes all the injured had been taken to the small infirmary built at the edge of the settlement. Leaning against the wall of one of the side rooms, Brandell watched as Zenton was stripped of his singed clothing and placed gently face down on an examination table. A path of angry redness ran from his left foot up the length of his body, across his shoulders, down his right arm and into his hand.

"Well?" Vemran demanded of the two apprentice-healers with him.

Grenath, the older of the two, moved closer to the unconscious prince. "At first sight the marks look like burns," she said, "but there's no blistering. I'm sorry, Master Vemran, I don't know how to treat this."

"It's as well to admit ignorance," said the healer. "Remember this, both of you. You could do more harm than good by pretending to have knowledge you don't possess."

"*Is* the skin burned?" asked Grenath.

The senior healer paused before answering. "I've seen three cases of people struck by lightning," he told his students, "but never anything quite like this." He looked up as Silmedd entered the room.

Brandell stepped forward. "What news of Renolth?"

"He's still unconscious," replied Silmedd. "His right hand is inflamed but I can find no other visible injuries."

"And the rest who were hurt?" Brandell asked.

Silmedd studied the marks on Zenton's body before turning back to Brandell. "I'm sorry to report that Halden is dead," he said. "The others are shaken but recovering quickly." He resumed his study of Zenton. "I've not seen marks like those on Prince Renolth's hand or Zenton's body before, Vemran. What do you suggest?"

"We need to treat the inflammation," Vemran responded. "I think we should combine silcan for burns with allamite for reducing the swelling and to ease any pain."

Silmedd nodded agreement. "I'll mix it now." He paused in the doorway. "We're running short of allamite, you know. We need to find an alternative soon."

Some two hours later, Donar and Irvanyal, leaders of the recently formed Settlement Council, came to the infirmary for the third time since the lightning strike had so devastatingly halted the coming-of-age ceremony. Finding Brandell sitting in the general waiting area, Donar asked, "Is there any improvement?"

Brandell sighed. "I said I'd send word," he reminded them, "but since you're here anyway – again – I suppose there's news of some sort. Zenton came round a few minutes ago. At least, he opened his eyes. He doesn't seem to be responding to anything though. He didn't react even when the healers checked the dressings on his burns – if they are burns. Renolth's still unconscious." He gave a short, humourless laugh. "I don't know which is worse, do you?" Without awaiting a reply, he rose and added, "I'm going to get some rest. Perhaps someone will send *me* word if there's any change here."

He headed towards the door but stopped and turned when Silmedd called, "Prince Brandell!"

"What's happened?" asked Brandell, "Are they worse?"

"No," Silmedd assured him. "In fact, Prince Renolth has just regained consciousness. Donar, Irvanyal – wait here, will you?"

The healer gestured to Brandell to accompany him and together they went to the small side room where Renolth lay. Grenath rose from her chair by the prince's bed, bowed to Brandell and Silmedd and quietly obeyed Silmedd's signal to move away to the side of the room.

"Brandell," said Renolth, his voice sounding weak but steady, "are you all right? Grenath tells me Zenton is hurt. What happened?"

"I'm fine," Brandell assured his uncle. "Do you remember the lightning striking at the end of the ceremony?"

Renolth struggled to sit up. Silmedd helped him upright and placed a pillow carefully behind him. Renolth closed his eyes briefly before he spoke again. "I remember feeling as if a gigantic aman had kicked me in the chest," he said, "and then I woke up here. Silmedd, I need to see my son."

"I'll take you to him later," said the healer. "You should rest for a while."

"No." The ring of command was back in Renolth's voice. "It's important that I go to him."

"He's not properly conscious yet, Renolth," said Brandell. "His eyes are open but he doesn't seem to see or hear anyone."

"I know. Grenath told me. Take me to him, Silmedd."

"I don't think that's wise just yet, Prince Renolth," the healer said firmly. "I doubt you're strong enough to be walking. Maybe in an hour or so."

"I'll crawl if I have to. Get me there, or bring him to me!"

"I'd prefer you to wait –" Silmedd began.

Brandell placed a restraining hand on the healer's arm. "I think, Healer Silmedd, you are forgetting the royal family bond."

Silmedd hesitated momentarily, then said, "Very well. But take your time, Prince Renolth. Don't try to hurry."

Though the night was mild and the infirmary warm, Silmedd wrapped a thick cloak around the Almari leader's shoulders before helping him to stand. Once on his feet, Renolth nodded his thanks for the healer's supporting arm as they made the short journey to the next room. Brandell and Grenath followed.

Vemran raised his bushy eyebrows as the group squeezed into the small chamber. He offered no comment as he eased Renolth into a chair next to his son's bedside. Zenton lay on his right side, eyes half open, staring sightlessly towards the door through which Renolth and the others had just entered. Renolth took his son's uninjured hand into his own bandaged one. "Leave me alone with him," he instructed, and Vemran began to usher everyone from the room.

Brandell hesitated then shrugged and went out with the others. "I'll wait in Renolth's room," he told the healers as they headed off down the narrow corridor.

"Master Vemran?" Grenath called as she hastened after the healers.

"What is it, child?" Vemran returned rather tetchily.

Having passed the twentieth anniversary of her birth, Grenath was no 'child', but she made no protest. "Prince Brandell seemed to think Prince Renolth could help, but he's not a healer, is he? Master Vemran, what is this 'bond' between members of the royal family?"

"Bond? Well, I suppose you could call it that. You'd do better to ask Maglin – he's the historian and teacher – but I'll try to explain."

Having come to the waiting area, Vemran waved Silmedd on and settled himself onto one of the chairs. Grenath sat down by him.

"How old were you when the earthquakes began?" asked Vemran. "Ten? Eleven?" Grenath had been older than that but she did not interrupt. Vemran went on, "You must have studied *some* of our history, surely? In times past, it is said in our legends, there were those amongst our people who had strange and wonderful talents. Some could heal by touch, others move objects by the power of thought alone. There were many gifts, too many to detail now. Legends tell how these people became Guardians of the Isles, working with the kings and queens to protect the land. Legends only, I fear. It's doubtful if such talents truly existed in the general population. However, history documents the real and proven powers of members of the Royal House of Almar, and the records tell us that, on the whole, they used those powers for the good of the people. There were a few notable exceptions, but you can go and talk with Maglin if you want to find out more. The point is, although these talents have waned considerably over the generations, they are still, we believe, latent in the royal family. Zenton certainly has exceptional sight, and he's also shown remarkable prescience on more than one occasion."

"But what about Prince Renolth?" Grenath asked.

"Well, he has no healing gift that I'm aware of, but if he believes he can help young Zenton in some way, then he probably can. At least, I hope he can, for I've seen nothing quite like this in all my years as a healer."

Chapter Twelve

Arrival

Most people said that Zenton favoured his father in features and mannerisms but to Renolth, at that moment, Zenton looked heartbreakingly like Ardelle.

"What happened out there, Zenton?" the Almari leader asked quietly. "I told Brandell I remembered being hit by something, and that was true, but I also saw the lightning. Did *you* see it? Light knows, I've seen enough storms in the past few years – but the lightning's always been that brilliant blue-white. This bolt was vivid green. Did you notice that? And it struck up through you, I'm sure of it. It came through you into my hand as we touched. Why should that be?"

He paused, watching for any reaction, but Zenton lay unmoving. Renolth sighed. His headache had cleared and there was little pain from his hand but he felt unutterably weary. "There's something strange here, son," he continued softly. "This land's good and yet there's something here I don't understand. I need your insights and your talents. Come back, son."

Using his uninjured hand, Renolth brushed an unruly lock of hair from Zenton's forehead. As he touched his son's face, there came into Renolth's mind a vivid image of the harbour with a huge creature soaring above white-crested waves. The mental picture lasted only a second and faded fast but it was enough to shake Renolth quite badly. He had never before experienced any sort of vision. Gently, he withdrew his hand and then, after taking a few calming breaths, placed his fingers lightly on his son's head again. There was no image this time, but Zenton's eyelids flickered and closed, his taut features relaxed and his breathing became deep and regular.

When Vemran came into the room a little later, Renolth was sitting leaning over his son's bed, head pillowed on folded arms. Both he and Zenton were sleeping soundly.

"Did you see the lightning?" Zenton asked three days later as he left the infirmary to return to the shelter built at the western edge of the settlement for Renolth and the two younger princes.

Brandell nodded. "I felt it too. Though at least I was far enough away to escape the worst of it." He slowed his pace to allow his cousin to keep up with him. "It's the first time you've mentioned anything about what happened. What do you remember?"

"Not much really. I just wondered if you'd noticed anything... unusual."

"Unusual?" Brandell thought for a moment. "I didn't see many clouds building up, so I suppose that was a bit strange. And there was only that one flash and thunderclap. Other than that, no, I don't think there was anything unusual – merely terrifying. Why do you ask?"

Zenton avoided the question by asking another of his own. "How's Merret? His brother was killed, was he not? Vemran told me."

"He seems to be coping well enough," Brandell replied. "I spoke to him after the farewell ceremony for Halden. I think Renolth's sent him out on a search, which is probably the best thing for him at the moment." He halted and gave Zenton a studied glance. "You don't look too well you know, cousin."

Zenton chuckled dryly. "Thanks."

"Did Vemran really release you from the infirmary or was this *your* idea?"

"Both Vemran *and* Silmedd said I could go," Zenton assured his cousin, "and I do feel a lot better, even if I don't look it. I'm just tired all the time. Anyway, Vemran is quite confident I'll soon recover fully."

Nearing the shelter, Zenton stumbled slightly on the uneven ground and could not quite manage to conceal a wince. Brandell put out a steadying hand. "Is your back still sore?" he asked sympathetically.

"A bit," Zenton admitted. "I'm stiff, too, but at least the marks have almost gone." He pushed back his right sleeve to reveal a pale streak of redness down the length of his arm.

Brandell grinned. "It must be something in the blood royal. Renolth's hand is healing fast as well." He stood back at the shelter entrance and gave a courtly bow. "And now, cousin, I've carried out my orders and escorted you safely home, so if you'll be so good as to go in and rest I'll go and find something more entertaining to do than act as a combined guard and apprentice-healer."

"My thanks, Brandell," Zenton responded, smiling. "Your duty is done. You may go."

Brandell saluted formally, aimed a mock blow at his cousin's shoulder and hurried away.

Watching Brandell stride away, Zenton found himself thinking yet again about the lightning strike. He had not been entirely truthful in saying he couldn't recall much of what had happened. He, like Renolth, had a clear memory of a vivid green flash of light. Unlike Renolth however, who had been deeply unconscious for over two hours, Zenton had a vague recollection of being carried to the infirmary and of hearing voices discussing his condition. Some time after that he'd felt himself drift into a dark labyrinth of some kind. He remembered standing in the blackness, eyes straining to see around him. Gradually a faint, warm glow had appeared and he'd begun to move towards it. The glow was emanating from a cave which he knew he'd been seeking for a long time. He'd been about to enter through the narrow opening when he'd heard his father's voice calling him back. The glow had faded as Zenton had struggled to wake and answer Renolth's call. The effort had proved too great just then and he had allowed sleep to claim him. When he'd finally woken properly, he'd found he was in a small room in the infirmary and it was afternoon on the day after the lightning had struck.

Zenton frowned. Why had he kept all this from Brandell? Was it simply that he was in no mood to appreciate the humorous remarks Brandell would undoubtedly make about visions and feelings? Shrugging slightly, and immediately regretting the rash movement, Zenton went into his room and lay down.

He dozed for a couple of hours, drifting in and out of a light sleep, and woke still tired. Deciding he might benefit from being out in the fresh air, he rose slowly, donned a light jacket over his tunic and trousers, pulled on his boots and ambled out towards the dunes overlooking the harbour. After stopping several times to chat to friends and acquaintances and to answer concerned queries about his health, he came at last to the edge of the dunes. He settled himself into a sheltered hollow where he could watch the activity either down on the sands or in the settlement.

A grey-blue lizard darted towards him, its feet and toes absurdly large in comparison to its tiny body. Keldries, the children called these small, harmless lizards, for Maglin had taught them the name meant 'swift ones'. Zenton kept still as the little creature clambered onto his trouser leg. It sat for a moment, purple tongue flicking, then it turned and leapt back onto the sandy ground. Zenton smiled as he watched it scurry off into the dunes.

The air was mild and the suns warm and comforting. Through half-closed eyes, Zenton stared out across the waters towards the cliffs of Mandano, north and west of the harbour. A shape, dark against the bright sky, appeared in the distance. Suddenly alert, Zenton sat upright, concentrating on trying to make out the details of what seemed to be a gigantic bird of some sort. It was so far away that even with his exceptional sight he could not be certain what he was seeing.

"What's so interesting?"

Startled, Zenton turned sharply – and flinched at the stab of pain across his shoulders. He might be healing rapidly but sudden movements still hurt.

"My apologies," said Brandell, sitting down by his cousin and gesturing for Drent and Chandrane to join them. "I didn't mean to surprise you like that. I thought you'd sense us coming. You'll have to work on that one."

Unsure for a moment whether or not to rise to Brandell's mocking tone, Zenton chose to ignore the comment. "Did you see that?" he asked, pointing out towards Mandano.

"See what?"

"I'm not sure what it was," Zenton admitted, "but it looked very big."

Brandell laughed. "I definitely haven't seen one of those. Have you, Drent?"

"Not recently," said Drent, joining in the laughter.

Chandrane remained silent throughout the exchange and then asked quite seriously, "Was it a creature of some kind?"

Disinclined to face further teasing from his cousin, Zenton changed the subject. "It was probably just a tennel or some other large sea-bird. I was half asleep. Anyway, Brandell, I thought you had better things to do than to keep checking on me."

"Actually," Brandell told him. "I went back to the shelter to talk to you. One of the servants said you'd headed out here." He jerked a thumb towards Drent and Chandrane. "These two tagged along to see how you're feeling."

"I'm fine, thanks," Zenton said. "What did you want to talk to me about?"

"Leave us, will you Drent? And you, Chandrane. I'll join you later." Brandell pulled up a blade of tough grass and chewed its end. He waited until the two young men had walked away and then asked, "Does he know what the people are saying?"

Zenton had no need to ask what Brandell meant. "I expect so," he replied.

"Someone should tell him how strongly the people feel about this," Brandell persisted. "You're his son; you should tell him."

"He considers you his son too," Zenton reminded him gently.

"Well – maybe so, but I'm not, am I?" He tossed away the grass stem. "Look Zenton, I really think you need to talk to him. I heard the Council Leaders discussing it this afternoon. They're going to go to him soon. It would be better if he was prepared."

Zenton sighed and stood up slowly. "He won't agree to it."

Brandell rose quickly and brushed sandy soil from his clothing. "I'll go with you," he offered. "Come on. He was in the meeting hall a short time ago. He'll probably still be there."

Brandell fidgeted with impatience as they made their way slowly through the busy settlement. He pushed open the meeting hall door to find that Renolth was indeed still there but that Donar, Irvanyal and several other members of the Settlement Council were there also, standing in a group in front of the table where the Almari leader sat.

Brandell and Zenton had arrived too late to hear what the Council Leaders had just said but they saw and heard Renolth's reaction.

"No." The prince pushed back his chair and stood to face those gathered in the hall. "It's too soon."

Valdrak, the respected and experienced sea-captain, stepped forward. "Your highness," he said formally, "it's nearing two years

70

since our ships left for the Homeland. With our charts to guide them, they should have returned months ago."

"I know that, Valdrak, but –"

"Prince Renolth," Irvanyal interrupted, "you led us here to safety. We respect your wisdom and authority. Be our High King."

Renolth raised a hand to silence the murmurs of agreement. "My brother may still live," he reminded them. "*He* is our rightful High King. Until I'm certain of Lantor's fate I shall continue only as your prince."

"Your highness –" Donar began.

"No, Donar," Renolth said firmly. "I value your trust and your loyalty, and I thank you all for the honour you show me, but the matter is closed." Leaving the documents he had been working on spread out on the table, he turned and left the hall.

Clearly disappointed, the Council members left to return to their various tasks. Zenton went to gather up the parchments.

Brandell followed him to the table. "He should have agreed to their request, Zenton. He *should* be our High King."

"Not yet, Brandell. He's right to wait. I feel Lantor *is* still alive."

"You and your feelings," muttered Brandell crossly. "He should – Zenton, where are you going?"

Leaving the papers still on the table, Zenton was heading out of the building. "I'm going to find out what that noise is all about. Are you coming?"

Brandell hastened after the departing figure of his cousin.

Following the many people who were hurrying towards the harbour, the two princes joined the men, women and children who had left their chores and were gathering along the quayside and on the sparkling sand. There the cousins found the source of the clamour.

A fleet of nine ships, bedraggled yet dignified, was sailing into Patoll's harbour.

Chapter Thirteen

Old Friends and Island Maps

Standing silently amid the noisy, excited throng at the harbour wall, Renolth felt his heart sink. The *Tennel's Flight* was not among the flotilla. Anxiously he scanned the main deck of the leading ship, the *Star's Reach,* as she docked at the quayside. There was no sign of his brother aboard the *Star* and it was unlikely he would have travelled on one of the smaller vessels. Renolth turned aside and went to check that the long-held plans to welcome newcomers ashore and to settle them into temporary shelters had been set in motion.

A little later, satisfied that all was proceeding smoothly with Donar and Irvanyal supervising the arrival of the Almari voyagers, Renolth took Zenton, Brandell and the *Star's Reach* captain for a brief meeting in his study in the royal shelter.

"Sit down, Jedron," invited Renolth, indicating a chair near the table. "I won't keep you long but I need your initial report. Details can wait till you're rested."

The stocky sea-captain waited until Renolth and the two younger princes were seated before he sank into the offered chair.

"They'd been working on rebuilding the fleet since we left. Those who were able," Jedron began, his eyes haunted. "I don't know how anyone survived. The Isles are devastated, Prince Renolth. There is no Homeland anymore."

Hiding his own distress, Renolth poured wine from a covered jug into a cup and passed it across the table to the captain. The wine was newly made, with a delicate aroma and a light, fruity taste but Jedron appeared not to notice the flavour. He sipped abstractedly at the golden liquid.

"The High King had sent ships round all the Isles," Jedron said, "taking on board all the survivors who could be found at any of the ports and at inlets where vessels could dock or rowboats land. When we finally assembled the fleet and left the Isles, there were seventeen mainships."

Renolth could contain his impatience no longer. "What of Lantor and his family?"

Jedron shrugged wearily. "The High King was aboard the *Tennel* with his wife and family, with Murl as captain of course. Their ship was leading the way. The *Star* was in the middle of the fleet. The voyage was relatively straightforward at first. Everything was going well. Too well, it seems." He took a longer draught of his wine. "We were close, Prince Renolth, so close. We were about two weeks' sail from the island here when a storm hit us out of nowhere. It went on for days, with heavy seas and a northerly gale. Visibility was down to a ship's length at times. When the storm abated we found that seven vessels were missing – including the *Tennel*." Seeing Renolth's stricken expression, Jedron added, "Every captain has a copy of the charts, your highness. They'll find their way back."

Renolth nodded, not trusting himself to speak for the moment.

"You said seven ships went missing," Brandell pointed out, "so *ten* should be here now."

Jedron scratched at the stubble on his chin. "One vessel was badly storm-damaged. She took on water despite attempts to repair her and she went down during the last day of the storm. Four people were lost but the rest were picked up by other ships."

"If you knew she was holed and sinking, you should have been able to save *everyone*," Brandell criticised, ignoring Renolth's placating gesture.

"We tried, Prince Brandell," said Jedron earnestly. "Conditions were appalling – and you know from your own voyage that there wasn't room for many rowboats. Still, volunteers went out despite the high seas. Four people drowned before we could get to them, including Captain Ballinden. She was last to leave her ship."

Renolth stood up. "Go and check on your crew and passengers, Jedron, then someone will show you to a shelter. You did well to bring as many people here as you have done. You have my thanks and my congratulations." As the captain left, Renolth turned to his son and nephew. "I think you'd better go and rest, Zenton. Brandell, you can help me greet the newcomers."

"I've *been* resting," Zenton protested. "I'll come with you and Brandell."

"Very well," consented Renolth, smiling, "but don't overdo things or Vemran's likely to have you straight back in the infirmary." He turned and led the way out of the shelter.

Back at the harbour the cousins went their separate ways and began the pleasant duty of greeting the new arrivals. It was past Oltan's set by the time all the ships' passengers had disembarked and, for those already settled in the new land, the joy of reunion with friends and family was tempered by sorrow on learning of the loss of loved ones in the Homeland and on the voyage.

The excitement of the occasion kept Zenton on his feet until the last of the nine ships had docked at the quayside. Then, hit by a sudden, overwhelming wave of fatigue, he decided he'd better seek his own bed. Passing a group of people being guided towards their assigned shelters, he noticed a familiar face among the newcomers.

"Aldana?" he called.

Hearing her name, the girl turned, her face lighting with a smile of recognition. Unusually embarrassed, Zenton tripped clumsily as he started towards her.

Aldana laughed. "Careful, Prince Zenton. I wouldn't want to be the cause of injury."

Recovering his balance and his composure, and not in the least offended by her laughter, Zenton greeted her warmly. "What news of your family?" he asked.

Aldana's dark eyes misted. "My mother died only a day after your fleet set sail. Father was killed during an earthquake as we prepared for our voyage."

"I'm sorry, Aldana," said Zenton. The words were heartfelt, not mere platitudes. Aldana's father had been Lantor's Chief Counsellor and a close friend of all the royal family, and Aldana, just a half-year younger than Zenton, had spent much of her time with the prince and his cousins.

"I must go, Prince Zenton," said Aldana, seeing her group moving away.

Zenton halted her with a hand on her arm. "Do you have any family or friends here?"

"I made some friends on the voyage, but –"

74

"You can stay at our shelter. We've a spare room. We're fortunate. I think only our shelter and the infirmary have more than two rooms." He realised he was beginning to babble and made a conscious effort to calm his excitement at finding her here. "Come on. Renolth and Brandell will be delighted to see you."

"Well, if you're sure..."

"Of course. Slen's leading your group. I'll send someone to tell him where you are. And by the way, it's still just 'Zenton'."

She stopped him as he reached to take her travel pack. "I'll take it, Zenton. It's not heavy and – I don't mean to be impolite – but you really don't look too well. Are you all right?"

"Lightning struck the ground near me a few days ago," he told her. "It knocked me out, and I'm still a bit sore and tired." Seeing her expression of concern, he added hastily, "I'm fine really. I just need to rest for a while. Don't tell my father, will you? He warned me about doing too much."

Aldana smiled. "Mother was a healer, remember? She taught me to keep confidences. Come on. Let's get to this shelter of yours."

Emotionally and physically drained, Renolth was heading towards his shelter when he saw a light burning in Maglin's workroom. The Almari leader tapped on the door and walked in to find the master cartographer and two of his apprentices working on a large map. The students stood immediately and Maglin waved Renolth to one of the vacated seats.

"Everything appears to have gone well with the landing," Maglin said.

Renolth nodded. "We'll celebrate the arrivals on the morrow. Today we just needed to find everyone somewhere to eat and sleep."

"It's fortunate the second settlement is well under way," Maglin commented. "I know *you* were convinced more of our people would come, but I'm afraid many of us had begun to doubt it." He set down his quillat carefully, so that no ink dropped onto the map, leaned his elbows on the table and steepled ink-stained fingers. "I'm sorry to hear our High King is not yet among us."

"There's time yet," Renolth said quietly. "Zenton believes Lantor still lives and I trust the lad's instincts." He pointed to the lamp on the table and observed mildly, "We're somewhat short of lamp oil, my friend. What's so important that you're working so late on a special day like this?"

"Ah, well," began Maglin, "it's something I overheard just a short while ago."

"Go on," urged Renolth, smiling at the cartographer's air of mystery. "You have my full attention."

"That makes a change," Maglin quipped. He ignored the horrified gasp from one of his students. "Well," he said again, "I'd just taken some of our newcomers to their accommodation and was on my way back here when I passed a group of children playing outside one of the temporary shelters. One child, one of the new arrivals, asked Jeya's daughter what we called this land. I must admit, I stopped to eavesdrop because, despite our deliberations on the matter, we've not reached any firm conclusion yet, have we?" Without waiting for any response from Renolth, he went on, "Anyway, Rannelle, that's Jeya's daughter –"

"I know who she is, Maglin," interrupted Renolth. "Do come to the point."

Quite unperturbed, Maglin continued, "As I was saying, Rannelle told the child that we live on the island of 'Zamara'."

"Zamara?"

"Yes. I went over to the children and asked Rannelle how she had come by that name."

"And?" prompted Renolth, now genuinely interested.

"Apparently she heard Prince Zenton call the land 'Zamara' and she and her friends all liked the name."

"Zamara." Renolth looked down at the map and smiled in sudden understanding. "*Zamara*. Well, it's close enough, and easier to say. So be it." He traced a finger gently round the charted outline and then turned from the table. "I bid you good eve, Maglin." He nodded to the two apprentices and left the shelter.

After a moment's silence, one of the students ventured, "Master Maglin, what's so special about the name 'Zamara'?"

"Look at the map," instructed their teacher. "What do you see?"

"Er… Patoll is mapped in fair detail and..."

"No. No. Look at the *shape* of the land."

The apprentices dutifully peered at the spread chart.

Maglin tapped the parchment with an ink-stained – but fortunately dry – finger. "The child misheard Prince Zenton. He must have said 'zamar arra' and she pronounced it 'Zamara'. That's what Prince Renolth meant about it being easier to say."

"But I still don't see…"

"Have you learnt nothing these past months?" demanded Maglin, losing patience. "Can neither of you remember your studies? In the Old Tongue, 'zamar arra' means 'the dragon asleep'."

Once more, the apprentices bent over the map and this time comprehension dawned. The outline of the land did indeed resemble a dragon curled in sleep.

Chapter Fourteen

Intimations of Danger

As day followed day in the new land, Renolth continued to organise work in the main settlement, to supervise the building of the second settlement and to deploy search bands. He worked closely with Donar and Irvanyal, finding as the weeks passed that he could delegate more and more tasks to them. The Settlement Council met regularly and though Renolth generally found the discussions and reports valuable there were times when petty disagreements among Council members drove him to the limits of his patience. After one particularly trying session, he finally decided to act on Valdrak's suggestion that a day's respite from his duties was long overdue. A break from routine would, he sincerely hoped, restore his energy levels *and* his fraying temper. Accordingly, he arranged to sail the next morning with Valdrak aboard the *Waves of Oltan* on her fishing trip out near the reef which guarded the harbour entrance and which had so nearly been the cause of the advance fleet's destruction when they'd first reached Zamara.

Somewhat to Renolth's surprise, Zenton failed to give the expected enthusiastic support to the proposal. "I'm due out on a search on the morrow," he reminded his father. "If you're set on sailing with Valdrak perhaps I'd better stay in the settlement."

Disappointed by his son's reaction, Renolth was more curt than usual. "We're neither of us totally indispensable, Zenton. Donar and Irvanyal can manage well enough for the short time we'll be away. Continue your preparations." He strode off, leaving his son standing thoughtfully by the harbour wall.

At Bardok's dawn on the following morning, Zenton sought out his father. "We're leaving shortly. I just came to wish you well. You deserve a time away from the pressures here."

Renolth sighed. "I feel as though I'm shirking my responsibilities," he admitted, "but I simply can't resist the opportunity to join Valdrak this time. Light knows, he's asked me often enough lately."

"You will take care, won't you? I know it should be safe, but –"

"You worry too much," Renolth interrupted, smiling. "Brandell will be there and he fusses over me even more than you do. Besides, it's only a day's trip."

"I didn't realise Brandell was sailing with you."

"Yes, he is. Why? Is that a problem?"

"No, not really. But if you're *both* away, maybe I *had* better stay. I can postpone this search or send someone in my place. I don't mind, you know. You do need some time to yourself, even if it is only one day."

"We've discussed this already," said Renolth, this time without irritation. "Go ahead with your search. I'll be back before you are. You're heading south again?"

Zenton nodded. "Aldana's joining our search band this time."

"Well," said Renolth, fastening a warm jacket over his tunic before reaching for his cloak, "I'm sure she'll prove an asset. Vemran speaks highly of her already and he's not easily impressed."

Zenton laughed. "How true. Mind you, he wasn't too pleased when Silmedd found she has a talent for using plants and herbs and asked you to reassign her to him!" Becoming serious again he added, "Please be careful. I know you hope to sight Lantor's ship while you're out past the reef. You might get distracted."

"I'll take care," Renolth promised. "Go to your search without fretting."

Zenton smiled and nodded, though he wondered, as he hastened to join his search band, if he should have said more. He could think of no valid reason for his concern over Renolth's plans. His father really did need a break and the sail would do him good. It was just that every time Zenton thought about the proposed trip a ripple of unease disturbed his stomach.

"Have you talked with your father?" Aldana asked quietly.

"No, not really," Zenton admitted. "He's always so busy. And, anyway, I was told often enough as a child that my vivid imagination coloured my judgement."

"I'm sure Renolth never said that," Aldana rebuked mildly.

"Well, no. Nor did my mother." He chuckled softly. "But Maglin and some of my other tutors certainly did."

Aldana smiled. "It's not your imagination though, is it?" She tucked her feet under her cloak, re-tied her long, fair hair and began to count off on her fingers the incidents he had just related. "You had a particularly vivid nightmare about trying to find a cave. You thought you heard someone telling you to seek the cave and later you went into the river by the Eye Lake, apparently trying to find this cave. When you stroked that young animal out on the grasslands, you thought it went dark and you felt a sort of earth tremor. Then, more recently, there was the green lightning which could have killed both you and Renolth."

Zenton gave a short, quiet laugh, his expression rueful in the flickering light of the campfire. "It doesn't add up to much, does it? A few strange happenings. Probably easy to explain if I could think rationally about them."

"Maybe," Aldana agreed. "But it has to be more than coincidence. Why *you*? No one else has been affected, have they?"

"Well, I wasn't the only one hurt by the lightning strike, so it must all be pure chance. And the first time I touched one of the creatures here – the nocturnal one I told you about – nothing happened, except that it stole my cloak brooch."

"But you've been at the centre of all the strange happenings. That little furry thief sounded enchanting, but as for the earth tremors and the nightmare..." She gave an exaggerated shudder. "Perhaps there's someone or something here that doesn't like you."

This time Zenton laughed out loud. He clapped a hand over his mouth and looked towards the nearby sleepers. No one stirred. Somewhere in the distance a night bird called twice, then fell silent. Zenton scratched at an insect bite on his wrist. He was glad of Aldana's presence. He had been able to talk to her without fear of ridicule.

"There are probably quite a few people here who dislike me," he said, still amused by her suggestion, "although as far as I know I haven't made any real enemies – at least, not ones who can throw lightning at me. Anyway, why should 'someone' or 'something' object to a coming-of-age ceremony?"

80

"I would imagine that your being acknowledged an adult might be deemed somewhat important, considering who you are," Aldana responded.

Using the toe of his boot, Zenton flicked an errant twig back into its place on the fire. His amusement faded. "I still believe Lantor's alive, and my cousins too, so I'm fairly low down in the line of succession. And I'm not exactly comfortable with the idea that there's someone on The Island – or some*thing* – with the ability to hurl lightning bolts. I think I'm missing some perfectly natural explanation."

Aldana shrugged. "Maybe so," she said doubtfully. She wriggled closer to the flames and drew her cloak more tightly around her. "That wind's getting stronger and wilder," she muttered disapprovingly. "I had enough of being cold on the voyage."

For a while, the only sounds were the crackle of flames disturbed by the strengthening wind, and soft snoring coming from one of the wrapped bundles off to the right.

Eventually, Aldana broke the silence that had fallen between them. "You should talk to your father," she said.

After a brief hesitation, Zenton nodded. "He left the infirmary the morning after the lightning strike but he came to talk to me later that evening. He said then that he felt we needed to discuss the land and our new lives here. I meant to take up his suggestion, but your fleet arrived and since then there just doesn't seem to have been a suitable opportunity."

"Make one," insisted Aldana.

"I will," Zenton promised. "As soon as we get back after this search." He sighed wistfully. "I wonder if they could be tamed and ridden."

It was Aldana's turn to laugh, though softly enough not to wake the sleepers. "You always used to do that."

"Do what?"

"Suddenly make a statement that has nothing to do with the current conversation."

Zenton was indignant. "It has, too!" he protested. "I was thinking about our journey back, and travel would be much faster if we could ride the tamans."

"Tamans?"

"Those creatures that came to the settlement. They live out here somewhere. I wonder if they'll ever let us ride them?"

He plucked a blade of grass, shredded it, tossed it into the air to judge the wind direction, and frowned.

"What's the matter?" Aldana asked.

"The wind's turned south-westerly. It's hard enough to negotiate the reef and the harbour entrance at the best of times with the prevailing northerlies. We hardly ever have winds from the south or southwest."

"What will Valdrak do?"

"It depends on the wind strength," Zenton answered. "He might be able to tack against it, or he might heave to, leeward of the reef, and wait for more favourable conditions. The *Waves of Oltan* is sturdy enough. She'll just be later back to land than intended. I suppose it'll give Father a little more time away from his duties, which is all to the good."

Aldana yawned broadly and mumbled an apology. The prince smiled at her. "I doubt you've walked this far in a day for some considerable time. I'll finish our watch. You go to sleep."

"I thought the search rule was that two people should be on watch."

"True enough. I'll wake Lissanne. She won't mind – unlike Slen. He'd doubtless complain for the rest of the search if he missed even half a minute of his allotted sleep time."

Aldana gratefully relinquished her place to Lissanne and, an hour or so later, Zenton roused a grumbling, bleary-eyed Slen to take his place.

Tired though he was himself, it was some time before Zenton fell asleep. It had been a relief to speak openly to Aldana, but their talk had raised more questions rather than answering any. He wished he'd mentioned how uneasy he felt about his father's trip with Valdrak. Still, that was probably yet more of his over-active imagination.

He woke abruptly, surprised to find he had been asleep. From the moons' positions, he judged that at least four hours must have passed. He lay for a moment, wondering what had disturbed him. The campsite was quiet and seemingly quite normal but to Zenton there was something badly wrong. He sat up quickly, slid out of his bedroll and hastily pulled on his boots. Snatching up his cloak, he rose swiftly.

"What's wrong?" Chandrane asked, leaving his place by the small fire and coming to stand near the prince.

"I don't know. It's just... I woke suddenly and..." Zenton struggled to find the words to explain what he was feeling. "Is everything all right here?"

"Yes, there's no problem. Drent and I took over the watch about a half-hour ago." Chandrane gestured vaguely towards the dark sky. "It's a while to Oltan's dawn. Go back to sleep, Zenton. I'll wake you if there's any cause for concern."

The prince nodded agreement and started back to his abandoned sleeping pallet. He had taken only two steps when he spun round, his heart hammering in his chest, his breathing ragged. "I have to get back to the settlement," he declared.

Woken by the sound of anxious voices, Aldana stumbled over to the group now gathering near the fire. "What's going on?" she asked sleepily. "Why is everybody up?"

"Zenton wants to go back to the settlement," Chandrane informed her.

"What? Now? It's still dark."

His pallet rolled and tied, and his travel pack over his shoulder, the prince stood ready to leave.

"What's going on?" Aldana asked again.

"There's something wrong and I'm going back," Zenton stated flatly.

"It's a six-hour walk, Zenton!" Aldana pointed out heatedly.

"I know that."

"It's still the middle of the night!"

"I know that too. I can see well enough with the moons out." He did not add that, lately, he could see pretty well even when the moons were hidden. It was just one more strangeness to add to an increasing list.

Slen, leader of their small team, stepped forward. "We'll strike camp and come with you," he said decisively.

"No," Zenton disagreed. "Silmedd told me he needs more of those plants you and I found on our last search out here. He said they're proving to make a good remedy for fever. You'll have to stay to collect them. Anyway, I can travel faster alone."

"Prince Renolth and the Council will have my hide if I let you go off alone," Slen argued.

Becoming annoyed, Zenton snapped, "This is wasting time. I'm going."

"I'll go with you," Chandrane said, his hurriedly gathered travel pack already slung over one shoulder, a shirt and what looked to be a crumpled edge of cloak dangling out. Catching Zenton's exasperated gaze, he dumped down the bag and hastily stuffed in the offending items. "You four carry on with the search," he suggested to the others. "Slen, you know what plants to look for and where they are." He shouldered his pack once more and smiled at the prince. "I won't slow you down," he promised, "but Slen's right. You shouldn't travel alone."

He barely waited for Slen's nodded agreement before he hastened after the departing figure of the prince.

Though Zenton set a challenging pace, Chandrane, true to his word, kept up well on their return journey – a task he found easier once the First Sun's light allowed him to stop stumbling over trailing roots or snagging his clothing on half-seen bushes. It occurred to him several times, as he limped on a jarred ankle or rubbed at scratched skin, to wonder how Zenton could apparently see with ease even when a thick patch of cloud obscured the moons' light and brought a brief but torrential downpour. He'd ask sometime, he decided, but not until Zenton was in a mood more amenable to questions.

Fit though they were, both young men were nearing exhaustion by the time they sighted the settlement. As soon as their return was reported, Donar and Brandell came out to meet them and Brandell told them about the tragic accident.

84

Chapter Fifteen

Storm

Murl glanced up at the rigging for the tenth time in as many minutes and bellowed for yet another adjustment to the sails. Too little canvas and they would have no control over the *Tennel*, too much and the capricious winds would have her over. Not that they had all that much choice in what they used, Murl reflected sourly; most of the sails were badly storm-damaged already. As if she was trying her best to alleviate her captain's worries, the vessel came about slightly, answering at last to the helm. Jerram, at the wheel, nodded his satisfaction and Murl called down his crew. He would send them aloft again as soon as the need arose but to be up there for long in these conditions was as good as a death sentence. He had lost three people already during the worst of the weather.

For days now they had been running before the wind, unable to steer the course they wanted, the *Tennel* and her two companion vessels struggling to stay afloat after the ravages of the worst storm Murl had encountered in all his years at sea. They had lost sight of over half the fleet during the first hours of the tempest. The sudden violent gales and mountainous seas had all but swamped even the sturdy *Tennel's Flight*. Of the seven ships driven south by the ferocious winds, just three now remained together. Murl could only guess at the fate of the others. Darkness and an impenetrable curtain of rain had obscured sight of them the previous night, and this morning's pale, grey light had revealed an ocean empty of all but the *Tennel*, the *Rays of Bardok* and the *Homeland Queen*.

One hand gripping the rail for balance, Murl went to inspect the most recent damage to the *Tennel*. They would have to make landfall soon and effect what repairs they could if they were ever to stand a chance of finding their way to the island. These seas were unknown to the Almari and Murl had no more idea of their exact position than did anyone else. Glimpses of stars and moons two nights ago had told him they were many leagues south of where they'd meant to be, but until this northerly gale let up there was absolutely nothing he could do about it.

Almost a third of the Almari travellers had died during the first two weeks of the voyage. Some had succumbed to injuries received during the quakes in the Homeland and some to illnesses that would have been treatable had healers and medicines been available, but by far the greatest number of those who'd perished had fallen victim to the plague. In the close confines of the ships the dreaded sickness had spread rapidly, causing panic amongst those who'd seen the tell-tale rash appear on the back of their own hands or on the hands of people near them. At times the ships' captains had been hard-pressed to maintain order. There had been a near riot aboard the *Tennel* – sparked off when a bereaved husband had reacted violently to a callous remark that at least the overcrowding problem was being solved. Order had been restored only by the intervention of the High King himself.

Lantor had worried constantly about carrying the plague to other lands. "We can't join Renolth if we still have the sickness aboard," he'd said, so many times that Ryella had given up telling him he was fretting too much, too soon.

By the third week, however, no new cases of the plague had been reported on any of the vessels and Lantor's anxiety had finally lessened. Tempers had cooled and life had started to take on some sort of routine. Once clear of inhabited lands and well-known waters, the fleet had begun to rely on the charts sent by Renolth. Three times they'd made landfall on small islands marked on the charts to take on fresh water and much needed fruit to help supplement the meagre rations aboard the ships.

A protracted period of calm had delayed them and then, when they'd finally managed to resume their voyage, contrary winds had sent them far off course, adding many more days to an already lengthy passage. Through the expertise of Murl and Jedron, the fleet had eventually returned to the newly charted waters. They'd been only a couple of weeks away from the sanctuary of the island they sought when the storm had struck.

Clutching a small, cloth-wrapped bundle containing cheese and some hard biscuits for Jerram, Amryl emerged through the hatch just as an ominous cracking and a yelled warning preceded the collapse of a splintered spar. She saw her father snatch Darrant out of harm's way as the spar crashed down. Frozen to the spot by terror, she watched helplessly as they both went down in a tangle of rigging. Darrant was on his feet and scrambling free almost immediately but the few seconds before her father emerged unscathed seemed an eternity to Amryl. She saw Murl hasten across the wet, slippery deck, shouting orders for the smashed wood and torn canvas to be cleared.

Her father looked angry. She hoped he wouldn't reprimand Darrant, not in front of Murl and the others on deck anyway. She knew Darrant had disobeyed their father, that he should have been below decks resting, but he only wanted to help, like Jerram – and it wasn't Darrant's fault the spar had fallen.

Amryl sighed. The months aboard ship had been hard on everyone, but of all her family Darrant seemed to have suffered most. Jerram, already a competent sailor before the earthquakes had begun, had put his skills to good use throughout the voyage. Her father, of course, had been a tower of strength, sometimes by contributing towards the physical work involved in sailing the huge vessel but mostly by inspiring confidence and hope in all those aboard the *Tennel* and the rest of the fleet. At each landfall, he had made a point of going aboard every vessel and speaking to as many people as he could and, in the few periods of fair weather when Murl had no urgent communications to send, her father had used the *Tennel*'s flags to signal messages of encouragement to the other vessels.

Amryl, fascinated by seeing the messages sent and received, had been quick to learn the intricate flag system. She was proud that she was now on the rota to decipher incoming signals and was sometimes even allowed to devise messages for her father. Along with her tasks as assistant to her mother, Amryl had more than enough to keep her occupied and feeling useful.

Her mother, too, had valuable skills. She'd been a healer before she'd married Lantor, and now she did what she could to treat illnesses and injuries of passengers and crew alike. With few medicines, Ryella could do far less than she would have liked but Amryl knew her mother's efforts made a difference.

Darrant was the problem, as far as Amryl could see, and she really felt he was not to blame. Younger than Jerram by six years, Darrant had never had the chance to hone his sailing skills. The earthquakes and the plague had seen to that. Back home he'd helped with all the administration involved in sending troops to the worst hit areas of the Isles and in sorting the rationing as supplies dwindled. Here aboard ship he was too inexperienced to be of much value to Murl, and rationing the paltry stores from the *Tennel*'s hold took up all too little of his time. Determined not to be a burden, he'd been willing to do even the most menial of tasks but he'd fallen badly quite near the start of the voyage. He'd suffered a concussion, and since then he had tired easily. It was a source of contention between the High King and his younger son that Darrant still tried to do as much as Jerram. Amryl knew her father worried about Darrant but the frequent rows did little to improve matters and only served to darken Darrant's mood still further.

Recalling her purpose, Amryl stepped out onto the deck as Darrant headed back towards the hatch. He was limping – and trying not to show it. He brushed past her without a word, almost knocking the bundle from her hand. Amryl hesitated, wondering whether or not to go after him, but Jerram turned and saw her, and he would be needing his food.

She started across the deck, noticing as she made her way carefully towards the helm that the ship was riding more smoothly than she had done for some considerable time. The wind had veered north-easterly and eased, and the taut, billowing sails were slackening.

"Land! Land ahead, south-south-east!"

The cry from the forward lookout drew the attention of all on deck. Shouting for Ryella to join him, Lantor followed Murl to the ship's prow. With the cloth of food clutched forgotten in her hand, Amryl hurried after them.

By the time the land came clearly into view, the upper deck was crowded. Jerram had stayed at the helm but Darrant, Ryella and Amryl stood close to Lantor as the blurred coastline gradually sharpened into focus. There were ships, six or seven of them, heading towards the battered Almari vessels and a faint cheer went up from some of the watchers. Surely they were saved at last. They would find refuge until they could be on their way back to the island they sought. An excited murmur rippled through the weary travellers.

At the ship's rail, the High King stiffened in sudden tension. He turned to the *Tennel*'s captain and asked quietly, "Murl, can we avoid them?"

Murl looked from the oncoming ships to the tattered sails and damaged planking of his own vessel. "Not a chance, Sire. Why?"

Lantor shook his head worriedly, staring out once more at the ships. "I have a terrible feeling about this, Murl. By the Light's mercy, I hope I'm wrong – but I think they're more of a threat to us than the storm."

Chapter Sixteen

More than a Dream

"The fishing went well at first," Brandell told his shocked listeners as they sat together in the royal shelter. "The wind was westerly and the sea swell only slight so Renolth asked Valdrak to sail farther out into open sea. We all knew he was hoping to find the *Tennel's Flight*, though Valdrak warned him there was little likelihood of that." He paused to refill his wine goblet before continuing. "We turned back at Oltan's set and were heading towards the harbour entrance when it happened. The wind veered south-westerly quite suddenly and strengthened within minutes. You know how treacherous those currents can be even on the calmest of days. The ship heeled to starboard. A spar broke loose. It must have been badly maintained. I'll have to speak to the master shipwright about that."

"Never mind that now," Zenton said impatiently. He stood up, shrugged off his wet cloak and dropped it to the floor. "What happened?"

Brandell took a long drink of wine. "Well, Valdrak and Renolth were standing together close by the starboard rail. The spar came crashing down and he was flung into the sea. We managed to turn about and bring him aboard but it was too late. He must have been killed instantly when the spar hit him."

Zenton sat down again and reached for a cup. He poured himself some banellin in preference to wine and sipped cautiously at the steaming liquid, feeling its warmth ease a little of his tension. The study was warm and bright, a contrast to the blackness he had felt on first hearing the news. "I'm sorry about Valdrak," he said, turning to his father, "but thank the Light *you* weren't killed as well! How bad is your shoulder?"

Renolth shrugged then winced. "Just bruising, I'm told. Nothing broken. It's pretty sore at the moment but it should soon heal. I was fortunate to escape so lightly. Valdrak was a brave man and a good friend. I shall miss him." He shifted position awkwardly. "It was strange though, Zenton. Just before the spar fell I could have sworn I heard a most peculiar, nerve-chilling cry from high overhead. I suppose it must have been some great seabird but it was like nothing I'd ever heard before. And Brandell said he didn't hear it. Anyway, I looked up because of the sound and that's what saved me. I grabbed for Valdrak but I was too slow."

Weariness and sorrow were etched deep into the lines of his father's face. "You should be in bed," Zenton observed, "and I could do with some sleep, too. I expect Chandrane feels the same. I'll have a few hours' rest then I'll make the arrangements for Valdrak's farewell ceremony. I really *am* sorry for his loss."

"It's all in hand," Brandell informed his cousin.

"Already?" Zenton leaned forward, surprised.

Brandell nodded. "Renolth was quite some time with the healers, and I didn't expect you back for several days. I've made the necessary arrangements with the Council Leaders."

"My thanks, Brandell," said Renolth, rising stiffly. "The ceremony is on the morrow? Then I'll check the details with you this evening." He accepted Brandell's steadying arm as he headed towards his sleeping room. "It seems you were right to have some concerns about the voyage, doesn't it, son?" he remarked quietly as he passed Zenton.

Chandrane held open the study door for Renolth and Brandell and closed it gently after they had left. He dabbed with his toe at the puddle his own soaked cloak had dribbled onto the study floor. "What did your father mean?"

Zenton hesitated before replying. He had not mentioned even to Aldana how worried he'd been before the voyage and he wondered now whether or not to give Chandrane any explanation.

"You don't need to answer," Chandrane said hastily into the silence. "It's not my place to question something that's between you and your father."

"I was uneasy about the trip," Zenton stated, deciding to confide at least that much information.

"So you knew something was going to happen?"

"Not 'knew' exactly. I just had a nagging feeling that something was wrong. I hadn't actually *said* anything, but I didn't show much enthusiasm. I didn't realise he knew how worried I was." He held up a hand to forestall any further questions. "I'm too tired to talk about it right now, Chandrane, and you must be just as worn-out. I'll see you this evening, if my father doesn't need me here." As Chandrane turned to go, the prince added, "My thanks for your company." He grinned suddenly. "It wasn't the most pleasant of walks, was it?"

Chandrane laughed. "It showed me I'm not as fit as I thought I was! Well, I'll bid you farewell for the present." He paused in the doorway. "You know," he added as a parting shot, "when Brandell told us about the accident, I thought at first Prince Renolth had been killed. He's safe, praise the Light, but I think you should start listening a little more closely to those 'feelings' of yours."

Zenton walked through a labyrinth of cold, damp, twisting passages, the only light an eerie, violet glow emanating from a strange fungus clinging to the tunnels' rocky surfaces. The cave he sought was somewhere deep in the heart of the winding maze. Sometimes he had to crawl, squeezing through low, narrow openings. Now and again he found he could pass through solid rock into yet another dim passageway.

He came at last to a long, straight tunnel which branched at its end into a right and left fork. Turning left, he saw a faint reddish light ahead and moved towards it, his booted feet making little sound on the uneven ground. He stopped at the entrance to a huge cave, the diffuse light curtaining the opening. Wary of entering, he rested one hand against the rocky wall and peered in.

A huge creature lay curled in sleep, enormous wings folded close to its body. The prince stared, spellbound. The shape was familiar. Gradually, he came to the realisation that in outline the creature resembled both the charted coastline of Zamara and the image on his medallion. Zenton's breath caught in his throat.

The dragon stirred and sighed. A twist of smoke curled lazily from one nostril. Despite the size and fearsome appearance of the great beast, the prince felt only a sense of peace and security as he watched it sleeping.

From someplace far below the cave there came a rustling, rattling, hissing whisper. Zenton shuddered. There was a feeling of wrongness here, a malevolence that made him break out in a cold sweat. The dragon's tail twitched. It opened one glistening eye and just for an instant seemed to stare right at the prince. Then it turned its huge head as if listening intently.

"Nad's teeth!" swore Brandell, close behind Zenton. "What's that sound?"

Zenton swung round, grazing his hand against the rough stone of the cave's entrance.

"Brandell? By the Light, you startled me! What's –"

The scene dissolved in a sharp clap of thunder and Zenton jerked awake. By the angle of the suns' rays, he estimated it was late afternoon. The wind had dropped and there was no storm. The sudden noise that had woken him must have been the slamming of a door. He flung back his light blanket and sat up, the dream still vivid in his mind. Glancing down, he saw that the back of his left hand was scraped and bleeding.

Zenton felt sick, not from the stinging pain of the abraded skin but from sheer fright. It had only been a dream. He must surely have knocked his hand against the wall or the low, wooden bed frame. When close scrutiny of the wall and his bed revealed no trace of blood, Zenton decided there and then that he needed to speak with his father.

He washed hurriedly, using the cold water in the washbowl rather than sending for heated water. Snatching up a clean shirt, he left his room, dressing as he went, and collided in the corridor with Brandell. Tugging his shirt on, Zenton offered a mumbled apology.

Brandell's response was not the expected teasing comment. "My apologies cousin," he said. "I wasn't looking where I was going."

"That's all right. It was my fault."

Brandell seemed not to have heard. "I'm going out for a walk," he declared. "I need some air."

"Why?" asked Zenton, responding now to his cousin's distracted manner. "What's the matter?"

Brandell grimaced. He scuffed the toe of one boot against the wooden floor, uncharacteristically hesitant. "I sat down to check some work rotas," he began. "I must have dropped off to sleep." His tone became defensive. "I'd been up most of last night, you know." When Zenton made no comment, he continued, "I had the weirdest dream."

Zenton stared at him, recalling how Brandell had spoken to him in *his* dream. "You dreamt about some rock tunnels?"

"Tunnels? No. What gave you that idea? I was out in the open somewhere. Someone kept calling me. He was offering me something. I don't know what it was but it seemed pretty special. I wanted to take it, but then the voice turned unpleasant – more insistent, demanding that I agreed to take whatever it was. That was when I woke. You know, cousin," he added, sounding aggrieved, "that's the fifth or sixth dream that's been clear enough for me to recall on waking. This never happened before we came here. You might be used to it but I don't like it happening to me. It's becoming hard to tell when I'm awake and when I'm sleepwalking!"

"Sleepwalking?" echoed Zenton in concern. "When? What happened?" But Brandell had already walked off down the corridor and was heading out of the shelter.

Feeling more unsettled than ever, Zenton knocked lightly on Renolth's door. He went in at Renolth's call and, keeping his promise to Aldana, he launched into a lengthy explanation of what had been happening to him from the time of their first landing and how he felt about it all. Now and again Renolth asked a question or made a comment, but for the most part it was Zenton who did the talking.

The telling took quite some time, and left Zenton feeling drained and badly in need of something to drink. He was about to suggest sending for some refreshments when a quiet knock sounded at the door.

It was Jennon, one of the servants. "Prince Renolth," he said, "my apologies for disturbing you, but Healer Vemran is here to check on your shoulder."

Renolth sighed. "Ask him to be good enough to wait in the study for a few minutes, Jennon. I'll join him there directly."

As the door closed behind the youngster, Renolth turned back to Zenton. "Well, son, you've certainly given me a great deal to think about. I don't see how we can possibly *prepare* for any more 'happenings' like those you've described. We'll just have to remain vigilant, will we not? But please, Zenton, come to me in future."

"I will," Zenton promised. "Aldana was right. I should have come to you sooner."

94

"Indeed you should," agreed Renolth, his smile taking any sting from his words. "We might not understand what's going on but at least we can try to puzzle it out together." He stood slowly, accepting Zenton's help. "Out of all that you've told me, I think I'm most astonished – and shocked – by the physical damage to your hand. Ask Vemran to check it while he's here."

"It's only a graze."

"Nevertheless I'd prefer it was properly tended, especially considering how you came by it."

"Very well, but – " Looking down, Zenton gave a short, humourless laugh and changed what he had been about to say. "Actually, I doubt there's much point bothering Vemran."

He held out his left hand, palm downwards. The injury had gone.

Chapter Seventeen

Festival Plans

As the months passed, life on Zamara settled into a routine of work, with exploratory searches sanctioned whenever time and resources permitted. Some of the people from the second fleet joined relatives or friends in the harbour area while most of the newcomers moved to the second settlement, a day's walk east, where they laboured with the first colonists there to bring some sort of order back to their shattered existence.

When a group of settlers came to Renolth one day complaining that many people were now calling themselves Zamaran rather than Almari, the prince surprised them by supporting the change.

"The land and the kingdom we knew are gone," he told them firmly. "We've made a fresh start here. Our heritage will always be important to us but it's time we looked forward instead of back. Our home is Zamara so we are Zamaran."

After that, those who continued to protest generally did so out of his hearing.

The Almari had been a proud race, seafaring traders for the most part, famed for their craftwork in pottery, clothing and jewellery, but fierce fighters when necessary. Though they had long ago lost the desire to conquer other lands, they had until quite recent times often been forced to defend the Isles against attempted invasion. A combination of a highly skilled, well trained fighting force and treacherous seas around their isles had allowed the Almari to claim justly that they had never been conquered.

Even though Renolth accepted change as being right and necessary in their new circumstances, he had since first landfall encouraged the traditional weapons training of all those able to bear arms. As the third anniversary of their finding sanctuary on Zamara drew near, he decided that a tournament of weapons skills, followed by a celebratory gathering, might provide a welcome relief for everyone from their usual chores and a distraction for those still inclined to grumble.

"Our first landfall anniversary passed almost unnoticed," he commented to Zenton and Brandell when he'd called them in to discuss his ideas. "We were too busy struggling to survive."

"True," agreed Brandell, grinning at Zenton as he added, "and the celebration plans for your coming-of-age ceremony went awry, did they not, cousin? So, it seems to me a good suggestion to have some sort of festival this year."

"I think the tournament idea would work well," offered Zenton, ignoring Brandell's jibe about the lightning strike. "It'd give purpose to the training we all have to do. I've heard quite a few people question why we persist with such skills when Zamara's uninhabited except for us and we've no neighbouring lands."

Renolth stood, signifying the short meeting was drawing to an end. "Well, I'm glad you both approve. And since we all agree on the basic outline for the celebrations, I'll leave you to organise the details, Zenton."

Brandell, too, rose but Zenton remained seated. "I was hoping to join the next search band," he said. "Now you've allowed longer searches, they're going north of the Eye Lake."

"I know where they're going," Renolth returned mildly. "I'd still like you to plan and supervise the anniversary events."

"Administration's not really one of my strong points," Zenton protested. "Wouldn't it be better if Brandell –"

"No. Brandell has managed rotas for settlement work and searches for nigh on a year now. It's time you did your share, Zenton."

Stung by what he considered an injustice, Zenton stood and faced his father. "I work as hard as anyone in this community!" he declared defensively.

"Indeed you do, and harder than many. I'm making no complaint about your commitment, but you're old enough now to help with the management of the settlements as well as the physical work. Since we're celebrating the anniversary of your birth as well as our third Landing Day, organising this tournament and meal seems a good place for you to start."

"I could help," ventured Brandell somewhat hesitantly.

"Not this time," said Renolth before Zenton had a chance to leap in and accept his cousin's offer. "Submit your plans to me, Zenton.

We'll discuss them as soon as you're ready. Brandell, I've received word from the second settlement that two of their people have gone missing. Go there and find out exactly what happened, will you? Offer them whatever help you can."

Zenton opened his mouth to protest again. He wanted to go on the search to the Eye Lake or to accompany Brandell. Either trip would be far preferable to organising a tournament and feast, particularly since the latter would have to take into account the rationing still in force. Renolth gave him no chance to voice his thoughts.

As Brandell hastened away to make his preparations, Renolth turned back to Zenton. "We seldom disagree, son," he said gently, "and I've no wish to quarrel with you now."

"I know. It's just –"

"Hear me out, Zenton. Over the past half year, since you and I discussed the possible strangeness of this land of ours, I've tried time and time again to persuade you to take a more active role in governing."

"But Brandell's so much better –"

Again Renolth cut him off. "He always *will* be better at organising and decision making unless you make the effort to learn." A sharp edge crept into his tone. "You're just as capable as your cousin. You're my heir, Zenton. And if anything should happen to me –"

This time it was Zenton who interrupted. "Are you all right?" he asked anxiously, the colour draining from his face. "You're not ill, are you?"

"No, of course not! I'm perfectly well!" snapped Renolth. Moderating his tone, he said, "I'm fine. Stop worrying. I just need you to realise how important it is to me that you start to share the duties of leadership. *Asking* you hasn't worked, has it? So now I'm *telling* you. Sort out this tournament." Picking up his light cloak, he fastened it round his shoulders as he concluded, "You never know – you might even find you enjoy it."

"That's it, really," Zenton finished, his enthusiasm waning suddenly when his father remained silent. "I'd have written it all down for you but Maglin says we're short of parchment. He's trying out a new writing material made from some reeds which grow round the Eye Lake, but there's not much of it yet." Realising he was beginning to babble, he closed his mouth and schooled himself to wait patiently for a response. It had taken him four days of hard work to prepare these ideas and, accepted as adult though he might be, at present he felt very much like a child again.

"That's interesting," Renolth said at last. "I must ask Maglin how he's progressing. As for your plans: they sound fine to me. Well done. Are they all your ideas?"

Zenton hesitated before opting for honesty. "No. Most of the suggestions are mine but I had help from Chandrane and Lissanne. I checked out the ideas with Slen and Aldana too. And I went to Jeya for advice about the food."

"Good. It's often useful to share the planning of something like this. The points system for competitions in different skills is well thought out and I particularly like the notion of contests spread over the week prior to Landing Day, with the final events on the actual day."

"We thought that would give time for our everyday work to be done and for more people to take part."

Renolth nodded agreement. "The celebratory meal is well planned too. We need to conserve our provisions but you and Jeya seem to have taken that into account."

Zenton began to relax. He hadn't realised quite how much he still needed and valued his father's approval.

"Has Brandell sent word yet?" Zenton asked as he prepared to take his leave.

"A messenger arrived from the second settlement a short time ago," Renolth told him. "Brandell's staying on for a day or two longer. I've no information as yet about what happened there. If there's no news soon I think I'd better go myself. It's a while since I've visited to check the progress there anyway." He pushed back his chair and stood up. "Well, I told Jedron and the other captains I'd meet them at mid-suns to make the final decision about which vessels we keep afloat."

"That's not going to be easy."

"No, indeed. It's a sad end for some noble ships. Nevertheless, we have no need of all eleven vessels, and we *do* need materials from them." He paused briefly before asking. "Will you attend the meeting with me?" Smiling, he added, "That's a request, not an order."

Zenton laughed. "I'll come willingly." Following Renolth out of the shelter, he remarked casually, "I hate to have to admit it, but you were right – again."

"Right? About what?"

"I *am* enjoying organising these celebrations. Please don't tell Brandell, though. It would doubtless give him cause to make some caustic comment about my finally growing up."

Chapter Eighteen

Cliff Edge

When a second messenger arrived with tidings that Brandell had led a search team into the forest region to seek the missing colonists, Renolth decided to go himself to the second settlement to discuss matters with the Council Leaders there. After the episode of his ill-fated trip aboard the *Waves of Oltan*, he broached the subject cautiously. Zenton surprised him by laughing.

"It's not a matter for jest, Zenton," admonished Renolth.

"My apologies," said Zenton, controlling his amusement with some difficulty. "I wasn't laughing at the idea of you going to find out what's happening. It's just that I can't help questioning your motives."

"My motives?"

"I show a glimmer of interest in helping to run things here and you take the opportunity to leave our settlement just before a Council meeting which I presume I'll be expected to attend in your stead. How very convenient."

It was Renolth's turn to laugh. "Would I really be that devious?"

"Indeed you would," his son informed him. Becoming serious, he added, "It's probably wise for you to go. The Council Leaders there will appreciate your visit. Besides, I think there's more to this tale of missing people than we've heard so far."

"Another of your 'feelings'?" There was no mockery in Renolth's tone. It was a genuine query.

Zenton shrugged dismissively. "Perhaps. Anyway, whether I'm right or not, it's still time you visited the Far Settlement, is it not? It's almost three months since you were last there."

"It's strange how the second settlement's become known as the 'Far Settlement'," Renolth observed, frowning slightly. "It's only a day's walk away. I hope there's no feeling of separation. We're still one community here."

"Well, Brandell and I go there quite often, and you usually visit every other month." He paused thoughtfully and then said, "Take Slen and Chandrane in your group this time, will you?"

"Certainly, if it will ease your mind." Renolth chuckled softly. "They won't thank me for it. I'm sure they'd rather be practising for the tournament."

"Maybe, but I'll feel happier if they're with you. Besides, the less practice those two get, the more chance the rest of us stand in the contests."

"Now who's being devious?" accused Renolth. "Still, I suppose it's highly probable they'll be amongst the finalists. How do you think *you* will fare?"

Zenton rubbed a hand through already disordered hair. "Well, I stand a good chance with the bow – although Lissanne's probably still the best archer we have, and Brandell comes pretty close after her. Brandell and I can both make Slen and Chandrane work hard for victory with sword or dagger but neither of us has actually beaten them in training bouts. I doubt we're ever likely to. Lajar's good as well. It should be an interesting contest."

"Merret's a possible contender too, isn't he?"

Zenton nodded. "He's changed, though. He's pretty surly most of the time these days."

"I suppose that's understandable," Renolth said. "It can't have been easy for him having to deal with his brother's death. He'd nursed Halden through the plague *and* kept him safe on the voyage only to see him killed by that lightning strike."

"I know. He won't even speak Halden's name these days. Several of us have tried to talk with him but he's so... angry... all the time. We've pretty much given up trying. Perhaps I should make more effort."

"The tournament contests might help him renew friendships. Let's hope so, anyway. And I'll take him along with me to the Far Settlement. Have Slen make the necessary arrangements will you, Zenton? We'll leave at Oltan's dawn on the morrow."

Zenton stood silently, a passive observer of a sea battle in which those around him fought for their lives against enemies who had boarded their vessel. Lantor was there, fighting alongside Murl, the

Tennel's Flight captain. Zenton watched with horror, unable to take an active role in the struggle, as his uncle and the captain were overpowered along with all the others.

The scene shifted, and Zenton was standing on bare, hard-packed soil, an icy wind blowing across open ground. Lantor, High King of the Almari, was digging, forcing his spade into unyielding earth to till the land for cultivation. His wife Ryella and Princess Amryl toiled nearby, picking rocks from the soil and carrying them to other Almari workers who laboured to build a dry stone wall along the field's perimeter.

Lantor paused in his task. He took off his ring and held it out.

"Here," he said. "You'll need this, Zenton."

The ring slipped out of his hand and vanished before it reached the ground. Lantor resumed his digging.

A guard stood overseeing the work, his or her face masked by a cloth. Zenton saw his youngest cousin falter, stumbling as she struggled to raise a boulder too large for her to manage. The guard stepped forward, whip in hand, and raised an arm to strike the girl.

"No!" Zenton yelled – and woke, sweating and shaken.

He lay for a while, his breathing gradually calming as he attempted to sort the images, wondering if this was merely a terrible dream or a vision which reflected reality. His first instinct was to seek his father's counsel, but Renolth was away in the Far Settlement and unlikely to return for several days. Disturbed though he was, Zenton could hardly leave his assigned duties and go to his father merely because of a vivid nightmare.

Deciding that sleeping again was out of the question just yet, the prince rose. He drew back the curtain to allow the moons' light to filter into the room and dressed slowly. He flung a cloak around his shoulders as he left the shelter.

The settlement was quiet and still. With the First Sun's dawn some hours away, all but the duty watch would be sleeping. Even the settlement guards tended to be less vigilant than in the first months after landfall, for there had been no threat to the colonists and nothing to cause alarm since that one incident when the herd of horned animals had ventured near. Perhaps it wasn't altogether a good thing that complacency had set in, thought Zenton as he made his way towards the harbour. What if a real threat occurred?

With a sharp drop in temperature following yesterday's heat, a thick sea mist had developed over the harbour waters. Zenton wandered past the quay and walked a little way farther west onto the cliffs whose steep slopes led down to a sharp rocky outcrop jutting from the glistening waters. He sat down to watch the play of the moons' light on the mist, fascinated by the contrast between the clear skies over the land and the fog-shrouded sea. Even in the poor light, he could make out the peculiar bluish tint of the harbour sands.

A slight breeze stirred the haze into dancing shapes, dispersing it enough to give occasional glimpses of the vessels bobbing gently on the smooth waters. They looked to Zenton as if they, too, were sleeping away the dark hours. The horror of the dream ebbed, though the memory of the images remained.

Little by little, the breeze strengthened, ruffling Zenton's hair and tugging playfully at his cloak. Absently, he pulled the medallion from beneath his tunic and ran his fingers over the raised image and faceted gemstone. Shivering slightly, he tucked the medallion away and drew his cloak more closely around his shoulders.

He was about to return to his shelter when his eye was drawn to a huge, dark shape gliding through the thinning mist above the harbour. He stared harder, trying to pierce the veil of cloud to determine what the creature might be. He was sure he'd seen it before. It had been flying over the far side of the harbour the day he'd left the infirmary after being injured by the green lightning. He'd not been sure then just what it was, and his next sighting of it had, after all, been only in a dream. Here though, as it flew closer, he could see it plainly.

Zenton's mouth went dry. His heart thumped painfully against his ribs. He made a deliberate effort to slow his rapid breathing. He knew now what manner of creature had its home somewhere on Zamara and was at this moment flying overhead. Knowing it and seeing it, he could still hardly believe it.

A strong gust of wind ripped a great hole in the fog. Zenton gazed, transfixed, at the awesome sight of the dragon silhouetted against the central moon.

The mist closed in again, obscuring his view, but Zenton knew beyond doubt that this was no figment of his imagination. The thrill of his discovery drove all other thoughts from his mind. He wanted

104

desperately to share his amazing revelation with Renolth and Brandell but neither of them was in the settlement. Still, Aldana was there. She would understand how very special this was.

The fog grew denser. Certain he would not see the dragon again this night, the prince surged to his feet. A haunting cry rang out, shattering the quiet calm of the harbour and sending a shudder down Zenton's spine. Unexpectedly, the memory came to him of his father's accident aboard the *Waves of Oltan*. He recalled Renolth speaking about hearing a strange cry from high above him immediately before that broken spar had crashed down claiming Valdrak's life and so nearly killing Renolth himself. Could it have been the dragon that his father had heard? If so, then by chance or design, the creature had saved Renolth's life.

The cry came again, a weird, drawn-out shriek made all the more eerie by the thick mist that hid the dragon from Zenton's sight. A third time the wailing call rang out – and Zenton felt a sudden, overwhelming sense of danger. He needed to get away from the cliff's edge.

He had taken just one step back when the ground gave way beneath him.

Chapter Nineteen

Contests

The rain which had drenched Patoll for the better part of two weeks finally ceased the day before the first of the pre-tournament contests was scheduled to take place. Casting a relieved glance at the clearing sky, Slen took his team of helpers to the eastern edge of the Harbour Settlement and began marking out areas for competitions, practice and spectators.

Though not particularly arduous, the work took most of the day. By late afternoon the suns' heat had taken the worst of the wetness from the sodden ground, though puddles and mud patches still abounded. Slen patrolled the marked sectors, surveying the layout critically before finally declaring himself satisfied.

Towards Oltan's set, several young men and women came out to the driest sections of the marked areas to start practising their various skills. Zenton sat quietly off to one side, on a rise of ground which gave a good view of the contestants, watching as Merret and Chandrane saluted each other and began their moves. The prince looked up and smiled as Aldana came to join him.

"How are they getting on?" she asked, nudging Zenton to one side so that she could spread a waxed cloak on the ground before sitting down beside him.

Zenton shuffled carefully onto the vacant portion of the spread cloak. "They've only just started."

"I didn't realise Merret was so good," Aldana commented after watching the pair for a few minutes.

"He *is* good," Zenton agreed. "Chandrane's better, though."

Aldana chuckled softly. "Spoken like a true friend."

"No," Zenton protested, wriggling into a more comfortable position, "I'm not saying that just because he's my friend."

"Of course not," Aldana teased. "You're probably right anyway," she added. "I think most people are hoping to see Chandrane challenge Slen in the swordplay final."

As they watched, Merret lunged forward unexpectedly. Chandrane's parry came barely in time. In defending himself against a renewed onslaught, Chandrane stepped back. His foot squelched in a muddy hole, causing him to lose his balance momentarily. His flailing arm caught Merret a glancing blow to the face, halting him in his tracks. He dabbed at a suddenly bleeding nose.

"Good thing Chandrane didn't have his sword in that hand," Zenton muttered, looking round for some clean cloth or a handkerchief he could toss to Merret.

"You did that on purpose!" Merret accused, drawing a sleeve across his nose in an attempt to staunch the flow of blood.

"No, Merret. I just slipped." Chandrane shrugged and smiled disarmingly. Unknowingly, he echoed Zenton's observation. "It's fortunate I didn't have my sword in that hand. Sorry about the nose. Are you all right?"

His opponent was not prepared to be mollified. "You're known for keeping your balance. Don't try to tell me you 'just slipped'!"

Chandrane's easy manner changed. "You were dangerously close on that move before I *slipped.*" He placed heavy emphasis on the last word. "Slen's taught us all how to keep the correct distance to avoid a return stroke after a thrust like you made."

"So you admit now it was a return stroke?"

"I didn't say that. I meant – "

Chandrane had no time to say what he'd meant. Sword in hand, Merret swung at him. Chandrane ducked and, within the space of a few heartbeats, the two were fighting in earnest.

As Chandrane twisted away from a vicious thrust, Zenton was horrified to see Merret bend swiftly to slide a narrow dagger from a hidden sheath in his boot. The blade glinted wickedly in the suns' lowering rays. The prince was on his feet and moving towards the two combatants when he felt Aldana's restraining hand on his arm.

"He's got a knife, Aldana!"

"I know, but you might distract Chandrane," she warned.

"I'll judge the moment, but I can't let this go on!"

He walked to the edge of the fight area, seeing to his added consternation that several people had left off their own practice sessions and were drifting over to find out what was happening. As

107

Chandrane and Merret drew apart momentarily, Zenton stepped into the marked sector and yelled, "Break!"

Trained by Slen to cease fighting on that command, the two antagonists hesitated. Zenton pressed home his advantage. "*Break*, I said!" he bellowed, trying to sound as authoritative as Slen.

To his relief, Merret and Chandrane lowered their weapons and turned towards him. Chandrane stood, breathing heavily, staring at Merret's dagger and looking partly angry and partly bewildered by what had just happened.

Merret rounded furiously on Zenton. "Stay out of this, Prince. It's not your fight."

"It is when you turn on one of your colleagues like that."

"He's well able to defend himself."

"True, but he shouldn't have to defend against the added threat of a boot knife."

"If you're so concerned about him, perhaps you'd like to step in and even the contest. Oh, my apologies, Prince, you're not able to fight at the moment, are you? How very convenient."

Angered and insulted, Zenton foolishly rose to the bait. "I can fight if I have to, Merret."

"Here, then."

Merret threw him the training sword. Without thought, Zenton caught it in his left hand. Pain shot through his wrist, arm and shoulder. Hastily, he transferred the weapon to his right hand. He felt sick.

"I'll take that knife, Merret," said a familiar voice.

The small crowd which had gathered parted as Brandell made his way unhurriedly past Zenton and came to stand facing Merret.

"I'll take that knife," he repeated, holding out his hand for the offending article.

Merret glowered, hesitating briefly before placing the dagger's hilt in Brandell's outstretched palm.

"My thanks," said Brandell casually. "Now, I suggest you consider yourself disqualified from this tournament. Find some tasks that will keep you well away from this area for a few days."

"Renolth should know of this," Zenton put in quietly but firmly, struggling against nausea and the urge to cradle his injured arm.

Brandell shrugged. "Perhaps. I'd say it depends upon whether or not Chandrane wants to take the matter further. Chandrane?"

Chandrane used his tunic sleeve to wipe some of the sweat from his face. He looked long and hard at Merret before saying, "It's over as far as I'm concerned."

"Good," said Brandell. "That's settled then." He placed a hand on Merret's shoulder. "Let's leave them to it, shall we, Merret?"

He guided Merret away, turning as he passed Zenton to advise softly, "Get that arm checked again, cousin. It wasn't one of your wisest moves to catch that sword, was it?"

The group of spectators closed in around Chandrane and Zenton, some wanting to discover the cause of the fracas, others eager to offer opinions on what they had witnessed. Snatching up her cloak, Aldana was about to push her way through to Zenton when someone called her name.

She turned as Wendrin, a girl some six or seven months her junior and a fellow trainee healer, came running up.

"What happened?" Wendrin asked. "Is Prince Zenton all right?"

"I think so, yes. Apart from being stupid enough to catch that sword and jar the arm he hurt at the cliffs."

"Aldana, what really happened to Prince Zenton? I mean at the cliffs?"

Aldana sighed. A full account had been given to the Councils and made public in both settlements, but still the rumours persisted.

Prince Zenton had been attacked by a dragon.

No, a dragon had caught hold of the prince and saved him from certain death.

The prince had fallen from the cliff but had used his powers to halt his descent and to leap back to safety.

Prince Zenton had fallen and had lain for hours before being found. It was remarkable that he had survived.

"He was on the cliff top just past the harbour," Aldana told Wendrin. "The ground gave way and he fell. He managed to catch hold of some straggly bushes growing out of the cliff sides and somehow climbed back up."

"He was hurt though, was he not? How did he manage?"

"The Light alone knows the answer to that one. He'd dislocated his shoulder and torn the ligaments and tendons in his wrist."

"Was there really a dragon?"

"He says he saw one, yes. But it didn't attack him, nor did it rescue him."

"Do you believe him? About seeing a dragon, I mean?"

"Yes, I do," Aldana replied without hesitation. She looked towards the slowly dispersing group. "I have to go now, Wendrin. I want to check that Zenton's all right."

Brushing aside the girl's efforts at further conversation, Aldana walked across to Zenton and Chandrane. Managing to extricate him with surprising ease from the few who had remained to talk, she steered the prince determinedly in the direction of the infirmary. Carrying the training swords, Chandrane tagged along.

"Injuries like yours often take longer to heal than a clean break, you know, Zenton," Aldana said.

"So Vemran told me. Look, Aldana, I know it was stupid of me –"

"Indeed it was," Aldana agreed.

"Well, I'm paying for it now. Can we please change the subject?"

"Not just yet, I'm afraid."

"Why ever not? I've already admitted –"

"*I'd* willingly talk about something else, Zenton," Aldana said sweetly, "but I think your father might want to know why you're heading for the infirmary."

"My father?"

Chandrane tapped the prince gently on his good arm and jerked a thumb to his right. Renolth was striding purposefully past the outer dwellings at the edge of the settlement, heading for the tournament area.

"If we hurry, he might miss us," Zenton suggested, sounding less than hopeful.

"Not a chance," said Chandrane.

He was right. Renolth had already seen the trio. He changed direction and came towards them.

"Zenton," he called as he approached. "I need to speak with you." He halted and looked appraisingly at his son. "You've hurt your arm again. What happened?"

"I... er... I... I'll explain later," Zenton said lamely.

110

Surprisingly, Renolth did not press him further. "Very well. Come on, then. I'll walk with you to the infirmary." He paused, his stern gaze encompassing all three young people before settling on his son. "I will, however, expect to hear a full account after Vemran has tended you."

Zenton nodded meekly.

"Leave us for a while, will you?" Renolth requested as the group set off again to the infirmary. "We'll see you at the evening meal, Aldana. Chandrane, you're welcome to join us if you'd care to."

With a few words of acceptance and thanks, Chandrane turned back towards the centre of the settlement. Aldana gave Zenton a quick, reassuring smile before following Chandrane.

"What did you want me for?" Zenton enquired, glad of the distraction from his throbbing wrist and aching shoulder. He guessed it must be something of importance, for Renolth could easily have sent for him rather than having come himself.

"The Council Leaders have approached me again about taking the title of High King. They seem to think the tournament final would be a good time to announce it."

Zenton halted. "And?"

Renolth walked on a step, then turned back. "I told them I'd give them an answer on the morrow. I wanted to speak with you and Brandell first."

Zenton smiled. "I think you've already decided, haven't you?"

Renolth responded with a question of his own. "Do you still believe Lantor is alive?"

"I'm not sure," Zenton answered truthfully. "There was that dream I had, but it could have been just that: a simple dream."

"If he *is* alive – "

"If he *is*, and if he finds his way here, you can abdicate immediately in his favour."

Renolth smiled now. "Succinctly put."

"Well?" Zenton urged.

"Well then, I'll tell them I'll accept the title."

Chapter Twenty

The Mandano Ridge

As predicted, Slen was declared overall victor at the conclusion of the tournament, though he later confessed just how close he felt Chandrane had come to taking the title from him. Having decided almost at the last minute to put his archery skills to the test, Brandell came second only to Lissanne in that particular contest.

Unable to participate, Zenton at least had the satisfaction of celebrating the seventeenth anniversary of his birth by presenting the small, beautifully crafted trophies to the winning contestants. Tegran, the former jewellery maker who had been one of Zenton's companions on the first search to the Eye Lake, had used wood, stone and shells to produce the much-admired awards.

During the celebratory feast which followed the presentations, Zenton slipped away from the crowd gathered round one of the blazing fires and made his way to a nearby copse of trees. It had been a long, tiring day and, despite the excitement of the tournament and celebrations, he felt a strange sense of isolation. He knew the feeling was probably a combination of relief now the tournament had been successfully completed and frustration at having been forced to watch rather than take part in the contests. Nevertheless, he suddenly wanted to be away from the noise and the laughter. Wine goblet in hand, he sat learning against the smooth trunk of a small, sturdy baltra tree.

"Abandoning the revels so soon?" Renolth asked, sitting down beside his son.

Zenton smiled a welcome. His father had always shown an uncanny knack for knowing when Zenton was troubled – and could usually find him when he wandered off.

"I needed a moment's quiet," Zenton explained.

"A rare luxury for those in positions of leadership, Zenton," his father said gently.

"I know that. More and more lately, whenever you are occupied, people come to me to make decisions for them."

"You're second-in-command here. You're expected to make decisions."

"I know, but what if I make the wrong ones?"

Renolth laughed softly. "You will, sometimes. We all make mistakes, son. Just listen to the opinions of others – especially if they know more about the situation than you do. Don't be afraid to ask for advice. Never be too arrogant – or too concerned about showing weakness – to take into account the views of others. The final responsibility will be yours, though, and you must accept that."

For a while, father and son sat quietly together, sipping their wine and listening to the sounds of the festivities. The stars glittered brilliantly in a sky devoid of cloud. Two of the moons were almost full, the third just visible in the west. A light breeze carried the smell of salty sea air along with a hint of smoke and food from the cook-fires.

"Your mother would have loved this island," Renolth said in a hushed tone.

Zenton felt his breath catch in his throat. He nodded but made no comment. He and his father could discuss any topic – any, that was, except Ardelle. Her death in a quake two weeks before the advance fleet's voyage had shattered them both. It was rare for either of them to speak of her, though their shared grief should have enabled them to offer each other some comfort. Perhaps this was the beginning, thought Zenton. Maybe the peace of The Island would ease the hurt and allow the happier memories to surface.

He took a deep breath, preparing to try to open a conversation about his mother. Before he could speak, however, Renolth laughed unexpectedly.

"What?" Zenton asked.

"Oh, I was thinking about Irvanyal's and Donar's reactions when I told them I'd accede to the people's request that I become High King – but not for another year." He chuckled again. "I suppose it was unfair of me to seem to agree at first."

"They *were* disappointed you wouldn't take the title sooner, but I think they accepted your reasons. It does seem a long time to wait, though."

"I can't bring myself to allow the ceremony any earlier, son. I have to give Lantor more time to find us."

113

"Well, I suppose we can always have another tournament to help celebrate your coronation."

Zenton had spoken in jest, but Renolth was quite taken with the idea of making some sort of contest an annual event. "We could alternate between fighting skills and crafts or farming skills," he suggested. "Without our crafts people and labourers we'd never have survived here. They deserve recognition."

He drained his wine goblet, then asked, "Do you still dream about needing to find that cave?"

Zenton smiled. "Aldana accuses *me* of jumping from topic to topic without warning. It must be something I've inherited from you! Yes, I still dream about the cave. Most of the dreams are meaningless, as far as I can tell – just jumbled images – but twice this past month I've felt something calling me there."

"To Mandano?"

Zenton nodded. "I want to search the northern cliffs. Kaldrina and her crew on the *Horizon's Edge* saw cave entrances, did they not? I think there must be passages within the Mandano Ridge. I can't explain it properly, but there's something in there I need to find."

"We'll go when that arm of yours is fully healed."

Zenton's face lit with excitement. "*We?*"

"Yes, indeed. I've rarely left the settlements, have I? I want to see more of this land of ours and I'm confident enough now in the Council Leaders to feel I can take some time away." He rose and stretched. "I remember the days when my mother was High Queen. She used to take the whole family and travel the Isles for weeks at a time. I doubt the assistant governors ever noticed we'd gone!" He reached down a hand to help Zenton to his feet. "Come on, son. Let's get back before someone organises a search band to find *us*."

"Speaking of search bands," said Zenton, accepting his father's steadying hand, "has there been any word about the latest search for those two who went missing from the Far Settlement?"

"No," Renolth answered, leading the way slowly back towards the cook-fires.

The tone of the reply caused Zenton to observe, "You've had news of some sort though, haven't you?" He moved up to walk alongside his father.

114

"You're too perceptive at times, Zenton," said Renolth in mild complaint. "Yes, there's news – from here, though, not from the Far Settlement. I had intended to tell you on the morrow rather than dull the shine on what has been a very successful day for you."

The implied praise was more warming than the wine, but Zenton responded to the seriousness of Renolth's tone. "I gather these are not good tidings?"

"I'm afraid not. Four of our people went missing from the settlement last eve."

"From *here*?"

Renolth nodded. "I've sent out searchers, of course."

There was a moment's silence before Zenton said softly, "You don't think they'll find them, do you?"

Renolth hesitated, then shook his head.

"Why? Because the other two haven't been found?"

Renolth sighed and shrugged. "I think there's more to it than we first suspected. The four who've gone from our settlement are all people who've spoken out against the change from the Almari name and against the loss of any of our former traditions."

"And the two from the Far Settlement?"

"They'd also made formal complaint to their Council on several occasions that the old ways were no longer adhered to."

"You think these six people have left by choice?"

"It's beginning to look that way. If they can survive away from the settlements, maybe in the forest – as I think they probably can – and if more join them, we could have problems in the future. A divided community is the last thing I'd wanted here."

Seeing Chandrane and Aldana approaching, Renolth said quietly, "Go and join your friends, son. We'll talk more of this on the morrow. And, Zenton – "

"Yes?"

"Mind you take care of that arm!"

It was Brandell who suggested attempting a coordinated search in Mandano. He put forward the idea of sending one search band across country to the cliff tops while a second team sailed to the northern coastline and then attempted to scale the towering cliffs to reach cave entrances which had been spotted by Kaldrina and her crew on one of their fishing expeditions.

Until recently, no safe landing site other than the harbour of Patoll had been found on any section of the Zamaran coastline. However, just a couple of weeks ago, Kaldrina had noticed a narrow ledge running almost the whole length of the northern coastline, part way up the cliff face. She believed that, if the weather conditions were right, it might be possible to lower a rowboat from the *Horizon's Edge* and land a group on the ledge. From there, they could climb up to the caves.

Brandell, Zenton, Renolth and Kaldrina worked together to plan the search. Zenton, his arm now fully healed, would be part of the group attempting to scale the cliffs from the seaward side. Perhaps one of the caves Kaldrina had seen would lead into the heart of the Mandano Ridge. Renolth and Brandell would take a second band to cross the river at its shallowest section, east of the Eye Lake, and make their way to the Ridge, hoping to find some other entrances to the tunnels Zenton believed were there. If all went well, Zenton's group would explore the caves and then climb the rest of the way up the cliffs to join Renolth's team for an overland return. Kaldrina would wait for two days, keeping her vessel near enough to sight a signal should the plan fail and Zenton's band need to chance the more dangerous return by rowboat from the ledge to the *Horizon*.

The *Horizon's Edge* hove to as near the rocky coast as Kaldrina deemed reasonably safe and a small landing craft was lowered. Ulven – Kaldrina's second-in-command – and a deckhand called Garris shinned down a swaying rope ladder to the boat. Lissanne followed, with Dallan and Pral close behind. Zenton and Tegran went next, but a sudden, violent gust of wind slapped the ladder hard against the ship's side, sending Zenton tumbling into the rowboat and causing Tegran to cry out in pain. Bruised but not badly hurt, Zenton hauled himself onto the rear thwart and looked up to see Tegran clinging desperately to the twisting ropes with one arm. The other dangled uselessly at his side. Pral and Dallan struggled to hold the ladder steady as Garris climbed to Tegran's aid. With Garris supporting him and Chandrane reaching from the deck above, the injured man was returned to the ship.

"Hurry, Chandrane," yelled Kaldrina. "The sea anchor won't hold much longer!"

Leaving Tegran in the care of Kaldrina's crew, Chandrane slid down the ladder into the plunging rowboat and Ulven cast off.

"Tegran?" Zenton had to bellow to be heard.

"Broken arm," Chandrane shouted back. "He'll be all right."

Battling the heavy swell of the seas and the strong, northerly wind, they rowed towards the cliff ledge. Only Ulven's expert seamanship kept them from crashing against the lethal, rocky wall. With no small difficulty, the search group threw lines around jagged outcrops of grey-blue rock to secure the rowboat long enough for them to scramble out onto the ledge. As Zenton clambered from the boat, a vicious blast of wind caught his jacket, billowing it out like a sail and yanking him towards the waves. Chandrane and Lissanne grabbed him just in time.

No sooner had the search group managed the tricky landing than both securing lines snapped, the ropes snaking away like angry sea-serpents. Ulven and Garris somehow kept the boat from overturning and, shouting a hasty farewell and good fortune, they bent to the oars and rowed back towards the *Horizon*.

Dallan, the most experienced climber in the group, checked the team's securing ropes and started up the cliff face. A chunk of rock came loose under his hand. Zenton ducked aside.

"The whole thing's unstable," Dallan yelled.

"We'll manage," Zenton called back. "Keep going."

"Make sure of your holds, then," Dallan shouted, and resumed the climb.

Moments later, dozens of tennels and smaller, black-backed feldrans swooped close, their harsh shrieks almost deafening. Dallan yelped in surprise. Chandrane and Pral cursed loudly as sharp beaks jabbed at them.

"We're near their nests," Zenton shouted.

Trying to protect their heads and faces, the climbers scrabbled onwards. Not until the team was well clear of the nest sites did the birds cease their attack.

Dallan was right about the unstable cliff face. Hand- and footholds crumbled away under the slightest pressure. Huge sections of chalky rock above them dislodged without warning.

117

A falling boulder caught Zenton a glancing blow on his arm. His hold loosened and he slithered downwards. The rope around his waist tightened painfully. He grabbed frantically at a rocky outcrop and halted his fall just above Lissanne.

"It's too dangerous," Dallan called down. "We'll have to go back."

"Not yet," Zenton shouted. "Give it one more try."

"Just one," Dallan replied. "If we can't make it this time, we go back."

"Agreed," Zenton shouted, though it galled him to think of abandoning the search before it had even begun.

They made a final attempt to reach the caves that lined a second, narrower ledge just a short, tantalising distance above and, to everyone's intense relief, they succeeded. They untied the climbing ropes and sat to rest for a few minutes.

Lissanne leaned close to Zenton. "That's three, so far."

"Three?"

"The rope ladder, your near dip in the water and that boulder."

Zenton shook his head. "Happenstance."

"Maybe so. All the same, take special care, will you?"

Zenton nodded and then pointed out to sea. "Look."

Far below, the *Horizon's Edge* appeared small and fragile, alone on the vast expanse of water. From the main mast flew a scarlet and yellow pennant, the pre-arranged signal that the second search band had been sighted on the cliff tops.

"We'll have to go back by rowboat," Dallan said. "There's no way we're going to make it to the top in order to meet the others."

Zenton nodded agreement. "I think you're right. Let's hope the descent's easier than the climb. Still, we can worry about that after we've explored the caves." He stood up. "We need to get moving."

The first four caves explored proved to be huge, damp caverns with no passageways off them. The fifth entrance, almost discounted as being too narrow to explore, opened up into a huge cave and thence to a passage which Zenton felt sure would lead deep into the heart of Mandano's cliffs.

Chapter Twenty-one

Grief and Responsibilities

Zenton and his four companions each took a few items of food and a water-pouch, then stacked their packs and climbing gear just inside the cave's entrance.

"I hope those work as well as you promised," Dallan said, pointing to the torches Chandrane and Lissanne were assembling.

"Should do," Chandrane said. "The packed reeds are slow burning and don't give off much smoke. They don't last all that long though, even with the wax coating – about a half-hour, if we're lucky. We'll need a fair number with us."

"The staves won't catch alight easily," Lissanne added, "but they tend to char if the reeds burn down too far so we'll take plenty of spare reed-heads."

Using a shaped piece of black angra and a tiny metal bar, she sparked alight one of the torches. She used this to light a second one which she passed to Chandrane.

"Sun-stone works better than angra and metal," he said to Dallan, "but it's too cloudy today, even at the passage entrance. No sun to focus onto the reeds." He held out his torch for the others to light theirs.

Ready at last, they began the search.

Zenton and Chandrane led the group, walking together whenever the way widened. Lissanne came next, followed by Dallan and Pral. The tunnel walls were damp and slimy, the air cool but fresh. Very soon they found side passages. Since the main passageway seemed to curve back upon itself, they branched off into a narrow rock corridor which they hoped would lead farther into the heart of the cliffs. Chandrane marked their route carefully. It would be all too easy to become disorientated and lose their way deep within the rocky maze.

The going was slow and difficult; the sides of the tunnels were often jagged, the ground slippery and uneven, and the air grew ever colder as they travelled on. Several times they had to press their way through narrow openings or crawl through low entrances to continue their journey. Whenever they came to an intersection, the rest of the group waited for Zenton to choose the path they should take. The first time this happened, Zenton stood pondering, trying to make a logical decision. There seemed no obvious answer so, in the end, he simply selected the way that felt right. After that, he let instinct guide him and found, as he had hoped and half-expected, something was drawing him on.

Whenever they stopped for a brief rest, Zenton fidgeted impatiently until they set off again. He had just begun to feel they were making good progress when Lissanne suggested they ought to turn back if they were to return before full dark to the cave where they had left their bedrolls and main provisions. She had an uncanny knack of judging time and Zenton knew she was right. Still, something was luring him on and he wanted desperately to continue.

"We'll just go a bit farther," he began, but Dallan sided with Lissanne.

"The tunnel's not too safe here," he said. "We need to be concentrating and we're all getting tired."

With ill grace, Zenton gave in and they turned to retrace their route.

Stumbling slightly on some loose rock, Zenton put his hand against the wall to steady himself. The tunnel seemed to spin slowly, just once, and he found himself alone in complete blackness. For a moment he was bewildered, then panic set in. He could feel the torch in his hand, the heat of it washed against his face, but he could see nothing. He called out to his companions but there was no answer save the soft, muffled echo of his own voice. He shouted again and his words faded off eerily into the darkness.

Taking slow, deep breaths in an effort to calm himself, he tried to work out what could possibly have happened. As he stood fighting the terror, a warm, rosy glow appeared off to his left. With the gentle light came a feeling of security, of comfort and of great wisdom. Knowing somehow that he was near the cave he sought, Zenton turned gratefully towards the glow.

"Zenton. Prince Zenton! Are you all right?"

Chandrane's voice came from a far distance. It took a moment for Zenton to realise he was in the rock tunnel with his companions. He still had his hand against the rough wall.

"Zenton? What's wrong? Is it your arm again?"

"What? No, my arm's fine." Straightening up, Zenton looked around, blinking in the light of the flickering torches. "How long was I standing there?"

Chandrane looked puzzled. "How long? Only a moment. You just tripped and put your hand against the wall."

"Did I call out?"

"Call out? No. I asked if you were all right but you didn't answer at first. *Are* you all right?"

"I think so, yes. The cave we want is that way." He pointed through solid rock.

Lissanne laughed. "After you, my prince."

"Oh!" Zenton smiled. "I see what you mean."

"Something happened when you touched the rock, did it not?" Chandrane observed.

Zenton nodded. "We need to take a passage that will lead us to the left."

"That's as maybe," Lissanne said, "but we're going to leave ourselves very short of time to reach the outer cave if we make too much of a detour now."

Torn between an almost overwhelming desire to go on searching and common sense that told him they really should go back and set up camp for the night, Zenton stood irresolute. Before he could come to any decision, he heard clearly from somewhere high overhead the same haunting cry which had sounded across the harbour waters the day he had fallen from the cliff top in Patoll.

"Did you hear that?" he asked, startled.

His companions looked puzzled. "Hear what?" Chandrane enquired.

"That sound. It was the cry the dragon made when I saw it over the harbour." When the others looked at him blankly, Zenton explained hurriedly, "When I was on the harbour cliff, the cry sounded like a warning. I started to move back, away from the edge. The ground crumbled and I fell. If I'd still been at the very edge, I'd have fallen the whole way and been killed."

"Are you saying the dragon warned you of the danger?" Lissanne asked, doubt clear in her tone.

Zenton shrugged. "It seemed that way to me. I –" He fell silent as the eerie shriek reverberated once more through the rocky tunnel. "Surely you all heard that!" he exclaimed, but it was clear from his companions' perplexed looks that they had not.

Zenton ceased trying to convince the others that the dragon's cry had sounded twice. It was enough that he himself had heard it, and he knew it was a warning of some sort. They should leave the labyrinth.

"We'll go back," he said decisively. "We can try this route again on the morrow."

They were nearing the end of their journey, with a hint of the Smaller Sun's light beginning to dispel the deep gloom of the tunnels, when Zenton halted abruptly. A wave of coldness washed over him, taking his breath away. He shuddered and gasped. Vividly and unexpectedly, he recalled his nightmare of fleeing from a terrifying, unseen enemy. Experiencing anew the horror of that chase, he felt sick and shaky. A sense of evil so powerful it defied belief momentarily swept all conscious thought from him.

Then, quite suddenly and distinctly, Zenton heard Renolth's voice behind him.

Zenton, I am proud to call you my son. Be true to the Light.

Zenton whirled round, almost colliding with Chandrane. There was no one but the search group in the passageway.

Careless of the lit torch and the uneven floor, Zenton raced on towards the outer cave.

When Chandrane and the rest of the group reached Zenton they found him kneeling at the cliff's edge, staring down in horror and disbelief at the still figure sprawled in a crumpled heap on a jagged spur of rock some distance below the ledge where the search group had landed earlier that day. Too stunned to argue, Zenton made no protest when Dallan and Pral insisted he remain where he was while they secured climbing ropes, abseiled down the steep cliff face and made the dangerous ascent back as far as the wide ledge, bringing with them Renolth's broken body.

Dallan climbed up again to help Zenton, Chandrane and Lissanne down to the ledge and Chandrane signalled the *Horizon*. Then, during what seemed an interminable wait for Ulven, Chandrane tried in vain to contact the search team on the cliff top. He and Dallan shouted themselves hoarse, and Pral made an abortive attempt to climb up the crumbling rock face, but there was only silence from above.

Eventually, Renolth was carried aboard the landing-vessel and the group returned to the *Horizon's Edge*. Kaldrina sent up an "abort search" signal for Brandell before they set sail for home. White with shock, but dry-eyed and outwardly composed, Zenton stayed by his father's body during the voyage back to Patoll's harbour.

Zenton sat in Renolth's study, listening with apparent calmness to all the details the overland search band could supply concerning the dreadful incident. Brandell and the others who had been on the cliff top spoke of sea-birds protecting their nests, of sudden, violent gusts of wind, of treacherous, loose rocks and, of course, of the dragon.

To Zenton, the reason for Renolth's fall to his death was not satisfactorily explained. All the accounts varied slightly. No one was clear about exactly what had happened. Slen told how they'd all seen the dragon and heard its weird, plaintive cry. He said that Renolth, without explanation, had ordered the team back down the steep, rocky ridge they had so recently climbed. Merret and Brandell had been the last to see and speak with Renolth. Brandell said they'd thought he was close behind them and they had only turned back on hearing him cry out. No one, it seemed, had actually seen him fall.

Zenton offered no comments on their accounts or on their expressions of sorrow and regret. Whenever his grief could be pushed aside for a moment, he could not shake the feeling that his father's death had been no mere accident. Zenton was coming to believe that, somewhere on the beautiful Island of Zamara, a force of great malevolence was beginning to exert its influence.

During the difficult days which followed Renolth's untimely death, Aldana was never far from Zenton's side. She helped him make the necessary arrangements and stood with him during the harrowing farewell ceremony. She stayed quietly by him when, away from the well-meaning but obtrusive crowds, he wept for the loss of the man who had been not only a beloved father but also a respected friend.

Over the next few weeks, the management of the settlements fell mainly to Brandell, for Zenton took little interest in any of the matters brought to him. More often than not, he wandered off on his own, out of the Harbour Settlement, seeking solace in the quiet beauty of the grasslands in southern Patoll or the windswept grandeur of the cliffs west of the harbour. He knew his friends were worried about him but could not bring himself to care. He needed to be away from the busy settlement, away from people carrying on their lives as if nothing of any great importance had happened. There was an emptiness inside him, an aching void distancing him from the routine of everyday work. He missed his father's solid, comforting presence, his wise counsel, his rare, deep laugh.

There was anger to deal with, too: fury that such a thing could happen, that a senseless accident could rob them of the man who had led them here. It was such a waste. All that knowledge and experience gone, lost forever on unforgiving, tide-washed rocks.

There was another feeling as well: Zenton was consumed by guilt. It had been *his* wish to search the Mandano Ridge in the first place. It had been *his* choice to tackle the seaward side of the cliffs rather than go with Renolth. Could the accident have been avoided? If Zenton had been up on the cliff top, would he have sensed the danger and given warning in time? The questions were useless, serving only to make the situation even harder to accept, but Zenton asked them anyway, over and over in his mind.

Resentment ate at his soul. This land *was* The Island (even in his grief, he maintained that certainty) and it was supposed to be a sanctuary for the Almari, a refuge in a time of great need – and what need could be greater than that for a new homeland? Why, then, had Renolth died? It hadn't been a sanctuary for him, had it? It was reputed in legend to be a good land, so why had something so evil happened? Zenton could find no answers, and he could not bring himself to go to Brandell or even to Aldana. Maglin had tried to talk with him several times, as had the Council Leaders, but on each occasion he had made his excuses and left. It was the wrong way to act; he knew that. As Renolth's heir he should be trying to fill the appalling gap left by the Zamaran leader's passing. Time slipped by, though, and he did nothing.

Some six weeks after Renolth's death, Aldana found Zenton sitting on the cliffs overlooking the harbour, not far from the spot where he had almost been killed in the landslide.

"Donar told me he'd seen you heading this way," she said, sitting down by him. "Is this part of the cliff safe for us?"

"Probably," Zenton replied disinterestedly.

The silence between them stretched for some time until Zenton said, "I suppose Donar also told you that I asked him to take his questions and problems to Brandell."

"No, he just said you'd come this way."

There was another pause, this time not quite so long, before Zenton spoke again. "I expect you're going to tell me that this isn't what my father would want."

"No, actually. I came to ask what it is that *you* want."

"What *I* want? What do you mean?"

"Well, Brandell's doing a pretty good job of leading us right now. Do you want him to continue?"

Zenton stared at her. "I... I don't know. I suppose so. I haven't really given it much thought."

"Apparently not."

Zenton's eyes filled with tears. Aldana reached towards him, then drew back her hand and waited for him to speak.

"My father would have wanted me to take command, would he not?" he asked softly.

"Yes, he would," Aldana agreed. "But he's gone now, Zenton. The choice is yours. What do *you* want?"

Chapter Twenty-two

Changing Roles

Brandell lay back on the warm deck and basked in the gentle heat of Oltan's early rays. Temperatures during the past week had been particularly high and it would doubtless be too hot to lie out like this later in the day. Relaxing in the rare moment of idleness, he hooked his hands behind his head, stretched out his legs, crossed his ankles – and frowned as his tranquil mood was marred by noticing the gap where the sole had worked loose from his right boot. Tharrentar was supposed to have fixed that two days ago. Brandell reached forward and grabbed his ankle, drawing the offending boot up a little. A neat row of stitches bore testament to the fact that Tharrentar had completed his work competently. It was another section of sole causing the problem this time. Nevertheless, Tharrentar should have seen that was about to happen and dealt with it, thought Brandell, not prepared to be placated. He sat up and sighed loudly.

"Is something wrong, Prince Brandell?" asked Jedron, pausing on his way across the deck.

"Not really," Brandell said. "I was just bemoaning the lack of decent footwear."

Jedron smiled. "I know what you mean," he said with a rueful glance at his own scuffed and torn sea-boots. "Still, we ought to be grateful the weavers have those new fibres to work with. Otherwise we'd be struggling for clothing as well as boots!"

Brandell glared at the young captain in mock anger. "I can see you're determined to be cheerful," he complained, rising to his feet and trying not to catch the loose sole on a rough section of planking. "That being the case, I shall withdraw and head back to the settlement."

Jedron laughed. "There's no need to go," he said. "I'll leave you in peace."

"No, it doesn't matter," Brandell responded. "I'd better not stay any longer. I've a meeting to attend and I'll need to change these boots first." He bent to retrieve his discarded jacket. "My thanks for the suggestion of coming out here, Jedron. It's a while since I've had even this amount of time to myself. You're due out on the next tide, are you not? Well, I'll bid you farewell and good fishing."

"Prince Brandell?"

Brandell halted and turned back. Jedron hesitated, clearly deciding whether or not to continue.

"What is it?" prompted Brandell.

"I was just wondering how Prince Zenton is. He's not been down to the harbour for a while and –"

"He's gone to the Far Settlement," said Brandell. He did not elaborate and his tone discouraged further questions.

He left Jedron standing where he was and strode off down the gangplank and onto the partially-completed new jetty. Pausing at the shore end of the jetty, Brandell took a few deep breaths to regain his poise. He had not intended to be curt with Jedron; it was just that the captain had touched a raw nerve.

When they had first come to this land, Zenton had still been little more than a child. Oh, he'd worked as hard as any adult, Brandell had to concede – and harder than some – but he had relied on others (Renolth and Brandell in particular) to make the important decisions. The change in him since that time had been quite dramatic, his competence and self-confidence blossoming as he matured. True, he'd lapsed now and then, but Brandell had never objected to taking control when required – and therein lay the present problem.

After Renolth's death, Zenton had reverted completely to his former ways; indeed, he had actively avoided shouldering the responsibility of leadership. Moreover, he had resisted all efforts to encourage him to resume any of his former duties let alone to take on those of Renolth. His lack of interest had been tolerated with understanding for quite some time by the Council Leaders and the rest of the settlers but leadership was needed and they had naturally turned to Brandell.

In truth, Brandell had not minded. He knew he was a good leader: decisive and sure where Zenton tended to be hesitant. Brandell's orders were generally obeyed promptly because that was what he expected and demanded. Zenton, in his cousin's opinion, was too inclined to ask for advice, too open to discussion. There was a time and a place for debate, Brandell believed, but prolonged

127

talking only led to dissent and delay. The ruling monarch ruled, and that was that. Life here might have changed drastically from that in the Homeland Isles but some stability had to be maintained and Brandell could claim without false modesty that the settlements had been well managed during the weeks of his leadership. He had enjoyed both the challenge and the status of the role, and he admitted to himself now that he did not welcome the idea of stepping down.

He didn't know what had brought about Zenton's recent change of attitude, and he didn't care to ask. He *did* know that his cousin had, only a few days ago, taken up the duties he'd neglected since Renolth's death. Brandell could give advice and suggestions but it was Zenton now who was making the final decisions. The fact that he consulted with Brandell on most issues was at least some consolation; it would just take a little time to become accustomed to being second-in-command instead of leader.

Shrugging off his irritation, Brandell decided to look on the positive side of the situation. He would be able to take the occasional short break from his duties – as he had done this morning – and, once Zenton was fully conversant with his role as leader, Brandell could take out more search bands and explore this fascinating land. The region to the west of the harbour had yet to be visited. As soon as Zenton returned from the Far Settlement, Brandell would take a team and venture out there.

With that decided, Brandell's spirits lifted. He spun on his heel and started off, only to find that the injudicious step had torn away more of the sole from his boot. "Nad's nails!" he swore crossly, flapping off the jetty.

A pace or two more and he gave up. It would be easier to remove his boots and carry the cursed things. Bending to do just that, he shivered suddenly as he recalled the time he'd pulled *on* his boots in a dream, only to find when he truly woke that he had in reality donned them during the night. Footwear in hand, he straightened up. He still dreamt now and again but it no longer distressed him as much. On the contrary, sometimes the images were quite intriguing. One of these nights he might actually see the figure so frustratingly hidden by that green glow. Perhaps in time he'd become so accustomed to his dreams that they would cease to bother him altogether – always providing he didn't start sleepwalking again.

Resisting the strong temptation to fling his boots into the harbour waters he set off for the royal shelter.

The infirmary had been the first permanent building erected to replace travel shelters and was still the largest structure in the Harbour Settlement. Built with wood from the fast-growing baltra trees, its main room held six low beds – only two of which were currently occupied – and a table and chair for the healer or assistant on duty. The other part of the infirmary was partitioned into sections, with a corridor off which were several small rooms. Two of these rooms were set aside for patients, a third for treatment of minor injuries, and a fourth and slightly larger room for storage and research. The final two narrow chambers were bedrooms for Silmedd and Vemran. Though the facilities were woefully inadequate when compared to those of the Homeland Isles before the earthquakes, they were a considerable improvement on what had been available during the voyage and the first year or so in the new land.

Leaving Silmedd to his current research on some strange, trailing fungi that promised to be quite an effective remedy for certain skin complaints, Aldana took a bound sheaf of parchments and returned to her post in the main room. With both patients resting comfortably, she had a little time to devote to studying the drawings and descriptions of the medicinal plants catalogued thus far. Each artist was required to mark his or her work and most of the pages were Lirreth's, though some of the entries bore Chandrane's signature and a good few the small, stylised z that denoted Zenton's work. Privately, Aldana thought the prince's drawings were better even than Lirreth's. But then, she admitted to herself as she carefully turned the pages, she was probably somewhat biased.

A noise and a discreet cough from the doorway behind and to her right caused her to turn from her studies. Brandell was standing there, uncharacteristically reticent. Usually he just barged straight into a room. Rising and going to him, Aldana saw that his left ankle and foot were stained with fresh blood.

"Come into the treatment room before you bleed all over the floor I've just cleaned," she said, ushering him ahead of her down the corridor.

"That's a fine way to speak to someone who's injured and comes to you for help," Brandell complained mildly, allowing himself to be guided along.

Aldana motioned him to a bench while she fetched a basin, cloths and fresh water. The blood washed away to reveal a short, deep gash just above Brandell's ankle.

"This could do with a couple of stitches," Aldana said. "I'll get Silmedd."

"Can't you do it?" asked Brandell.

"Well, yes. But I'll have to ask permission first."

"Aldana, you have my permission," Brandell said grandly.

"Fool!" muttered Aldana as she went to speak with Silmedd.

Returning moments later with a small jar of pale, greenish ointment, Aldana dipped a piece of cloth into the stuff and knelt to smear it around the cut.

Brandell drew his foot away. "That smells foul," he observed, wrinkling his nose in disgust.

"True," agreed Aldana, "but it helps to deaden the skin for a short time." She smiled sweetly up at her patient. "You can put up with the smell or with the pain while I stitch the wound. It's entirely your choice, Brandell."

The prince grimaced. "I'll take the ointment," he said.

Aldana laughed. "A wise decision." She coated the skin of his ankle and settled on the bench next to him to wait for the substance to take effect. "How did you gash your leg?"

Brandell held up the cause of the trouble. "I couldn't walk properly in this so I took off my boots. I caught my ankle on a rough stone down near the harbour." He shifted round to face her. "Aldana, you're off duty this afternoon are you not? I thought perhaps we could take a walk out onto the grasslands and see if we can spot any of those creatures Zenton insists on calling tamans."

"I'd love to, Brandell," Aldana told him, "but I really need to learn to recognise some more of the herbs and flowers we use. And Zenton's due back."

Brandell shrugged and smiled. "Ah well," he said, "I just thought I'd ask. One of these days you might say yes." He bent forward and tapped his ankle quite hard. "Seems numb enough. Go ahead and stitch. I've a meeting to go to and I'm already running a bit late because of this ridiculous excuse for footwear."

He sat motionless while Aldana sewed the small wound and bound a clean bandage around it. "My thanks," he said when she had finished. He rose, gathered up his boots and headed towards the door. "You know," he said, glancing back over his shoulder, "that young cousin of mine must be blind if he hasn't yet noticed how you feel about him."

Leaving Aldana blushing a bright scarlet, he padded out of the room.

Chapter Twenty-three

A Shield Against Evil

Zenton was with Brandell and Aldana in the royal shelter when the Council Leaders came requesting that he accept the title of High King.

Zenton repeated the answer his father had once given. "It's too soon."

"Prince Zenton," Donar said, "it's more than a half year since Renolth's death."

"I didn't mean that," explained Zenton. "I just need to know Lantor's no longer alive to claim his true title here."

"Your father had agreed to the coronation," Irvanyal reminded him. "Will you not follow his example?"

The prince did not respond immediately and Donar tried again. "You've earned our respect and our trust over these past months, Zenton."

Seeing Donar look across at Irvanyal, Zenton asked, "What is it you're not telling me?"

Donar smiled. "Renolth used to do that."

"Do what?"

"Know when there was more to be said."

"Well," urged Zenton, "say it."

Usually confident and forthright, Donar was uncharacteristically hesitant. He glanced at Irvanyal again, obviously seeking her support, before he said in a rush of words, "Many of our people are uneasy. Some are deeply afraid. There are rumours that there's some harmful force here on Zamara."

"They might well be right," Zenton pointed out calmly. "We've discussed it freely in open meetings, haven't we?"

"Indeed," Irvanyal agreed, "but this adds weight to our argument that you should accept the crown."

"How so?"

"You're of the Almari royal line. Our history tells us that the royal family had powers to defend their people against danger."

It was Zenton who smiled now. "I know it does, but that was in the past."

"Perhaps it's because Maglin has been reviving the old lore," Donar said, "but it would be comforting to feel we have the protection of a High King here on Zamara. Since Lanna's time, the people have considered the High Monarch our shield against evil forces."

Brandell snorted. "Superstition. As far as I'm aware, there'd been no evidence of any 'evil forces' in the Homeland for many generations."

"No, indeed," agreed Donar, "and mayhap their absence was due to the High Monarch's latent power."

"No evil in the Homeland?" Irvanyal said. "The earthquakes and plague –"

Brandell cut her off. "They were natural disasters. Appalling catastrophes, but natural. And there's no malicious force at work here, either."

"Nevertheless," Donar persisted, "the people need reassurance. They trust in the monarch's special abilities. And the royal seal symbolises those abilities, does it not?"

"Maybe so," said Zenton, "but I don't have Lantor's ring, do I? Nor do I want it. I'm still hoping he'll find his way here. And I don't think I have any special powers that could help us, Irvanyal."

"The people believe you have. And who's to say they're wrong? You've certainly shown some gifts of vision, both with actual sight and with prescience, since we came here."

"Special powers or not," Donar insisted, "it's the wish of the people that you take the title."

Zenton pressed his fingers against the raised image on the medallion beneath his tunic, the shape so uncannily like The Island of Zamara. He loved The Island and he wanted to help govern and protect it. Still, accepting the title of High King seemed a huge step.

He turned to his cousin. "What do you think, Brandell?"

Brandell shrugged. "You've taken up most of Renolth's duties now. I can help and advise where needed. It's clear the people want this."

Aldana had remained silent up to this point. Now she said quietly, "Renolth always said he'd abdicate if Lantor arrived here. You could do the same, Zenton. It was your suggestion anyway."

"I'm being manoeuvred hard against the ship's rail here, am I not?" said Zenton, though there was no real rancour in his tone. He sighed, forcing aside the useless wish that he was not facing this dilemma, that Renolth was here, still the Zamaran leader. "I'll accept –"

"You have our thanks, my prince," Donar said hastily. "With your permission, I'll make the announcement immediately and –"

Zenton held up a restraining hand. "Hear me out, Donar. I'll accept, but not until the eighteenth anniversary of my birth. That's our fourth Landing Day. My father wouldn't take the crown until then. Neither will I."

Donar began to protest at the delay. Irvanyal elbowed him hard in the ribs. "It's only a couple of months hence," she said reasonably. "If you'll allow us to make it known, we can at least all to look forward to the celebration."

Zenton forbore to mention that it was not a ceremony *he* anticipated with any great joy. "Sit down again, will you please Donar? You too, Irvanyal. There's one more thing you should know." He waited until the two Council Leaders had complied and then announced, "I intend to take a search team to the Mandano cliffs again, and I want to leave within the week."

Donar and Irvanyal stared at him in stunned silence. Even Brandell and Aldana were taken aback.

"But Dallan and Pral said the cliffs and that ledge are very dangerous," Donar pointed out when he could speak again.

"Landing there again isn't possible anyway," returned Zenton. "Kaldrina reported that huge sections of the ledge collapsed in the storm last week. She said no landing-vessel could get close to the cave entrances now. I'll take an overland search."

The debate that followed was long and heated, and Zenton found it hard to keep his temper. At one point he came close to dismissing the Council Leaders from the study, telling them he would listen to no more of their protests and that he intended to explore The Island whenever he could, both now *and* when they made him High King.

134

Indeed, he opened his mouth to do so when Brandell solved the problem by suggesting a compromise.

"Send a team to the cliffs, Zenton," he said. "You know full well you'll cause too much anxiety here if you insist on going yourself. No, listen a minute," he added as Zenton started to object. "I know how much you want to discover more about Zamara. Come with me on *my* search."

That gave Zenton pause for thought. Brandell planned to head westward into territory previously unmapped and Zenton longed to discover what lay out there. He would go back to the northern cliffs himself sometime in the future he decided, but for now he would agree to Brandell's proposal.

"Very well," he said, and saw both Council Leaders sigh with relief. "And even though it's long out-dated, I'll abide by the old 'three-days out, then turn back' rule if that will help."

Brandell cleared his throat noisily.

"What?" said Zenton.

"I was under the perhaps mistaken impression this was *my* search," Brandell said.

"Oh," said Zenton. "Of course. In that case –"

"We'll abide by the three days out rule this time," Brandell said with a grin.

Donar and Irvanyal expressed their thanks and took their leave.

"There could just be one problem," Brandell stated as the door closed behind the Council Leaders.

"And what might that be?" Zenton asked.

"I assume you'll want Chandrane along on this search of ours?"

"Yes. Lissanne and Aldana too, if that's all right with you, Brandell. You'll come, Aldana?"

Aldana nodded her consent. "I'd love to. It's been months since I've been out on a search."

"So," said Zenton, "what's the problem, Brandell?"

"Ah, well, you see, I mentioned the possibility of a search to Merret. He was pretty keen to be included. That was before these changed arrangements of yours."

"You mean it could be a bad idea to have Merret and Chandrane in the same band?"

"Precisely. They've kept pretty much apart since that incident before the tournament last year. I'm not sure how they'll react to working closely together."

"I doubt Chandrane holds any grudge," said Zenton, "and I trust Merret takes the same attitude. If they're both assigned to the search band they'll have to make the best of it, will they not? Anyway, it might give them the chance to repair their friendship."

"Spoken like Renolth," stated Brandell. He rose, stretched, then ambled out of the study, leaving Zenton wondering whether the comment had been an accusation or a compliment.

Throughout the night prior to the search band's departure, dense clouds obscured the moons and stars, and driving rain swept in from the north. By Oltan's dawn, however, the rain had eased to a fine drizzle and, as Bardok climbed lazily into the sky, the thinning clouds dispersed and fled. Zenton strolled across the settlement, heading for the quayside. Wandering down onto the azure sands, he stood looking out across the harbour to the high, rocky ridge of Mandano. The peaceful waters glistened under morning suns that turned the sand-grains to miniature jewels. How strange the blue sand had appeared at First Landing, how different from the greenish-yellow Homeland shores. Now it seemed quite normal to see the many tiny, blue-shelled creatures inhabiting the rock pools and scavenging at low tide on the sands they matched so well.

From the awakening settlement came sounds of shouting, laughter and someone whistling a familiar tune. For the first time since his father's death, Zenton felt a lightening of his burden of grief. The beauty of The Island was working its magic and he could not help but respond to the magnificence of the scenery. He took a few deep breaths of the clear sea air, turned slowly away from the water's edge and went to join his search group.

For the first day's journey, the band made good time travelling the now well-mapped route towards Mandano. After an overnight camp, they turned west, heading towards low hills indicated on the charts but as yet unexplored. The hills proved easy to traverse, the crossing to lower land on their far side taking just half a day. Brandell's misgivings about Merret and Chandrane seemed to be unfounded. Though neither actively sought the comradeship of the other, they were at least civil enough when they spoke.

Throughout the second day, the group found the weather growing noticeably warmer and more humid. They crossed several narrow streams and discovered as they travelled that the firm, dry land of Patoll and Mandano was gradually giving way to softer, marshy ground.

Brown, shaggy-coated animals roamed the area, half-hidden in the tall grasses. They looked up curiously before ambling away, streamers of vegetation dangling from blunt muzzles, whenever any of the search group approached. Zenton came closest to touching one, but it shied away at the last minute and bounded off, its splayed hooves allowing it to move swiftly over the damp ground.

As Oltan began to dip low in the sky, Zenton called a halt to give the band an hour or so of light by which to set up camp near the banks of a slow-moving rivulet.

Brandell dumped down his travel pack and sauntered over to his cousin. "You're obviously becoming quite used to this leadership business," he observed mildly.

Zenton reddened, then laughed. "My apologies. I keep forgetting – it's *your* search, is it not?"

"It was when I first planned it."

Zenton hefted his pack again. "Lead on," he offered. "We'll camp when you say so."

"Right. Just so long as we have that settled." Brandell retrieved his own bag, walked on a few paces, then stopped. "This looks a good place. We'll camp here."

He turned and grinned at his cousin. Zenton sighed in mock exasperation before dropping his travel pack down once more.

Looking around for the best site for the travel shelters, both Brandell and Merret paused to admire a clump of low-growing flowers shaped like sail-wings, their striped petals of scarlet and amber glowing iridescent in the lowering rays of the suns. Brandell reached out to touch a velvety stem.

"No! Brandell, wait!"

He snatched back his hand. "What's the matter?"

137

Aldana hurried over to stand by him. She knelt to examine the plant, then rose, brushing grass and soil from her clothing. "I've seen flowers like that before," she explained. "A search band brought some back from the grasslands."

"I gather it's unwise to touch them?"

"I think the flowers are safe enough, and the stems, but I didn't want you to take any chances. There's a sticky fluid inside the roots that's highly toxic. Two of the other trainee healers touched just a drop of the stuff and became ill."

"Well, my thanks for the warning but, by Nad's cloak, Aldana, you certainly startled me!"

"Hush, Brandell," Aldana cautioned automatically. "He'll wake if you call him."

Brandell gave a short laugh. "Really? What makes you think he's still asleep?"

Aldana went white. Brandell patted her gently on the arm. "I was joking, Aldana. Come on; help me decide on the layout of this campsite."

The following morning, Brandell, Merret and Lissanne set off to track the course of the narrow river while Zenton, Aldana and Chandrane concentrated on sketching the plants along its bank. Towards mid-suns Lissanne came trotting back, her usual taciturn manner replaced for once by near enthusiasm.

"You must come, Prince Zenton," she urged. "Beyond those next hills the river widens. There are strange trees and vines of some sort. Merret and Prince Brandell are waiting for us."

Hastily gathering up their sketches, Zenton and the others made a final check of their cleared campsite before heading westwards with Lissanne.

They walked at a brisk pace, talking little as they concentrated on making their way over increasingly difficult ground. Zenton pondered the fact that Lissanne, like many of his friends in the Harbour Settlement, had taken to giving him his title when addressing him. He felt it distanced him from them. He supposed it was their way of showing acceptance of his position and leadership but it saddened him that the old familiarity seemed to be slipping away.

Seeing the group arriving, Brandell threw away a half-chewed grass stem and rose lazily from the fallen log on which he'd been sitting. "We'll need to take care," he said, strolling over to meet his cousin. "The ground ahead seems a bit treacherous. I think there may be a swamp of some kind not far on."

Brandell was right. The nature of the land changed with surprising abruptness, with numerous small streams meandering across increasingly marshy ground. With Chandrane leading, the group forged cautiously onwards.

As they moved deeper into the swamp, the vegetation became dense, the air moist and steamy. There were some sections of safe, dry ground where travelling was relatively easy but the farther the group journeyed the more hazardous it became. Tall, broad-leafed trees and thick, creeping vines effectively cut out much of the suns' light. Firm-looking ground often turned out to be nothing more than thick algae on the surface of deep pools. High overhead, colourful birds flitted among boughs weighed down by huge, pale flowers, twisted gourds or pendulous, fleshy fruits. Unseen creatures chattered and called in the leafy canopy.

It was difficult to judge the hour in the gloom of the swamp, but when Brandell finally asked her, Lissanne reckoned they needed to head back straight away if they were to make their way out of the marshy jungle before Oltan's set. Accepting her estimation of the time, Brandell agreed that the band should begin the return journey. Fascinated as they were by the amazing vegetation and tantalising glimpses of unfamiliar creatures, no one wanted to chance an overnight camp in the swamp if it could be avoided.

Their journey into the swamp had been slow due not only to the nature of the terrain but also because Zenton had been mapping their route and Aldana had been taking small samples of plants. Travelling back out should, they all thought, be somewhat swifter. It proved not to be so.

To their astonishment and dismay, the mapped paths could seldom be found. Streams had unaccountably altered course. Previously firm ground was sodden and impassable. Bewildered and alarmed, the search group came to a halt on a narrow stretch of reasonably dry ground.

It was Merret who broke the uneasy silence. Turning to Zenton, he said, "Well, your highness, Brandell might be leading this search but you're the one who's supposed to have special powers. What do we do now?"

Chapter Twenty-four

Plants, Felines and Pools

Zenton bridled at Merret's tone. Sorely tempted to snap back a cutting retort, he clamped his jaw shut. Starting an argument was hardly going to improve the chances of Merret regaining former friendships. Besides, only a few hours ago Zenton had been silently bemoaning the lost familiarity of his companions. He couldn't have it both ways, could he? Resenting Merret's lack of respect was contradictory. Anyway, now he came to consider it, he *did* feel as if he knew the direction they should take to leave the swamp.

"I don't know what's happened to the paths," he said at last, his temper in check, "but I think I can get us out of here."

"You can?" Aldana sounded both sceptical and relieved at the same time.

Zenton nodded. "We need to head east, and –"

"I could have told us that," interrupted Merret sourly. "But how exactly are we supposed to know which way is east? If you hadn't noticed, it's clouded over and we can't see the suns."

Zenton shrugged. "I was about to say I just have this feeling that we have to keep going *that* way." He pointed off through the undergrowth. "We'll probably have to detour round pools and marshy ground but that's the way back."

"Well," said Brandell, "if no one else has any better suggestion, we'll try it your way. I certainly hope you're right, cousin of mine. Come on, everyone. Let's get moving. Lead on, Zenton."

For the first half-hour the going was relatively straightforward; then the problems began. Firm, safe ground became a rarity, and time and time again they were forced to turn aside from their intended route, seeking ways to cross streams, bypass pools and avoid treacherous ground. Fading daylight found them still within the humid confines of the swamp, all of them bemused and frightened by the way the area had changed its configuration since they had entered it.

"How much farther?" Merret asked. He sounded as scared as Zenton felt.

"I don't know," Zenton admitted. "I thought we'd be out by now. It's just that we've had to backtrack so often. We *are* generally heading the right way though."

"Oh, good." The surliness was back in Merret's voice. "That makes me feel a whole lot better." He slipped the travel pack from his shoulder and hooked it over a low branch. "We can't go on like this. It'll be full dark soon."

Brandell concurred. "It's become appreciably darker since that last rest stop and what light there is will go fast in here. We'd better start looking for a place to camp while we can still see what we're doing."

"I could scout ahead," offered Chandrane. "As long as I keep – Ouch!"

Aldana pushed carefully past Brandell and Zenton. "What's wrong?"

"I think something bit me!" Chandrane declared crossly, rubbing his wrist.

Aldana moved closer to him. "Here, let me see."

Chandrane obediently rolled up his sleeve to reveal a deep cut, long but very narrow. He poked at the wound and winced.

"Don't do that," Aldana chided. "You'll get dirt in it." She peered at the thin, bleeding gash. "It doesn't look like a bite mark. It's too straight and narrow. You must have scratched your wrist on something."

Chandrane tilted his head and peered at his injury. "Well it *felt* like a bite."

Zenton laughed at his friend's aggrieved tone. "You've had far worse injuries in training. And complained less."

"True," Lissanne said, "but then at least he knew the cause."

"My thanks for your comforting words, Lissanne," Chandrane muttered, tugging his sleeve back farther from the wound.

"Actually," Lissanne announced calmly, "I think I've found your attacker."

"What? Where?" Chandrane turned to look and the others crowded closer.

Lissanne pointed to the grey foliage of a large bush growing at the side of the muddy track they had been following. There was blood on one of the big, stiff, razor-sharp leaves. "That, my injured friend, is what *bit* you."

Chandrane made an exaggerated pretence of examining the plant. "Just checking it's not carnivorous," he quipped. Declaring himself satisfied, he turned back to Aldana.

She rummaged in her pack and drew out a small jar of ointment and some clean strips of cloth. "This should help stop any infection," she told Chandrane, dipping a piece of cloth into the ointment and daubing it onto the deep scratch. "Hold still, will you?"

Grimacing at the smell of the sticky substance, he sat on a moss-covered tree stump while Aldana bandaged his arm.

Zenton watched for a moment then wandered off from the group, searching for the source of a gentle gurgling noise. A meandering rivulet they'd recently crossed forced itself through a narrowed section of streambed and down a shallow dip, and this tiny waterfall, he discovered, was the source of the sound. A short way ahead, the water drained into a large, algae-covered pond, just visible through thick undergrowth. The pool's surface glimmered faintly, a strange, compelling, violet glow shimmering in the darkening swamp. Fascinated, Zenton peered through the vegetation at the gleaming water. He turned as he sensed his cousin approaching.

"Now what have you found?" asked Brandell.

Zenton pointed. "Look there."

"Nad's teeth," Brandell swore softly. "What's *that*?"

"I wish you'd stop using his name like that," Zenton complained.

"Oh, don't *you* start. I've had enough of that from Aldana *and* our revered Council Leader Irvanyal."

Zenton turned from his contemplation of the shifting, violet light. "My apologies, then. It's just something that makes me uncomfortable."

Brandell laughed. "Well, we'll be a great deal more uncomfortable if we don't find somewhere to camp soon." He pushed back an obscuring branch and studied the area around the pool. "Actually, it looks quite promising over there on the far side of the pond. You go back to tell the others, will you? Merret and I will check it out."

He called Merret over and they set off past Zenton towards the pool, shoving carefully through the plants alongside the bank of the slow-moving stream. Zenton watched, tempted to argue that since he had found the pool he should be the one to explore there first. Remembering it was supposed to be Brandell's search and not his, he controlled the urge to take charge, turning instead to do as Brandell had asked.

It was strange how things changed, he mused as he retraced his steps to where the rest of the group waited. Here he was, wanting to take over when not so many months ago he had actively avoided any form of leadership.

By Lissanne's reckoning, Brandell and Merret were away for less than a quarter-hour but to Zenton the wait seemed much longer than that. Like the cave in Mandano's rocky ridge, there was something about this pool that called to him – a more gentle summons, to be sure, but present nonetheless. When Merret returned to lead the way, Zenton found it hard not to rush past him.

The glow, it turned out, emanated not from the water itself but from the film of algae covering the surface. Over to one side of the wide pool grew an enormous, misshapen tree with distorted branches overhanging the water, its gnarled, twisted trunk thicker than four people could encircle with outstretched arms. Vines and creepers decorated the trunk and limbs, dangling down in places to trail in the sluggish water below. One huge branch had broken away – some time ago to judge by its mossy covering – and now formed a makeshift bridge spanning the pool. The algae concentration was greatest under and around the fallen branch, the glimmering luminescence brighter than elsewhere on the pool's surface.

Before anyone could stop him, Zenton knelt by the pool's edge and dipped his hand into the gleaming water. Immediately his fingers began to tingle. He withdrew his hand, though the sensation had been unusual rather than unpleasant. A slight phosphorescence glinted on his skin, glittering there for a few seconds before fading away completely.

"Don't do it again," Chandrane warned softly as Zenton reached forwards once more.

Zenton looked up at him. "It's quite safe."

"All the same, my prince, I'd rather you didn't take the chance." Concealing his reluctance to leave the water, Zenton stood up.

"There's not a great deal of room for us to camp here, Prince Brandell," Lissanne observed as the team closed up together on the only stretch of firm ground along the pool's rim.

"True," agreed Brandell amiably, "but there's a relatively dry clearing just beyond. We can't go around the pool because there are too many of those razor-leafed bushes blocking the way, but we've checked out that log over the water and it's safe enough to cross if you're careful. Watch out though; some of the smaller branches sticking out from it are pretty jagged. It's somewhat slippery as well, so take care." He edged past Zenton and began organising the group. "You go first, Chandrane. Use that famous balance of yours! Then you, Lissanne, then Aldana. There's a narrow track to the left once you're over. You'll have to duck down under some low branches but it opens up a few paces farther on. Zenton, you follow Aldana, and Merret and I will come last."

Chandrane raised his eyebrows and sighed slightly. He was at the back of the group and would have to squash past to take the lead.

About to step forward, Chandrane hesitated as a low, plaintive whimper sounded close to their right. From the bushes emerged a small creature, a young feline of some sort by the look of it, its grey-green fur speckled for camouflage. Large, oval eyes stared out of a round, fur-fringed face as the animal, apparently quite unafraid, regarded the interlopers who had invaded its habitat. Long, dark whiskers and pointed ears twitched as it sniffed the air. Its tail beat a gentle tattoo on the soft ground. For several moments, animal and search team stared at each other, then the little creature padded a few steps nearer to Aldana.

"Don't touch it," advised Zenton in a whisper. "Its mother's probably nearby and she could well be a great deal larger and far less appealing!"

Seemingly irritated at being ignored, the youngster mewed softly, then suddenly let out an ear-splitting yowl.

Barely had the cry died away than a huge, tawny, snarling shape erupted from the dense vegetation, lips drawn back menacingly to reveal wickedly sharp fangs. Instinctively, Zenton stepped in front of

145

Aldana. Poised to leap, the mother feline halted and stared up at the prince. Zenton froze, his heart thudding painfully as he tried to control his fear. Behind him he heard the whisper of metal as someone – Chandrane in all probability – drew a knife from its sheath.

"No," Zenton said aloud. "Don't hurt her."

The tableau broke as the creature snatched up hers wayward infant by the scruff of its neck, spun lithely on her haunches and fled into the undergrowth. Zenton exhaled in relief and began to laugh.

"What's so amusing?" Brandell asked sourly.

His cousin shrugged, still chuckling. "This was supposed to be a *safe* search remember? Move on, Chandrane. If that's all right with you, team leader?"

Brandell ignored him.

For the second time, Chandrane started off, only to freeze in his tracks as an eerie, shrieking cry sounded high overhead.

"It's the dragon!" exclaimed Zenton, startled. He looked round to see his companions staring up, trying to peer through the thick, leafy canopy. "At least you all heard it this time."

The cry had been a warning again, he was certain, but surely no danger threatened now the feline had taken her cub and vanished. Perhaps the dragon was simply reacting to what had nearly been an attack, or maybe they should be continuing to make their way out of the swamp instead of going to the clearing. Unsettled and unnerved, Zenton stood where he was, trying to decide what to do.

"It's no good standing here," Brandell declared. "It's almost dark and there's nowhere else to camp but that clearing. Go on, Chandrane. If the dragon wants us for its supper it's going to have to find us through all this greenery."

It wasn't hunting them, Zenton was sure. There was something wrong; he just didn't know what it could be.

"Get moving, Chandrane," Brandell ordered. "We need to cross before the light goes completely."

With a muttered and somewhat perfunctory apology as he trod on Merret's foot, Chandrane began to squeeze his way to the front of the group, causing chaos as the team tried to maintain their footing on the narrow, slippery stretch of mud while jostling in near darkness to take up the positions Brandell had assigned to them.

146

Zenton felt a sudden, sharp pain in his left side, and then a hard push to his shoulder knocked him off balance and sent him tumbling into the brackish water of the swamp pool. His head struck the log bridge and he lost consciousness instantly.

His companions cried out as he slipped beneath the algae-covered surface.

Chapter Twenty-five

A Night in the Swamp

Brandell shed his travel pack and kicked it to one side. He knelt by the pool's edge and delved into the murky water.

"I can't find him!" he yelled, standing and shrugging off his jacket. "I'm going in."

Chandrane beat him to it. He threw down his pack and slid swiftly into the slimy pond. The water came almost to his shoulders. He forged forward, splashing through water-weeds and algae. He reached down blindly.

"I've got him!" he shouted, hauling something from the water.

It was a just a huge branch. He swore and tossed it aside. Again he went under, this time snagging hold of clothing and dragging Zenton to the surface. Brandell, by this time also in the pool, struggled across to help.

Chandrane spat out a mouthful of algae. "He's unconscious."

"So I see. Let's get him to the far bank." Brandell turned and shouted to the others, "Meet us on the other side."

Lissanne and Aldana dropped their packs and scrambled across the log bridge. Side by side, they knelt on the muddy bank. With them tugging, and Brandell and Chandrane shoving, they managed to get Zenton's inert form out of the water. Brandell and Chandrane clambered out and carried him to the small clearing. Merret made several trips over the slimy log to retrieve the packs.

Chandrane knelt, panic-stricken, beside Aldana. "He's not breathing, is he? I tried to get to him quickly, Aldana. I really tried!"

Just as terrified, and trying not to show it, Aldana sought inner calm as she was taught to do in her training. Chandrane was right: Zenton wasn't breathing.

A sea-faring nation, the Almari had long experience of water mishaps, and techniques aimed at reviving those rescued from drowning were amongst the first skills taught to new apprentices. Still, it was one thing to practise such skills in training and quite another to be faced with reality. She tried to distance herself from the knowledge that it was Zenton lying limp and unresponsive before her, that he was not only the High King in all but title but also, and of greater importance to her, her friend. More than a friend, if she was honest.

"Get his pack off him," she ordered.

Working swiftly, she cleared trailing weed from Zenton's throat, tilted his head back, pinched his nose closed and blew gently into his mouth, breathing for him until at last he jerked and gasped in air. She turned him on his side then, holding him close while he retched swamp water from his lungs. For a moment he seemed aware of her, then his eyes closed once more as he lapsed into unconsciousness.

The hours that followed were like a nightmare to the young trainee-healer. Even Brandell looked to her for instructions as they set up camp in the small clearing and tried to tend Zenton. His pack, like his clothing, was soaked and filthy. Merret provided dry garments for him and Chandrane and Brandell helped with the difficult task of drying and re-clothing him before changing out of their own sodden clothes. In the dampness of the swamp it proved impossible to light a campfire. The spluttering torches gave off smoke enough to keep at bay most of the biting night-insects but gave scant light for Aldana to assess Zenton's injuries. The head wound was obvious though, with dark, sticky blood matting his filthy, algae-coated hair and smearing his face, and this she cleaned as best she could. There was little else she could do until the suns rose, and the feeling of helplessness was almost more than she could bear.

Zenton slept fitfully, his breathing shallow and ragged, his skin hot with fever. The others took turns sharing the watch over him but Aldana stayed awake most of the long night, frightened that he might stop breathing again. Brandell was there often, asking each time if Zenton was conscious yet.

The night swamp was alive with noise: the buzz and drone of insects; chitters and squawks of unseen creatures; rustlings in the undergrowth and the occasional soft splash as something plopped into the nearby pool. Once, Aldana heard a chillingly familiar snarl from the bushes close by and knew that the large feline had returned. The animal stayed hidden though, disappearing off into the dense jungle sometime during the night, Aldana presumed, for she did not hear the growl again. Most frightening of all were the high, wailing screams that sounded as if some creature had fallen victim to a predator and was in mortal agony. The few times she did drift into a light doze, some noise would wake her sharply.

The faint glow from the pool added to the eeriness. The shifting, violet glimmer danced in weaving patterns each time the surface was disturbed, brightening sometimes but never enough to give any useful light.

It was with immense relief that Aldana became aware of the gradual lightening as dawn broke over the dense swamp. That relief, though, was tempered by worry. They could not remain here for long; their supplies would not last and Zenton would need proper care. They should, she hoped, be able to use the suns' positions to help them keep travelling east until they were out of the swamp. They'd have to make a carrier of some sort for Zenton.

Her thoughts were interrupted by Brandell's approach. He squeezed his way into the small travel shelter and sat down by her. "It's starting to rain," he observed, brushing a hand through his damp hair and tying it back from his face. "If we can't tell which way is east, how in Nad's name are we going to get out of here?"

Too tired to reproach him for his choice of language, Aldana stared up at him.

"I can get us out," Zenton asserted quietly.

Brandell and Aldana turned to him at once. "Welcome back, cousin," said Brandell. "You gave us all quite a scare last night, you know."

"Last night?" Frowning, Zenton put a hand up to his head.

Brandell stared at him. "You don't remember what happened?"

"No. I thought we were leaving the swamp. Why are we still here?"

Brandell glanced at Aldana then said to Zenton, "You had an accident, Zenton. You fell into the pool and banged your head."

"Pool? What pool? Brandell, we should get back to the settlement. I promised the Council Leaders..."

"He must have concussion," Aldana whispered as Zenton sank back on his sleeping mat. "I'm not sure we should move him after all."

"We certainly can't stay here," Brandell said decisively. "I'm breaking camp and we're leaving while he's alert enough to tell us the way." Without waiting for a response, he wriggled out of the shelter.

Aldana sighed and bent close to the injured prince. "Do you feel up to travelling, Zenton?"

"Yes," he lied. "Help me up, will you?"

Aldana wanted to make a carrier but Zenton's insistence that he could walk prevailed. Still, he needed Chandrane's help every step of the way. The swamp paths had changed yet again, so that there was now a fairly wide and relatively dry route around the pool into which Zenton had fallen. Brandell led, turning frequently to check the direction with his cousin.

It took them only a half-hour to reach the fringe of the swamp. The clouds lifted and Oltan's rays set the vegetation steaming as they emerged at last from the gloom into the brightness of the grassland. A half-hour. The unspoken thought was in everyone's mind. If they had continued last evening instead of seeking a campsite, Zenton might not have been hurt.

"There's no guarantee we'd have got out this quickly last night," Brandell said, as if someone had voiced the thought. "Those paths could have led us round in circles for hours. Come on. Let's keep going as long as we can."

Brandell wanted to reach the first low hills before calling a halt but soon after they had left the swamp it became obvious that Zenton could go no farther. Lissanne spread a waxed cloak and Chandrane eased the prince down to the ground where he sat hunched forward, breathing jerkily and clutching his side.

Seeing blood on Chandrane's hand, Aldana asked, "Have you knocked your hand, Chandrane, or has that cut on your wrist opened again?"

Chandrane gave his hand and arm a cursory examination. "Neither," he told her. "Look to Zenton, Aldana. I think the blood is his."

The young healer dropped her pack and knelt by the prince. With Bardok now adding its rays to those of the First Sun, it was at last easy to check Zenton properly. His right temple was discoloured by a purpling bruise extending above and below his eye but the actual gash had not reopened. In fact, the cut looked as if it was healing already. Aldana had no time to ponder the puzzle. In the bright light of the two suns, she noticed now an ominous, dark stain spreading across the left side of the prince's borrowed shirt.

"Move your hand and lie down, Zenton," she ordered. "I need to take a look at your side."

Unable to suppress a gasp of pain as the movement pulled at torn muscles, Zenton lay back on the gently sloping ground. His head ached fiercely and his abdomen felt as if it was on fire. He was cold and shivery, although he presumed the suns must be giving warmth since others in the group were stripping off cloaks and jackets. He tried feebly to push Aldana's hands away as she peeled his blood-soaked shirt away from his injured side. There was something he needed to tell her, something vital about the wound he'd somehow received. He couldn't form the words though; it was too much effort. Abandoning the attempt, he concentrated instead on trying to deal with the appalling pain.

"Oh, Zenton," Aldana scolded gently as she delved in her pack for water and ointments, "why didn't you tell me your side was hurting?" She was angry with herself though, not with him. If only she had noticed earlier – but she'd been so concerned about that head wound, and Zenton had been covered in mud, and it had been so *dark* in the swamp.

"How is he?" asked Brandell, wandering over after a hasty conference with Merret.

"Not good," Aldana replied, sitting back on her heels and looking up at Brandell and the others who had formed a loose semi-circle around the injured prince. "His side's a mess. He must have torn it on a branch when he fell. I'll be able to tell a bit better when I've cleaned the wound."

"Has he remembered what happened to him?"

"I don't think so."

"If we find some way to make a carrier, can he travel?"

Aldana placed a hand on Zenton's hot forehead. "I think it's too dangerous to move him any farther. He's burning with fever and his side's still bleeding. I should have noticed it last night. He's probably already lost a lot of blood."

152

"You can't be blamed for what you couldn't see," Brandell said. "None of us knew he'd hurt his side as well as his head."

"I didn't notice his side when we dried him," Chandrane said, obviously feeling just as guilty as Aldana. "He was covered in muddy slime."

"Standing here wondering about it isn't going to get us anywhere," Brandell said brusquely. "Merret and I will go for help. The rest of you stay with Zenton. Chandrane, sketch a copy of the route for us. We'll leave most of the supplies here, including the shelters, so we should be able to travel pretty fast. We'll bring one of the healers back as quickly as we can. If Zenton improves, set off back, but keep to the mapped route so we won't miss you."

Waiting only long enough for the travel packs to be hastily reorganised and for Chandrane to finish the sketch-map, Brandell and Merret headed off at a brisk pace back towards the Harbour Settlement. Aldana barely noticed them go. Using herb-water, she bathed Zenton's head, pressing gently around the cut in an attempt to check for any fracture, then she set about cleaning the wound in his side. He tolerated her touching his head but fought her weakly when she started to cleanse the wound beneath his ribs. In the end, she called Chandrane to hold him still so she could tend him properly, and both of them gasped aloud as they saw the extent of damage revealed when the worst of the dirt and blood had been washed away.

"I'm no expert," said Chandrane, "but that looks to me remarkably like a knife wound."

Chapter Twenty-six

Desperate Measures

"A *knife* wound?" Lissanne came hurriedly to crouch next to Chandrane, her normally impassive features creased with concern. For a long moment she stared down at Zenton. He was unconscious again, or perhaps just sleeping; it was hard to tell which. He looked dreadfully ill, though. "Chandrane's right, you know," she said quietly to Aldana. "That's no tear from a branch."

The young healer nodded unhappily, looking at the oozing wound. "I did wonder as I cleaned away the blood."

"*I* didn't do it," Lissanne stated firmly. "I'd never harm him. He's our shield against the coming evil."

"*What*?" Chandrane and Aldana spoke together.

Lissanne shrugged and her tone became slightly defensive. "That's what some people in the settlements are saying. I happen to believe them."

"And I certainly wouldn't hurt him!" Chandrane protested heatedly as Aldana stared hard at him. "He's not just my sovereign, he's my friend!"

"I wasn't accusing you," Aldana assured him. "I was just wondering..."

"Wondering what?"

"Well, it all happened so fast, didn't it? We were crowded together, and you were trying to get past. Who was next to him?"

"Merret!" Lissanne spat out the name.

Chandrane was aghast. "No, Lissanne. Surely not even he would do this."

"Who else?"

On his feet at once, Chandrane stared off the way Merret and Brandell had headed. The two were long out of sight. "I'm going after him." There was cold fury in his voice.

"Chandrane, no!" said Aldana. "I need you here."

"He's hurt Zenton, and Prince Brandell might be in danger."

Lissanne stood and placed a restraining hand on her colleague's arm. "I doubt he'll attack Prince Brandell," she said calmly. "Think about it, Chandrane. Are we sure it was Prince Zenton he was after in the first place?"

Puzzled now, Chandrane frowned. "What do you mean?"

"Well, if you recall, Prince Brandell had just mentioned your innate balance – and that was part of the trouble back when you and Merret fought, was it not? Merret never believed you slipped. Anyway, perhaps that reminded him of the fight. Then you trod on his foot."

"But that was pure accident."

"Maybe so, but Merret might have thought it deliberate."

"So you're saying *I* was his target and he stabbed Zenton by mistake?"

Lissanne shrugged again. "It's possible. He'd hardly be likely to admit it, would he? And he certainly left quickly enough when he had the opportunity."

"He must have known we'd see the wound eventually," Aldana said. "So why did he chance staying with us?"

"Maybe he thought we'd attribute it to one of those sharp leaves," Chandrane suggested.

"Perhaps so," said Aldana. "But that leaf made a very narrow cut on your arm. This wound's wider and much deeper."

"Who knows what goes on in that man's mind?" Lissanne said evenly. "I suppose there was no danger to him while we didn't know about Prince Zenton's injury – and he'd need to stay with us to get out of the swamp."

"He could still turn on Brandell," Chandrane pointed out.

"He could, yes," agreed Lissanne.

Chandrane gave a snort of contempt. "He's too much of a coward, is he not? He's far more likely just to make a run for it when Brandell's sleeping."

"Probably," said Lissanne equably.

With a muttered oath, Chandrane knelt down and turned his attention to helping Aldana tend Zenton.

Aldana packed the deep, angry wound with a herb poultice before wrapping bandages around to hold the main dressings in place. The cut would need stitching but she hoped the herbs would stop the bleeding and reduce the swelling and infection first.

Finished at last, she rinsed her hands and covered Zenton with a light blanket before settling herself down wearily beside him. Chandrane went to assist Lissanne set the rest of the camp and they came to join Aldana a short time later, bringing her a welcome cup of steaming banellin.

For a time, the three of them sat in silence. It was Aldana who spoke first. "You remember me telling all of you about that plant near our campsite on the way here?"

Chandrane looked perplexed. "The flowers Brandell nearly touched?"

"Yes."

"You said the roots were toxic."

"A fluid in the roots, yes."

"You told us one of the trainee-healers touched it and became ill," Lissanne prompted when Aldana fell silent.

"Actually, I said *two* people touched the fluid," Aldana reminded her. "Wendrin's hand came out in a nasty rash and she had a fever for a couple of days. Grenath was really ill, though. Silmedd feared we were going to lose her."

"What's your point, Aldana?" asked Lissanne.

"Grenath had a slight cut on one finger," Aldana continued steadily. "Silmedd reckoned she was affected so badly because the poison entered her bloodstream through the cut and not just through the skin like it did with Wendrin."

Chandrane leaned forward and placed his cup carefully on the grass. "I take it this has something to do with Zenton," he said worriedly.

Aldana nodded. "Grenath's whole arm became badly swollen," she told them. "Her hand turned an awful mottled purple, with red streaks of infection all up her arm."

Reaching out, she drew back Zenton's blanket. The flesh around the dressings was inflamed, blotched purple and red, an angry mass of tissue. Telltale livid threads patterned his stomach and chest.

Lissanne drew in her breath sharply. "Merret wanted to make certain of the outcome, did he not?"

156

The question was rhetorical. Chandrane merely gazed in horror at his injured friend before rounding on Aldana. "You're the healer! Do something!"

Stung into silence by the injustice of the outburst, Aldana sat mute. Tears filled her eyes. She blinked them back angrily, brushing her sleeve across her face.

Immediately contrite, Chandrane knelt and put his arm around her shoulders. "I'm sorry, Aldana. That was unfair and wrong of me. I know you're still in training. You've been amazing. You have, really. It's just that I feel so... so helpless!" He rose suddenly. His hand going to the dagger at his belt, he faced the direction Merret had taken. "I'll kill him for this!" he vowed. "By the Light, I'll kill him!"

As the day wore on, Zenton's condition deteriorated. His fever worsened so that at times he was delirious. Now and again, in brief periods of lucidity, he asked where he was and what was going on. Most of the time, though, he slept uneasily, restless with pain. Towards mid-suns, Chandrane prepared some travel rations, urging Aldana and Lissanne to eat and forcing himself to do the same. Becoming weak and ill themselves would hardly benefit Zenton.

"There's no improvement, is there?" he asked anxiously as Aldana checked Zenton's side yet again.

"No. He's worse. The poison's spreading through his body."

"There must be *something* we can do?"

Aldana sighed wearily. "Even Silmedd and Vemran didn't know how to counteract the toxin. They just used potions to ease the pain and inflammation. They gave Grenath plenty of water and kept her warm and quiet. I can't even coax Zenton to drink when he does wake, and I'm frightened of choking him if I try when he's unconscious."

"We can't just let him die!"

"I'm doing my best, Chandrane! If I could think of something else to try –" She stopped in mid-sentence, looking from Zenton to Chandrane.

"What?" Chandrane demanded. "What is it?"

Aldana chewed at her upper lip. "No," she said after a pause. "It's a silly idea. It couldn't work."

"What idea?" Frustration laced Chandrane's tone. "Tell us, Aldana."

"How's your wrist?"

Chandrane stared at her. "My wrist? It's all right. What's that got to do with anything?"

"Roll your sleeve back and let me see where that leaf cut you."

"Aldana, I said it's fine!"

"Please, Chandrane."

With a grimace of annoyance, Chandrane rolled up his sleeve and ripped the bandage from his arm. "See," he declared triumphantly, "I told you it was all right."

"It's better than all right," Lissanne observed placidly. "There's barely a mark there. That's pretty fast healing, my friend."

A quick study of the injury site showed Chandrane that Lissanne was right.

"Well, yes," he conceded. "It *is* a bit surprising. Then again, I'd believe anything of that swamp after the changing paths and those night noises."

"So what were you thinking, Aldana?" prompted Lissanne.

Gazing into the dancing flames of the small campfire, Aldana hesitated before answering. "I've been wondering about the swamp pool."

"The one where Zenton fell?"

Aldana nodded. "The one with that strange algae. Perhaps it's... special."

"The water or the algae?" Lissanne wanted to know.

"Both. Either. I'm not sure."

Chandrane looked sceptical. "Special in what way?"

"Your wrist's healed amazingly quickly," Aldana said. "I'd expected there might be infection because you'd been in that stagnant water."

"Are you suggesting the water's helped in some way?" asked Chandrane.

Aldana nodded again. "The water or the algae – yes."

"If you're right," Chandrane said doubtfully, "wouldn't the pool have helped to heal Zenton too?"

"Perhaps it has," Aldana responded. "At least in part. His head's badly bruised but the gash itself has already started to close. It

158

mightn't even need stitching now. He went under water too. People who breathe water into their lungs like he did usually develop a chest infection. At least, that's what Vemran's taught me. He hasn't started coughing and I can't detect any congestion in his lungs. And another thing: I don't think missing the cut in his side was totally my fault after all." She sipped absently at her rapidly cooling drink. "I really *couldn't* see properly in the swamp, but I'm sure I'd have noticed blood on his side as soon as it was light enough. Maybe the wound had begun to heal but walking tore it open again."

"There's still the poison to consider," Lissanne said.

"I know. And that's where my theory comes unstuck. He's really ill, and he's getting worse. So why hasn't the pool done something about the poison? Unless..."

"Unless what?" demanded Chandrane. "Come on, Aldana. We have to try something. Anything. We can't just let him die."

Aldana took another sip of her drink, then set it aside. "What if the pool *has* helped? Grenath touched only a drop of the fluid, and she washed it off as soon as it started to sting. The Light alone knows how much poison was on that dagger. What if the water or the algae has kept him alive so far but simply isn't strong enough to go on working?"

Ever practical, Lissanne stated calmly, "Then we need more of the pool water."

"I'll go," Chandrane volunteered immediately

"Those paths could well have changed again," Lissanne pointed out. "How will you find the pool?"

"I'll find it somehow," Chandrane said, clambering to his feet.

"No, there's no need," Aldana told him. "I took a sample of the pool water during the night. The container's in my pack."

Lissanne fetched the young healer's travel pack and held out three sample bottles for Aldana to choose the one she wanted. Exposed to the light when the container was opened, the algae in the water glimmered faintly with the now familiar violet sheen.

Aldana hesitated, then knelt by Zenton and drew back the blanket. The web of scarlet threads had spread alarmingly, reaching almost to his throat. "Hold him still for me, Chandrane."

"Are you sure about this?" Lissanne queried worriedly. "That water smells foul."

159

"No, of course I'm not sure." Aldana was close to tears. "I just don't know what else to try."

"He's going to die anyway if we leave him," said Chandrane, his voice catching in his throat. "Do it, Aldana."

Aldana gave the bottle to Lissanne to hold while she removed the bandages and blood-soaked dressings. Her hands shook as she retrieved the container and poured the contents over the livid wound. The liquid trickled sluggishly across the prince's body, gleaming with sudden, startlingly bright iridescence before rapidly losing all trace of light and colour.

Zenton's eyes snapped open. He cried out, struggling weakly against Chandrane's restraining hold.

"Light help us," cried Lissanne as Zenton's whole body went into spasm.

The pain was all-consuming. There was an enormous pressure on his chest, constricting his lungs and throat. He gasped desperately for breath, feeling as if he was under water again, burning and drowning at the same time.

Abruptly, he was no longer lying on the grass near the campfire but walking through the long, dark, rocky passages deep within the cliffs of Mandano. His head throbbed; every step hurt his side, yet he knew he must continue his search. The tunnel forked ahead of him, one branch bright with a clear, white light, the other lit only by a misty, rosy glow. He wanted to go on but he needed to rest. Perhaps if he slept for a while he would feel better. He looked around for a place to stop.

"No, son. Don't stop now."

The voice was Renolth's, unmistakably.

Zenton started forward again. "Father?" A movement in the bright passageway drew his attention and all his desire for sleep fled. "Father?" he said again.

"Not this way, Zenton," said the silhouetted figure. "Take the other passage."

"But that leads to the dragon's lair," protested Zenton, not questioning how he knew.

"Yes, it does, but the dragon won't harm you. Find the cave, son. Use the knowledge there."

160

"There's something else there too," Zenton argued. "Something near the cave. Something evil."

The figure nodded. "I know, and you must be strong and face it."

A scraping sound, like long claws drawn across stone, caused Zenton to turn to the darker tunnel. Intrigued, he walked slowly towards the source of the sound. Glancing back, he saw that his father had gone. He forced himself to move on.

There came a gentle, snorting breath, and the passage began to fill with smoke and fire. Wary, but not truly afraid, Zenton walked into the searing flames.

Beneath Chandrane's hands, the prince's convulsions ceased. His eyes closed and his body went limp. Aldana knelt with her hands flat on the grass in front of her, silent tears streaming down her cheeks.

"What have I done, Chandrane?" she whispered. "What have I done?"

Chapter Twenty-seven

Poison

Out foraging for morrenna berries to supplement the last of their travel rations, Lissanne plodded steadily up the gentle slope of a low hill east of their small campsite. Aldana had pointed out the bushes to the group on their way to the swamp and Lissanne knew they were somewhere in the hills. If only the terrain didn't look so similar around this area, she might, she was sure, have more success. The sketch-map was some help, of course, but even so it was hard to pick out the noted landmarks. Oddly-shaped boulders, copses of silvery-leafed trees and thin streamlets abounded just here. It would be all too easy to become lost even with the map. Now and again she glanced back to check her direction and distance from the camp.

The sought-after bushes appeared without warning, almost hidden in a cleft she had nearly bypassed. Lissanne took two cloth pouches from her pocket and set to work gathering the sweet, juicy fruit. There were fewer berries than she had hoped for but any extra food was welcome.

She was on the point of returning to the others when she heard voices. She froze, listening. Yes – it was definitely voices she was hearing, not the chattering calls of the brown, shaggy creatures that roamed hereabouts. Fastening the partly filled pouches to her belt, she scrambled to the top of the rise.

Six or seven people – it was difficult to be sure with them walking close together and the tall grasses hiding their outlines – were heading for a prominent copse some way off to the north-west. Through narrowed eyes, Lissanne studied the group. The leader must surely be Brandell, the dark hair and easy stride marking him out even at that distance, and there was the tall figure of Silmedd at Brandell's shoulder. They were going in the wrong direction. Following the path they were on at the moment, they would miss the camp completely. Shouting as loudly as she could, Lissanne began to run towards them.

The sound of voices caught Aldana's attention. Looking up from the fire where she'd been heating some water, she saw Lissanne leading a group of people towards the campsite. Silmedd was with them.

Aldana ran to meet the Master Healer. "Thank the Light you're here at last!" she exclaimed. "What took you so *long*? He's conscious now but, oh, Silmedd! – he's still so very ill. The poison's stopped spreading, I think. Has Lissanne told you about the poison? I ran out of pain relief for him two days ago and I –"

"Peace, Aldana. Draw breath and then we'll talk." Favouring her with one of his rare smiles, the healer took both of her hands in his. "Now," he said, "come with me and tell me exactly what happened and how you've treated the prince thus far. Then you can take me to him." He walked a few paces away from the rest of the group and Aldana followed him meekly.

Chandrane hastened across to Brandell. "What kept you?" His tone was carefully neutral. "Where's Merret?"

Brandell handed his travel pack to Lissanne. "There are some provisions in there," he said. "Lajar and the others have more. Sort some food for us all, if you will Lissanne. Now, Chandrane, before I answer *your* questions, I've some of my own. Lissanne told us you all believe Zenton was stabbed, and she said the dagger used was poisoned. Is this true?"

Chandrane nodded.

"That explains it," mused Brandell.

"Explains what?"

"Has Zenton remembered what happened?" asked Brandell, ignoring Chandrane's query.

"I don't know," Chandrane told him. "He's spoken very little since he came round the other day. He's in the shelter over there if you want to see him."

"I do, but I'll wait until Silmedd's tended him." He wandered close to the campfire and sat down wearily. "I can't believe it, you know. If I'd known what had happened, I'd never have left him. And as for Merret..."

Chandrane sat down next to Brandell. "What of Merret?"

Brandell shrugged. "He's gone. He took off sometime in the night during our first stop. Now I know why."

He plucked a grass stem and rolled it in his fingers before setting it between his teeth. He pushed it to the corner of his mouth where it bobbed up and down as he spoke.

"We'd travelled pretty fast and we were tired. None of us had slept much the night Zenton was hurt, had we? Anyway, we made camp as Bardok set. I'd hoped to start off again at Oltan's dawn but I'm afraid I overslept. When I woke up, Merret was gone. And he'd taken the map with him." He paused to throw away the piece of grass and accept a cup of banellin from Lissanne. "It was easy enough for me to get myself back to the harbour and the settlement but finding you again was quite another matter. I lost us a whole day by following the wrong branch of a stream and having to backtrack, and another half day by mistaking the contours of the first set of hills. I'd have gone astray again if Lissanne hadn't spotted us when she did." He sipped his drink and scowled. "Too weak," he complained. "What's Lissanne used? Banellin or old tengra leaves? No, Chandrane, don't bother changing it. I'll drink it. At least it's warm and wet. Oh, look; Aldana's coming over. And Silmedd's going in to see Zenton at last."

When it had become obvious that they would need to stay and wait for help, Chandrane had joined together two shelters to give more room to tend Zenton. It was still a small space, though, and Silmedd went on his hands and knees to enter. The flap of the improvised tent had been fastened back to allow in fresh air to keep Zenton cool. Silmedd set down his bag and knelt by the prince.

Zenton's face was ashen, his skin coated with a sheen of sweat, but his eyes showed awareness and he nodded slightly in response to the healer's greeting. Silmedd took his time, examining Zenton thoroughly. The knife wound, neatly sewn, was angry and the skin across the prince's hips, stomach and chest was discoloured and tender, but the evil, purple mottling Silmedd had feared to see was barely visible. Zenton flinched when touched but did not cry out. Reasonably satisfied, the healer turned his attention to the head wound, gently moving Zenton's hair back off his forehead to check the injury. He pressed carefully around the scar, testing under still-bruised skin for any fracture at the temple or cheekbone, explaining to Zenton what he was doing.

"I can't detect any fracture," he said at last, "though that's been a nasty injury. I'm surprised the cut's healed so well." Perhaps Aldana was right about the powers of the pool water. Open-minded about the mysteries of Zamara, he was quite prepared to give credence to the idea. "As for your side, young man," he continued, "you're fortunate to be alive, you know. Left untreated, that knife wound could have proved fatal, even without the poison in your system." He watched carefully for Zenton's reaction to his words, pursing his lips thoughtfully when the prince showed no astonishment at the mention of poison. "You knew?" he asked.

"I guessed as much," Zenton murmured, speaking with visible effort. "I felt it in me. I think I tried to tell Aldana but she worked it out for herself anyway."

The healer regarded him steadily. "Aldana tells me you recall the journey out of the swamp but you can't remember anything of what happened when you fell."

"I can remember some of it now," Zenton told him. "It's come back in sort of flashes. Bits at a time."

"Can you tell me?" Silmedd pressed.

Zenton shifted position, wincing as he did so. "I remember the pool with the algae. There was an animal near the pool. I remember that, too. It was a baby feline and its mother came for it."

"That's good," Silmedd said encouragingly. "Go on."

Zenton sighed. "I think we were getting ready to cross the pool, to find a campsite. I heard the dragon and... and... I'm sorry Silmedd. I don't recall anything more."

"You've done remarkably well," the healer assured him.

"Silmedd?"

"What is it, my prince?"

"I want to go home now, but..."

"But what?"

"I... I don't think I can walk that far just yet."

Silmedd chuckled softly. "You won't be walking anywhere for quite a while, your highness. Don't fret. We'll get you home. Here, drink this." He slipped a supporting arm round Zenton's shoulders and carefully dribbled a sweet, syrupy liquid into the prince's mouth. "This should ease the pain and help you sleep. I'm going to speak with Aldana and the others. I'll be back shortly."

As soon as Silmedd had left the small shelter, Brandell crawled in to take his place. "Well, cousin," he said, slipping off his jacket and using it as a mat, "this wasn't quite what I had in mind when we set off to explore the swamp."

"Nor I," Zenton responded quietly. "Brandell, I was stabbed, was I not?"

"I'm afraid so."

"By Merret?"

"Yes."

Zenton was silent for a moment. "Why?" he said at last.

Brandell gave a short, humourless laugh. "You were in the way."

"In the way?" Silmedd's potion was starting to take effect. Zenton's concentration was waning.

"We think Merret was trying to kill Chandrane, not you. Leave it for now, Zenton. We'll talk more when you're feeling better. Rest, cousin. We've quite a journey ahead of us on the morrow."

"Brandell –"

"Hush. No more questions. I'll sit with you until Silmedd comes back. Go to sleep, Zenton."

Lissanne glanced up as Chandrane wandered over to help her finish preparing the food. "I know that look," she declared. "What's troubling you?"

Chandrane picked up a cleaned stick and idly stirred the concoction in the cooking pot. "Brandell's sent Slen and Drent and some others after Merret."

"Good."

"I doubt they'll find him."

"Probably not."

"He'll be long gone by now."

"Probably."

"I wonder *where* he's gone."

Lissanne shrugged. "The forest? The plains? Who cares, Chandrane, as long as he *has* gone?"

"*I* care," said Chandrane with quiet passion. "I want to know what really happened back there in the swamp."

"We *do* know."

"I suppose so. I just overheard Brandell telling Zenton that Merret had been trying to kill me, not him."

"What of it? I told Prince Brandell that. I thought we'd decided that's what had happened."

"It *is* the logical explanation, is it not?"

Lissanne sprinkled a few herbs into the pot and frowned. "I hate cooking." She turned to her colleague. "You don't believe it, do you?"

"What? Yes, I believe you hate cooking."

"Fool. You know very well what I mean."

Chandrane smiled briefly, then became serious again. "You know, Lissanne," he said slowly, "I think Zenton might well have been the intended target after all."

Lissanne pondered this statement for a moment before asking, "Why should Merret want to kill Prince Zenton?" She slapped Chandrane's hand away as he went to add a whole fistful of extra herbs.

"Halden was killed by that lightning strike," he said, replacing the herbs in their bag and rubbing his hand. "Renolth and Zenton lived. Merret's nature changed after his brother died. And..."

"And what?"

"Merret was on the cliff top when Renolth fell."

Lissanne stared at him, aghast. "You're surely not suggesting – "

"I'm not certain *what* I'm suggesting," interrupted Chandrane, "but it bears thinking about doesn't it?"

Taking the stick from Chandrane, Lissanne took over stirring the stew. "Well," she said at last, "we'll never know the truth, will we? Merret's gone. And I shouldn't think it's all that easy to survive here on your own, so perhaps he's dead by now."

Chandrane straightened up and gazed across the small encampment, looking east towards Patoll. "I hope Slen finds proof of that," he said softly.

Chapter Twenty-eight

A King's Task

Amryl was working alongside her mother, lifting stones for a boundary wall, when she stumbled, made unsteady by the weight of the rock she was trying to move. An overseer laid a whip across her back – and Lantor saw it. Whether the spells which bound him to servitude had simply weakened over time or the Almari powers of old still ran in his veins, Lantor did not know. Whatever the reason, he was sure that Amryl's beating had been the catalyst for his awakening.

Had the overseer touched her again, Lantor would doubtless have killed the man, and been executed for doing so, but the whip was coiled and Amryl resumed her task before the High King found the will to act. Despite the burning desire for revenge, Lantor had the presence of mind to conceal his new awareness lest his captors discover him and reinforce the fading enchantment.

With lucidity came the painful memories of the boarding of the ships and the capture of his people. He recalled how they had all been taken ashore and stripped of their few possessions. He remembered someone forcibly removing the royal seal from his hand. Glancing down, he could see the faint mark on his finger where the ring should be.

He knew now how his people had been treated since their capture and he fought to contain his fury. He dared not show any change in behaviour. He could not help the Almari if he fell victim again to the enchantment that had stolen his mind. Though his whole being cried against doing so, he turned away from his wife and daughter and continued his work.

For many days, Lantor sought a way to break the spell which held Ryella in its thrall. Quite apart from his desire to restore her free will, he needed her counsel and her expertise if the plans he was forming were to stand any chance of success.

In the early hours of one rainy morning, Lantor woke to the sound of Ryella weeping softly in her sleep. Moved to pity and rage, he touched her forehead, stroking away the tangled hair and whispering words of comfort, speaking in the Old Tongue so that the others in the hut would not understand. To his surprise and utter delight, Ryella cried out and woke from her sleep and from the spell.

Having Ryella back gave Lantor hope and renewed purpose. Using the method of touch and words that had restored Ryella, he 'awakened' more of his people, selecting first those like Murl and Tallin who could be relied upon to pursue the idea of escape without betraying anyone involved in the plotting. He chose to leave Darrant and Amryl for the time being. He felt that awakening them to their true plight would be both unkind and useless. He worried about Jerram, too, for they had been separated on coming ashore. Night after night, as he made his way through the nearby camps and villages to restore mind and memory to his people, Lantor searched in vain for Jerram.

It was a difficult and dangerous time. The Almari were not the only race to have fallen victim to the powerful southerners and Lantor knew that any false move on his part would be reported by another worker to an overseer. He tried on three occasions to 'wake' someone who was not Almari but who could, he believed, be trusted. He failed each time. Lantor gave up and concentrated his efforts on the Almari.

Sometimes his agents were able to bring people to him but more often than not the High King had to go out to them, and he could only travel so far in a night if he was to have some rest and be back at his work by morning. It helped that many of the Almari had been kept together and were guarded by just one overseer at a time, their southern captors presumably being so confident in the spell of binding that rebellion was not expected.

Never had Lantor been so exhausted in his life, nor so determined to complete a task. He would free all those of his people he could find. He yearned to find every one. He knew he must work as swiftly as possible; the longer he took, the more chance there was of betrayal. His burden finally eased a little when he roused Darrant and Amryl. He bitterly regretted not waking them sooner, for both

169

proved able to clear the minds of enslaved Almari once he'd shown them what to do.

Ryella's help was invaluable too. Although she did not possess whatever power Lantor, Darrant and Amryl used, she called upon her store of medical knowledge to produce a special blend of herbs that could bring about a deep and seemingly natural sleep. Without these herbs, Lantor's task would have been impossible, for someone would surely have sounded the alarm at his unauthorised presence. As it was, his trusted agents had to ensure that any overseers in the vicinity due to be visited by Lantor on any particular night were well dosed with Ryella's sleeping potion.

Three hundred and seventy-two people had been aboard the captured Almari vessels. By the time Lantor was ready to put his escape plans into action only one hundred and forty-nine had been traced. Some, he learned from his growing network of spies, had died under the harsh regime of captivity. Others had been taken aboard vessels and transported elsewhere. Fifty or so could not be accounted for and these, the High King reluctantly decided, would have to be abandoned to their fate. He found this decision particularly difficult since Jerram was still amongst those missing.

On the night Lantor set in motion his plans to take his people to freedom, he received a report that a new group of workers had been brought in from a village many days' walk away. In this group was one Almari. Though it threatened to spoil the careful timing and thereby ruin all he had worked for, Lantor could not bring himself to abandon any Almari who could be helped. Leaving Ryella to begin the movement of their people, he and Tallin hastened to the huts housing the newcomers. Finding Jerram was, Lantor felt, the Light's reward for his dedication.

Jerram woke to the feel of strong hands pinning him down and a piece of cloth being stuffed into his mouth. Instinctively he struggled, trying to fight his way free and call out to the overseer that there were intruders in the camp.

"Be still, son," said a quiet, authoritative voice near his ear.

There was something familiar about the voice, something he should recognise. His thrashing ceased as he tried to think through

170

the fog that was clouding his mind and his judgement, and in that moment of calm someone placed a firm hand on his forehead and spoke some strange words. He felt an instant of blinding pain and the gag muffled his agonised cry as the haze was ripped from his mind like a curtain being torn violently aside to let in the brilliant light of the suns. The hand lifted from his head, the pressure on his shoulders eased and the cloth was pulled gently from his mouth. Someone leant forward with a lantern, lifting the light so it illuminated the face of the man bending over him.

"Jerram? Son? Can you understand me?"

Jerram peered up at the figure looming above him. "Father?"

The hands that had pinioned him now supported him as someone just beyond the light's range helped him to sit up.

"Father?" he said again. "What's going on? Where...?"

The words died in his throat as he recalled in vivid, horrifying detail their attackers boarding the *Tennel* and her sister vessels, the brief, desperate, hopeless fight against overwhelming odds and then... and then... What had happened next was not so clear.

He vaguely recollected being herded ashore but everything after that was just a jumble of images and feelings: working in fields and villages; eating but always being hungry; sleeping, and waking still tired. What he did know with utter certainty now the restraining fog had been banished was that not only had his body been captured but so too, in some horribly disturbing way, had his mind.

"How long have we been here?" he asked.

Lantor's shrug sent shadows dancing grotesquely on the wall of the small hut. "I'm not sure, Jerram. A year, I think, judging from how the children have grown. Perhaps nearer two."

"*Two years?*" Jerram glanced down at his hands, seeing calluses and scrapes beneath the grime. His face was sore and, reaching up with grubby fingers, he traced a raised scar running from his left cheekbone to his jaw. He had no idea how or when he'd been hurt. "By the Light, Father, what happened to us? Where's Mother? Where're Amryl and Darrant? Where's your ring?"

"Keep your voice down, Prince," admonished the second person in a hoarse whisper, moving into the lantern's meagre light.

"Tallin? Is that you, Tallin?" Jerram asked, recognising the man who had been one of the senior royal guards at the palace.

"Aye, Prince Jerram, and you'll have an overseer down on us if you persist in raising your voice." The burly guard turned to Lantor. "We should go, Sire. There's not much time."

Lantor nodded. "Come," he said, taking hold of Jerram's arm and urging him to stand. "I'll explain what I can later. For now you must trust me and come quickly and silently. We've a fair walk ahead of us and we must not be seen or heard." He shuttered the lantern and led the way outside.

The night was cold and breezy, with thin cloud scudding across a sky brightened by two half-moons and one thin, orange crescent. There was light enough to see, and therefore there was danger of being seen. Cautiously, the three men made their way northwest towards the main harbour, picking up their pace once the huts were well behind them. Burning with questions, Jerram found it hard to remain silent. Twice he opened his mouth to speak and twice he was prevented from doing so – the first time by Tallin grabbing his arm and gesturing for him to stay quiet, the second by a near-encounter with an overseer on routine patrol. Finally controlling his desire to learn more, he turned his attention to their hurried journey.

Lantor stumbled on the uneven ground. Tallin and Jerram caught him in time to prevent a fall and he thanked them with a nod. Tired though he was, this was hardly the occasion to become careless. He would need his wits about him this night if they were to stand any chance of escape.

By now, the overseers on duty should have been dosed with Ryella's sleeping herbs, as should all the nearby non-Almari who could raise an alarm and any Almari children too young to understand the need for stealth. Lantor prayed fervently that those charged with adding the herbs to the food or drink had been thorough – and if the mixture used on the overseers turned out to be a little too strong, well, he for one would harbour no guilt about that.

Murl should already be at the docks, ensuring firstly that the guards there were dealt with and then supervising the boarding of the *Tennel's Flight* and the *Rays of Bardok*. The Almari vessels, repaired months ago by supervised workers, had been riding at anchor with no southern crew aboard for the past week and Lantor could only pray that this situation had not changed. He regretted the necessity of leaving the *Homeland Queen* behind but there were simply not enough trained sailors to crew three ships.

The southerners' vessels were the main danger. Lantor had delayed the escape attempt until most of the enemy fleet had sailed, seeking more victims to enslave in all likelihood, but five ships remained, as did their crews. The alarm would most certainly be sounded as soon as the Almari sails unfurled. Larger and faster than the Almari vessels, the enemy ships would doubtless give chase. Lantor and Murl were relying on surprise and the greater manoeuvrability of the *Tennel* and the *Rays* to see them as far as the harbour entrance. After that, the other ships should not be a problem. If the men and women sent ahead to hole the hulls of the southerners' vessels had succeeded in their sabotage mission, those ships should take on water at a prodigious rate.

Lantor glanced up at the positions of the moons relative to the stars and fought back panic. Had they left someone awake who should have been drugged? If so, the alarm would be raised before all his people were aboard. He reckoned they would have at best a two-hour margin of relative safety. If their escape attempt was noticed, a fast runner from one of the camps could reach the southerners' barracks in about an hour and guards would be mobilised swiftly. They *had* to be well under way before reinforcements came from those barracks. Two hours, if the Light favoured them.

Ryella met them before they reached the ships. She flung her arms round Jerram and held him close for several moments. "Thank the Light you're safe," she said. "We thought we'd lost you." Turning to Lantor, she asked worriedly, "Is Darrant with you?"

"Darrant? No. I though he was with you."

Ryella shook her head. "No. I told him to make sure Amryl was aboard, then help Murl. I've just been on the *Tennel*. He's not there."

Lantor cursed softly. "What's the lad up to now? We've no time for this. Jerram, go ahead with your mother. Go with them, Tallin. I'll check our sleeping quarters and meet you at the harbour." He hastened away before any one of them could protest.

He had almost reached the huts when Darrant came hurtling towards him. Lantor grabbed his son and shook him. "Your mother's

173

frantic with worry for you," he hissed. "Let's get moving. You can explain later."

Darrant resisted his father's shove. "The new overseer had this," he whispered, holding out his hand. Dirt-encrusted but still recognisable, the royal seal lay in Darrant's palm.

Lantor's eyes filled with tears. He took the ring and slipped it onto the middle finger of his left hand, finding that it fit as neatly as it always had. Perhaps it would reach the new homeland after all. He drew Darrant into an embrace. "My thanks, son," he said softly before pushing him gently away. "Now, we must run."

With Darrant at his side, Lantor set off. He needed to be there at the docks, to make certain everything went according to plan. He was under no illusion about their peril; all the fugitives knew just how slender were their chances. Fierce determination and pride burned in his chest as he ran. They might not succeed – but they would die rather than be recaptured. If it did come to that, at least they would die free in body and mind.

Chapter Twenty-nine

Reflections

The coronation ceremony was planned to take place at the First Sun's set. The preparations were complete: the ground made ready; accommodation arranged for those from the Far Settlement staying overnight; the great banquet organized; speeches practised; entertainment rehearsed. Zenton had run through the coronation oaths so often that he'd found himself repeating them in his dreams. He would be glad, now, to have the matter over and done with. The waiting was preying on his nerves.

Maglin had done a fine job of combining the traditional Almari vows with words appropriate to the start of a new reign in a new homeland. Brandell, too, had blended tradition and innovation into the overall organisation of the whole event so that even those still resentful of change would surely approve. Zenton had taken surprisingly little part in the actual planning of the day, his offers of assistance having been courteously but firmly rejected, with the standard response being words to the effect of, "You'll have enough to do on the day itself and you must not tire yourself out beforehand. Leave all the arrangements to us."

Sitting in a chair beside his bed, he watched as pale light filtered through the chamber window, heralding Oltan's dawn. The quality of that early light held promise of a fine, clear day. For his own part, Zenton truly did not care if the ceremony was washed away by a freak flood but he hoped for the sake of Donar, Irvanyal and all the others who had worked so hard that everything would proceed smoothly. His sombre mood was, he knew, the combination of apprehension and fatigue. He had not slept well for the past few nights – hardly surprising, considering the step he was about to take – and he was afraid of the future. It wasn't just the responsibility of leadership that frightened him; he was fearful of proving unworthy, of being inadequate for the task, of letting everyone down and, worst of all, of failing to live up to his father's reputation. He missed Renolth greatly.

He rose slowly and wandered over to the window, trying for calmness, for the poise and confidence everyone else seemed to think he possessed. He didn't feel confident this morning. At this moment, he bitterly regretted having managed to persuade the healers to declare him fit enough to face the long ceremony. Perhaps he should go to them and say he felt ill again.

Silently, he chided himself for his cowardice. He *was* better. Not completely recovered yet, it was true, but certainly well enough for the coronation to take place.

It had been a slow process, his recuperation – frustratingly so at times. The healers had assured him all along that he was doing well, that his strength and energy would gradually return, and they were proving to be right. The violent headaches were gone and the dreadful pain in his side had eased to a discomfort he noticed only if he moved too quickly or became overtired. His limbs ached less these days and debilitating fatigue no longer plagued him as often or as severely as it had in the first weeks after the stabbing. As long as he took care (and Aldana made sure that he did), he could cope with most of his duties as Zamaran leader. It had taken time, though, to reach this stage.

Still convalescing – finally out of the infirmary and back at the royal shelter – he had spent the eighteenth anniversary of his birth in bed instead of being able to keep his promise to take the title of High King on that day. Much as he might wish it, he could not allow the rite to be postponed a second time.

A movement past the window caught his wandering attention. The duty guards were changing shift. Zenton sighed. Slen had badgered him until he'd consented to the establishment of a Royal Guard Company, based on the traditional Almari Palace Guard, and all because Chandrane believed Zenton had been Merret's target all along. Even though there had been no trace of Merret, one or two members of Slen's newly-formed unit always accompanied Zenton whenever he left the royal shelter. Brandell was guarded too, although, unlike Zenton, he seemed not to mind.

Zenton had thus far refused to sanction any return visit to the swamp. That the water or the algae in it had been instrumental in saving his life, Zenton did not doubt. Had Aldana not made her brave decision to use it on him, he was certain he would have succumbed

176

to the poison. He could well imagine Silmedd's desire to test the pool water and discover the truth about its properties, but Zenton was not prepared to risk lives if he could avoid doing so. The swamp, with its changeable paths and streams, was simply too dangerous. Perhaps in the future a way might be found to search and map the area but for now Zenton would continue to withhold his permission.

The Mandano Ridge, though, was another matter. Until quite recently, Zenton had felt too ill to bother about sending more search bands there, let alone to consider going back himself. He doubted that his workload as High King would allow him much time for joining extended searches even when he was well enough to travel far, at least until he had grown familiar with the role and the increased responsibilities. Sometime in the near future, though, he would ensure that the ridge was explored more thoroughly. The need to find the cave he now believed was the dragon's lair had diminished of late but it had not subsided altogether.

Zenton sighed again. It seemed to him that Brandell was still better than he was at administration. Indeed, Brandell had slipped back easily into the leadership position while Zenton had been out of action. For a fleeting moment, Zenton was tempted to pass overall control to Brandell, to abdicate in his cousin's favour and opt for a supporting role in the government of The Island. He dismissed the notion almost as soon as it formed in his mind. The ultimate responsibility was his alone.

Anxious suddenly to be outdoors, he turned from the window and strode towards the door. Crossing the room, his glance lit on the coronation garments hanging near his bed. He had no idea how the clothiers had managed to produce such rich-looking fabrics. When he'd asked, he had been told politely that the clothes were the gifts of those who had made them and the process need not on this occasion concern him. Some secrets, it appeared, could be kept even from kings.

Smiling at the memory, Zenton left the shelter, nodded a greeting to the two guards who stepped forward immediately to accompany him and strolled through the awakening settlement to his favourite spot overlooking the harbour. He dropped his cloak onto the dew-damp grass and sat watching the light on the rippling water as Oltan rose lazily in the eastern sky. The vessels at anchor bobbed

177

gently on the incoming tide, their motion rhythmical, almost hypnotic. The knots in Zenton's stomach began to ease and he felt some of the tension seep from the tight muscles in his neck and shoulders as he gazed idly across the glistening expanse of water, shading his eyes against the morning glare.

There was something out there.

He stood and pointed out towards the harbour entrance. "What's that?"

Both guards moved forward alongside him and stared dutifully in the direction indicated. It was obvious from their expressions that neither one could see the harbour entrance clearly at that distance let alone make out any object on the water.

"There's a ship coming into the harbour," the prince said.

"Oh, it must be Kaldrina, Sire." Tillek – young, tall, auburn-haired and eager – sounded relieved at being able to give an easy explanation. "She said she'd bring the *Horizon's Edge* back in time for the crew to join the ceremony today."

Zenton shook his head. "That's not the *Horizon*. Dannen, fetch Brandell and Aldana, then find Slen and Chandrane. Tillek, go and bring Silmedd and Vemran and the Council Leaders. Rouse them from their beds if you have to."

"But, Prince Zenton," Dannen protested, "we're not supposed to leave –"

"Go!" commanded Zenton in a tone that brooked no argument. "Now!"

The two guards sped off to do his bidding. Through narrowed eyes, the prince watched the distant vessel negotiate the treacherous currents of the harbour entrance and advance smoothly into the calm, enclosed waters.

Before the ship had covered even half the distance to the quayside, Slen had a string of armed guards arrayed along the harbour wall. Chandrane and Lissanne flanked Zenton, while Slen stood at Brandell's shoulder. The Council Leaders and healers waited a few paces behind Zenton, while the gathering crowd, on Slen's orders, was kept well back.

For some time, the watchers stood in anxious silence until Zenton instructed, "Stand down your forces, Slen. We want a welcoming committee here, not a defence line."

"You're sure?" Slen asked cautiously.

Zenton nodded. "I'm sure, yes. That's Murl's ship." He gestured to the incoming vessel. "That's the *Tennel's Flight*."

Chapter Thirty

Murl's Tale

Despite the early hour, the crowded study in the royal shelter was already warm and slightly stuffy. Zenton opened the shutters to allow in the cooling breeze before seating himself in the chair he still regarded as his father's.

"What happened?" he asked Murl.

Murl tugged gently at his untidy beard. "Prince Brandell told me about Renolth," he said. "You have my condolences. He was a good man."

Zenton responded with a brief nod of acknowledgement. "What happened?" he asked again.

"You'll know from Jedron how our fleet became separated during a storm," Murl said. "Never have I known such a gale. Ten vessels were lost to us within the first half-hour of the storm's onset. I've been told that nine of those reached safety here under Jedron's command. The seven of us left were driven south. We kept together for a time but conditions grew still worse and we lost sight of four of our ships. I take it none of those made safe landfall here?"

"No," said Brandell. "Just Jedron's nine."

Murl took the goblet Healer Vemran held out to him but did not drink. Cradling it in gnarled, scarred fingers, he continued, "The storm lasted for days, and even after its main force was spent the strong wind persisted, driving us ever farther southwards. When the wind finally abated and the weather cleared, we could see land. Ships came out to us. At first we thought they would help, but as they came closer High King Lantor warned us we were in danger. There was nothing we could do. The *Tennel* was badly storm-damaged and we couldn't outrun them in the state we were in."

"You were boarded, weren't you?" said Zenton quietly. "They took you all as captives."

Murl turned to him in astonishment. "You knew?"

Zenton gave a slight shrug. "I saw as much in a dream some time ago. I'd hoped it wasn't true."

The sea-captain took a sip of his drink before setting the goblet aside. "They took us to their land and made us slaves."

Into the hush that greeted Murl's words, Brandell queried, "Did you not resist?"

"Not at first. They had a power of some kind that robbed us of independent thought. There were others there, too. People from races we've never encountered before. Whatever enchantment our captors used held them as it held us. Time lost all meaning. I'm still not sure exactly how long we spent there."

He fell silent until Brandell prompted with a hint of impatience, "Go on, Murl."

The captain shivered slightly and rubbed his hands together as if to warm them, though it was hot enough in the study. He looked gaunt, his jacket hanging loosely on shoulders and chest which had once been muscled and strong. "It was the High King who saved us," he said quietly. "Whatever power they had over us faded from him first. I don't know how he broke their hold, but somehow he gradually freed our minds. Many of our people had already died in that land, and some were transported elsewhere, but we gathered all we could."

He reached for his goblet and stared into the liquid, swirling it gently before draining the cup.

"They relied too heavily on their sorcery," he said at last, "and that was our salvation, such as it was. They must have thought their magic was sufficient to hold us to our tasks. There were few overseers, and we drugged them with a concoction of Queen Ryella's devising. We took two of our ships – the *Tennel's Flight* and the *Rays of Bardok*. At first, all went to plan, but we'd not quite cleared their harbour when they fired on us." Murl's voice became thick with grief. "Their arrows killed the two princes. They used fire-arrows too, and it was fire that claimed the lives of Princess Amryl and Queen Ryella before we could control the flames on the *Tennel*. The *Rays* went down near their harbour entrance."

In a hushed, strained tone, Zenton finally voiced the question he had feared to ask before. "And what of my uncle?"

Unheeded, a single tear rolled down Murl's swarthy face. "He'd taken an arrow in his shoulder during the first volley and then he was badly burned trying to save his wife and daughter. He tried. Oh, how

181

he tried!" The captain looked round at his shocked audience and declared softly, "Despite his grief and his injuries, it was he who ensured our escape."

"How so?" Brandell wanted to know.

Murl took a grubby square of cloth from his pocket and noisily blew his nose. The scars on his hands stood out, testament to the fact that he, too, had fought the flames. He sat with the grimy rag clenched in his fist as he said, "We'd already holed their vessels, and the *Homeland Queen* so they couldn't have her, and that slowed them, but two of their ships came after us anyway. Lantor ordered us to use their own fire against them and we set their sails alight." He ran his hand over his face and scratched at a healing scar on his cheek. "We cleared the harbour and a south wind – the first we'd known in all our time in that land – sped us on our way. Lantor set the direction we should sail, though how he knew it is beyond my understanding. We came at last to the chain of small islands we'd passed on our first voyage with Prince Renolth. I'd destroyed our sea-charts when we were first boarded but the maps were clear in my mind and I told the High King the way was now known to me."

Again it was Brandell who spoke out. "If you were near those islands then you were less than ten days' sail from here."

Murl nodded agreement. "Indeed so, and I firmly believe our High King had waited only for the knowledge that the last of his people would be safe." Quite unashamedly, the burly sea-captain began to weep freely as he said in a choked voice, "He died that same night."

He delved into an inner pocket and, reaching out with a trembling hand, set onto the table in front of Zenton the High King's ring: the royal seal of the Almari.

Chapter Thirty-one

High King

Standing by the window in his room, Zenton gazed unseeing across a settlement emptied now of people, for they had left to gather on the sloping field marked out for the coronation ceremony. His life in the Homeland seemed to belong to the dim and distant past, the last ties severed by the tidings of the deaths of Lantor and his family.

The realisation came to Zenton that he would not go back even if he could. He was Zamaran now – Almari no longer. He loved The Island with its strange beauty, its amazing diversity of plant and animal life and its intriguing mysteries. Perhaps he was not yet as good as Brandell at management tasks, but he would learn. Doubtless he would make mistakes but he would do his best to be the leader his people needed. Surely they could ask no more of him than that.

A quiet tap at the door interrupted his reverie and Aldana entered when he called permission. He turned to face her.

She stood looking appraisingly at the slender, dark-haired young man in front of her. The weavers, dyers and clothiers had done their work well. Zenton was dressed in deep-purple trousers, so dark they were almost black; his tunic was of the same material, with silver-grey trim at throat and cuffs; his old, soft, black boots gleamed – cleaned, carefully patched and newly polished. The only pieces of jewellery he wore were the dragon medallion given to him by his father and, on the middle finger of his left hand, the royal seal.

"Renolth would be proud of you," Aldana declared softly.

"I hope so."

"Are you nervous?"

"A little. Mostly I feel sort of numb, as if all this is happening to someone else and I'm merely a spectator." He chuckled quietly. "I suspect this detachment will vanish – unfortunately! – as soon as I set foot outside the shelter." He rubbed absently at the faint scar on his temple. "I didn't sense Lantor's passing, you know. I thought I would know if he died, but I didn't. I didn't know about my aunt or my cousins either."

He twisted the ring around on his finger, wondering anew at the way it had fit without alteration even though Lantor had been larger and heavier than he. He wished he could ask his father about it. It was the symbol of the monarch's authority and, supposedly, of his or her special powers. Was there more to it? Perhaps he should study the legends more closely. Maglin would be able to help him.

"Why didn't I know?" he whispered. "I should have known they'd died."

"You've been very ill, Zenton," Aldana reminded him gently. "It's no wonder you weren't able to sense what happened. It's only this past week or so that you've started to look more like your old self."

Zenton glanced towards the window again. "It's almost time, is it not? Ah well, at least I know now that the title is mine by right."

He drew in a slow, deep breath, released it and stepped towards the bed, reaching for his coronation cloak. Aldana took it first, running her fingers across the shimmering, violet fabric, its grey lining and trim matching the edging of Zenton's tunic. Carefully, she placed the elegant garment around Zenton's shoulders and fastened the jewelled clasp before standing back to check his appearance.

Zenton's hand went to his chest, touching the clasp and the medallion beneath it. The medallion's raised image of a dragon curled in sleep represented for him leashed power – guarding The Island that bore its shape. The cloak clasp, with the Almari emblem of a dragon in flight, had been Renolth's. Zenton smiled as he recalled another cloak clasp, not so fine as this but well-crafted for all that, lost to the thieving hands of that enchanting little creature by the Eye Lake.

Before Aldana could ask what was amusing him, another knock sounded at the door and Brandell strode straight in. "Are you ready, little cousin?" he demanded, grinning at Zenton's finery, though he himself was dressed in new garments for the occasion.

"Not so little," Aldana pointed out. "He's taller than you now."

Brandell laughed. "Not by much."

"I'll have to go, Zenton," Aldana told him, adjusting his tunic collar so that it lay neatly over the neck of his cloak. Panic flared in his pale eyes and she added soothingly, "I won't be far away. I'll be right near the dais, next to Vemran and Silmedd." Then, with a gentle touch to his face, she was gone from the room.

"Well, cousin," Brandell said, "now's your last chance to change your mind. Once the deed is done, there's no turning back."

Responding to the levity in Brandell's tone, Zenton said with mock seriousness, "I'd stand down but I can't think of anyone else around here who'd be capable of doing the job competently."

"Oh, I don't know about that," Brandell retorted. "I reckon I'd muddle along somehow – and that outfit of yours would look pretty good on me." He opened the bedroom door and stood back. "After you, your well-dressed Majesty."

With Brandell at his side and an honour guard as escort, Zenton made his way unhurriedly through the waiting crowds to the sloping field and the decorated dais. His earlier detachment had indeed deserted him but he managed well enough, speaking out loudly and clearly during his short speech to the assembled gathering and meaning with all sincerity the oaths he took before his people.

The ceremony drew to its climax as Brandell raised the newly-forged crown, holding it aloft for all to see. Zenton knelt to receive the metal circlet.

Darkness descended so abruptly that Zenton gasped aloud. The people near him, those he could still see in the eerie dimness, appeared frozen, caught in different postures like living statues. For the space of a few heartbeats there was utter silence. Then came a deep, rumbling murmur, like the menacing growl of some gigantic creature. The pent fury in the sound lifted the hairs on the back of Zenton's neck and the wash of evil that swept across the dais made him feel physically sick.

He fought against the nausea. This brooding, threatening presence had assailed him before, he remembered. He'd felt its malign touch in some of his dreams and in reality in the labyrinth on the day his father had died. He'd had vague recollections of having felt the same evil sometime during the worst of his illness after the stabbing – and now a hazy memory surfaced of a dream involving Renolth, the dragon and this terrifying menace whose identity he felt he ought to know but whose name slipped from his mind even as he searched for it.

He peered into the stifling gloom but could see little beyond the first rows of people around the dais. Brandell stood close to him, the crown held in perfect stillness.

Do not accept the crown.

Zenton's breath caught in his throat. His mouth was dry and his heart thudded painfully in a chest suddenly tight with fear.

The voice was quiet and sinister yet horribly compelling as it warned him there was something wrong with the crown. The crown was dangerous. It was deadly. If he accepted it, he would die. It would settle around his brow, pressing down and contracting, squeezing, constricting until it killed him.

Terrified, Zenton's first instinct was to reject the crown and all it represented. Someone else must take it – anyone, as long as it was not Zenton himself. Brandell was standing right there; he could have it. He was next in line of succession anyway; he was the obvious choice.

The nausea abated the moment Zenton considered giving up the crown but it returned with renewed vigour as he realised he could not let anyone else to face such peril. If the crown was dangerous, it might kill Brandell.

Still, he could not allow the metal to touch his head. He did not want to die, to leave The Island and the people – *his* people. He did not want to lose Aldana.

Give it away, insisted the voice. *It will not harm Brandell. Give it to him.*

Perhaps he should obey. Brandell was a good leader. He would serve the people well. The awful sickness faded again. Why not let Brandell become High King? The crown wouldn't hurt him.

The ring grew warm on his finger: the royal seal – emblem of his family's past powers and continuing responsibilities. He would need this ring. As High King, he would need it.

Why was he thinking about being High King? If he was to be the monarch, he would have to accept the crown, and that would be fatal.

Faintly, distantly, a new sound penetrated his bemused thoughts. From high overhead came the haunting cry of the dragon, and Zenton recalled with utmost clarity hearing his father's voice in the Mandano Ridge tunnels. He could almost hear again the pride and encouragement in the well-loved voice as Renolth had urged him to remain true to the Light.

Zenton brushed a hand wearily through his hair. He could not be certain the crown was safe for Brandell. He could not take the chance of it harming his cousin or anyone else. He must take it, as his father would have wanted, though it would surely kill him. He felt saddened, defeated and desperately frightened. He was going to die. His reign would be over before he'd had the chance to prove his worth to himself or the Zamaran people. Nevertheless, he knew he would not be able to live with himself if he abandoned his Light-given role as High King and, for self-preservation, let another person risk taking the crown in his place. The ultimate responsibility for The Island and its people was his alone. The crown was his. He would accept the consequences.

He had made his decision.

As if in furious response to his inner certainty about the path he must take, a violent tremor shuddered through the ground, rocking the dais and pitching him forward. Catching himself on outstretched hands against the slender rail, he held his balance as a second tremor, weaker this time, shook the platform beneath him. The ground ceased its trembling and, as he knelt upright once more, the darkness lifted as suddenly as it had descended.

"Zenton?"

He looked up to see Brandell staring at him.

"Zenton, what's wrong? You've gone very white."

Zenton frowned. No one else seemed aware of anything amiss. The ground was steady and the threatening aura had receded somewhat, taking with it much of his feeling of sickness, but the evil was still there, waiting, hovering in the background, expectant – and wholly malevolent.

He'll wake if you call him. The Evil One sleeps, don't disturb him. The old sayings came unbidden to Zenton's mind. Brandell used the name lightly enough and casually dismissed the idea that Nad existed. What if Brandell was mistaken? Was Nad here on the Island? Had he followed them here? Had he been here already, sleeping until they had woken him? Was it Nad trying to prevent this coronation?

"Do you want me to halt the ceremony?"

Brandell's whispered question jerked Zenton back to his present situation. Why did no one else sense the wrongness here? Why hadn't they noticed the tremors and the darkness? They were all looking his way, smiling and untroubled. He gazed fixedly at the crown in his cousin's hands.

"Zenton, shall I call the healers?"

Unable to tear his gaze from the glinting metal circlet, Zenton shook his head. "No," he whispered back hoarsely. "Just finish it, Brandell."

His cousin hesitated briefly, then nodded. Bending forward, he settled the crown on Zenton's head.

The gathered crowd might have been ignorant of the experience Zenton had just endured but every man, woman and child at the ceremony heard the single terrific thunderclap which resounded across the whole settlement, shaking buildings and sending sea-birds squealing into the air. When the shrieks of fright from people and birds alike subsided and it became apparent there was no further danger, reaction to the scare caused chatter and nervous laughter.

Utterly astonished to find the evil presence gone and himself completely unscathed, Zenton could not immediately summon the energy to stand. He felt Brandell's steadying hand under his arm and finally made the effort to rise to his feet. Surprisingly, he received no joking comment from his cousin. Indeed, Brandell looked as shaken as Zenton felt.

A long, eerie call and the thrumming of huge wings caused heads to turn skywards and hands to point up. Blue and bronze scales glinted in the light of the setting suns. The Zamaran dragon circled directly overhead.

Parents grabbed their children. People near the dais turned to Zenton, many of them calling out for him to save them. Some of the crowd started to run away.

There was no need for the panic. They were not under attack. Zenton knew with utter certainty that the dragon's shriek was a cry of victory, not aggression.

"Wait!" he ordered. "Stay where you are!" Though the crowd was large, his voice carried above the clamour and the people obeyed him. "We're in no danger!"

188

A hush fell upon the assembly. The dragon stretched out its neck and emitted another piercing, triumphant cry before wheeling away, winging lazily ever higher, heading towards the cliffs of Mandano. Only when it was lost to sight did attention turn once more to the raised dais and their newly-crowned monarch.

With a hand that trembled considerably more than he would have liked, Zenton reached up to adjust the circlet. It was warm to his touch, comfortable on his head – and he was unharmed. He let out the breath he had not realised he'd been holding and looked up, his gaze following the direction the dragon had taken. It had gone now. The sky was empty but for a few wispy clouds floating like blown sea-foam across its evening red-gold expanse. Oltan was dipping below the distant horizon, leaving Bardok's gentler rays to light the proceedings for another hour or so.

A trifle unsteadily, Zenton stepped down from the dais. True to her promise, Aldana was nearby. She left her place at his beckoning and came to stand beside him.

"Are you all right?" she asked quietly.

Zenton nodded. "I am now."

"Zenton, first High King of Zamara," Aldana said, savouring the words. "It sounds... right, somehow."

With a conscious effort, Zenton put aside the horror he'd experienced just before he had accepted the crown. He would explain to Aldana later what had happened. It was enough that he was sure, for the present, that The Island and its people were safe from the evil that had threatened. If it was indeed Nad, the ancient enemy from Almari legend, then somehow the completion of the coronation ceremony had defeated him.

Right now, Zenton had a new life ahead of him and, rather to his surprise, he found he was actually looking forward to it. He smiled at Aldana, then turned to acknowledge the cheers of the Zamaran people.

~ The End ~

From **Gandeel** by Sue Hoffmann

The dragon's laugh rang out across the crowded market square.

"Shut up," hissed Meb, stuffing the pendant back down the neck of her tunic and hastily buttoning her jacket. Muffled chuckles accompanied her as she sauntered toward the jeweller's stall, trying for nonchalance. *Nothing to do with me,* she thought, concentrating fiercely and waving her hand as if brushing away a troublesome fly. *Everything's fine. Nobody heard a thing.*

A muffled guffaw almost spoiled her focus. She thumped a fist into her chest, to be rewarded by a grunt that matched her own slight gasp of pain, then blessed silence. She breathed a sigh of relief and weaved her way onwards.

"Tamas?" she called softly, reaching the stall and seeing a figure crouched over some boxes in the shadows at the rear of the booth...

'Gandeel' is one of the 13 stories shortlisted in the Earlyworks Press fantasy challenge, published along with a selection of fantasy-related poetry and artwork in the anthology *The Sleepless Sands*

The Sleepless Sands   UK £7.50

ISBN 978 0 9553429 3 6
Pub Earlyworks Press 2006

From **The Eye of the Beholder** by Sue Hoffmann

Adam blinked hard to clear his vision.

"That's it for now," he said. "I'll check the rest after lunch."

Giving his client no time to protest the early break he strode out of the gallery, rubbing surreptitiously at the unpleasant ache in his temples.

Ensconced in the safety of his office, steaming coffee and a Waldorf salad set in front of him, he gingerly fingered the tender area above his right ear. Good thing his hair was still strong and thick – the Restorate tablets were an expense he had never regretted – for the swelling and redness had definitely increased of late. It wouldn't do for anyone to see the inflammation and speculate as to the cause. Going public about the implant had been spectacularly good for business but any rumours about a possible software malfunction would surely set his profits plummeting. Not that there was any real cause for concern. After all, the authentication protocols still worked fine, didn't they?

It was only shutdown that was sometimes a little problemmatical...

'The Eye of the Beholder' is one of 23 shortlisted works from the Earlyworks Press Sci-Fi challenge, published in the anthology *The Road Unravelled*

The Road Unravelled   UK £9.75

ISBN 978 0 9553429 9 8

Pub Earlyworks Press 2007

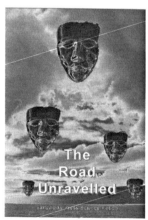

The
Road
Unravelled

More from Circaidy Gregory Press

The Freak and the Idol
by Katy Jones

Gorgeous, red-haired Shona is worshipped by her boyfriend, his best mate and... well, most of the men who've ever clapped eyes on her. She is the envy of her friends, but Shona has a problem - and this time it's not which lipstick to wear.

Set in a youthful world of city bars and student digs, this quirky debut novel is a postmodern fable exploring issues of image, subjectivity and identity.

The Freak and the Idol
ISBN 9781 906451 28 8
Pub Circaidy Gregory Press

Forest Brothers
by Geraint Roberts

1918, a squadron of royal navy ships prepare to return home, and a young navy officer jumps ship, sacrificing his career for the love of a woman.

Years later, the world is at war again. He joins the Forest Brothers, the partisans living secretly amongst the silver birches of Estonia.

There, with killers on his trail, ghosts of his past life emerge...

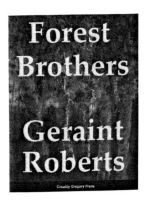

Forest Brothers
ISBN 978 1 906451 69 1
Pub Circaidy Gregory Press

Available from your library, independent bookshop or online direct from...
www.circaidygregory.co.uk

Herm's Secret
by Kate O'Hearn

Come to Herm now, or you'll die!

Lori Watson is just a normal teenage girl until she hears the strange voice warning that her life is in danger. Her only chance of survival is to get to the tiny channel island of Herm, a remote, mist-shrouded place that holds the key to her true nature.

Gunrunners, kidnappers, and a fight for the survival of a rare species: her arrival on Herm is only the beginning of a terrifying ordeal that will change her life forever…

Herm's Secret £7.49
Paperback ISBN 978-1-906451-31-8
Ebook ISBN 978-1-906451-38-7
Order from www.circaidygregory.co.uk